Praise for Deb Caletti's

Honey, Baby, Sweetheart

★ "Readers will immediately fall for Ruby with her humor and her wry way of looking at the world. . . . A story full of heart, fun, and energy."

—*School Library Journal*, starred review

"Caletti writes a compelling, multigenerational story about teens and parents who simultaneously weather heartbreak and find new self-worth, enriching the telling with the Northwest setting, folksy wisdom, and Ruby's strong, sure voice."

—*Booklist*

"Caletti explores the conflicting, complicated impulses of the human heart with polish and penetration. Her portrait of Ruby, aware of her own weakness even as she succumbs to it and hurts those she loves most, is delicate and authentic, conveying a sensitive understanding of character and of our ability to surprise ourselves in ways good as well as bad. . . . This is a stylish and perceptive account of a young woman's developing perceptions of human frailty and human strength."

—*Bulletin of the Center for Children's Books*

"Tender and poetic. . . . Caletti has the gift of voice and tells her story with humor, insight, and compassion."

—*Kirkus Reviews*

"Caletti is a top-notch writer. . . . Her smart writing packs keen observations on love, boys, and life in general."

—*Romantic Times BOOKclub*

"Caletti fills the pages with wonderful images, sharp dialogue, and memorable characters."

—*KLIATT*

A National Book Award Finalist • A Book Sense Pick
A *School Library Journal* Best Book of the Year
An International Reading Association Children's Book Award Notable
A New York Public Library Book for the Teen Age

also by deb caletti

The Queen of Everything

Wild Roses

The Nature of Jade

The Fortunes of Indigo Skye

Honey, Baby, Sweetheart

DEB CALETTI

SIMON PULSE
New York · London · Toronto · Sydney

▧ SIMON PULSE
An imprint of Simon & Schuster Children's Publishing Division
1230 Avenue of the Americas, New York, NY 10020
Copyright © 2004 by Deb Caletti
All rights reserved, including the right of reproduction in whole or in part in any form.
SIMON PULSE and colophon are registered trademarks of Simon & Schuster, Inc.
Also available in a Simon & Schuster Books for Young Readers hardcover edition.
Designed by Ann Sullivan
The text of this book was set in Goudy.
Manufactured in the United States of America
This Simon Pulse edition March 2008
10 9 8 7 6 5 4 3 2 1
The Library of Congress has cataloged the hardcover edition as follows:
Caletti, Deb.
Honey, Baby, Sweetheart / by Deb Caletti.—1st ed.
p. cm.
Summary: In the summer of her junior year, sixteen-year-old Ruby McQueen and her mother, both nursing broken hearts, set out on a journey to reunite an elderly woman with her long-lost love and in the process learn many things about "the real ties that bind" people to one another.
ISBN-13: 978-0-689-86765-1 (hc)
ISBN-10: 0-689-86765-4 (hc)
[1. Interpersonal relations—Fiction. 2. Love—Fiction. 3. Old age—Fiction. 4. Self perception—Fiction.] I. Title.
PZ7.C127437Ho 2004
[Fic]—dc22   2003018331
ISBN-13: 978-1-4169-5783-6 (pbk)
ISBN-10: 1-4169-5783-9 (pbk)

For Sam & Nick.

You are the joy and the meaning.

∎∎∎∎∎∎

*Heartfelt thanks to Ben Camardi, as ever,
and to Jen Klonsky, editor and friend.
Appreciation, as well, to the good people of
Simon & Schuster, especially Jennifer Zatorski
and Samantha Schutz. A note of thanks again
to Anne Greenberg for starting the engine, and to
Scholastic Ltd., UK, for their overseas kindness.*

*And gratitude to the family and friends who are always
there with love, support, and enthusiasm. You continually
make me realize what a lucky woman I am. Evie Caletti,
Paul & Jan Caletti, Sue Rath and Mitch, Tye & Hunter,
Renata Moran & gang, Ann Harder, the Harper family,
Irma Lazzerini, Joanne Wishart, Mary Roukes, and the
memory of Jim Roukes—love to you all.*

■■■■■■

Chapter 1

The first thing I learned about Travis Becker was that he parked his motorcycle on the front lawn. You could see the tracks of it all the way up that rolling hill, cutting deeply into the beautiful, golf course–like grass. That should have told me all I needed to know, right there.

I'm not usually a reckless person. What happened the summer of my junior year was not about recklessness. It was about the way a moment, a single moment, could change things and make you decide to try to be someone different. I'm sure I made that decision the very moment I saw that metal, the glint of it in the sun, looking hot to the touch, looking like an invitation. Charles Whitney— he too made a decision like that, way back on August 14, 1945, just as he ground a cigarette into the street with the toe of his shoe, and so did my mother when she decided that we had to steal Lillian.

Reckless is the last thing you'd call me. *Shy* is the usual word. I'm one of those people doomed to be known by a single, dominant feature. You know the people I mean—the Fat Girl, the Tall Guy, the Brain. I'm The Quiet Girl. I even heard someone say it a few years ago, as I sat in a bathroom stall. "Do you know Ruby McQueen?" someone said. I think it was Wendy Craig, whose ankles I had just whacked with too much pleasure during floor hockey. And then came the answer: "Oh, is she That Quiet Girl?"

I blame my quiet status on two embarrassing incidents, although my mother will say that I've always just been a watchful person by nature, doing my own anthropological study of the human race, like Jane Goodall and *The Chimpanzees of Gombe.* She is probably right that personality plays a part. I sometimes feel less hardy and cut out for the world than the people around me, too sensitive, the kind of person whose heart goes out to inanimate objects—the sock without a partner, a field of snow interrupted by footprints, the lone berry on a branch. But it is also true that humiliating experiences can wither your confidence sure as salt on a slug.

I was reasonably outgoing in the fifth grade, before I slipped on some glossy advertising circulars in our garage, broke my tailbone, and had to bring an inflatable doughnut to sit on at school. Before this I would actually raise my hand, stand at the front of a line, not be afraid to be noticed. My stomach seizes up into knots of humiliation just remembering that doughnut. *It looks like a toilet seat,* Brian Holmes cracked, and the above mentioned Wendy Craig laughed. And he was right; it did—like those puffy ones that you see in tacky, overdecorated bathrooms.

I had begun to put it all behind me, pardon the pun. I'd nearly erased the memory of Mark Cummings and Dede Potter playing Frisbee with the doughnut during lunch, trying instead to remember what my mother told me, that Brian Holmes would no doubt end up prematurely bald and teaching remedial math, and that Mark Cummings was gay, only he didn't know it yet. Then it happened again: humiliating experience, part two. Just when you thought it was safe to get back in the water. This time it was my own fault. I'd placed a pair of minipads in the armpits of my blouse so I wouldn't soak my underarms with nervous sweat during a science speech, and one sailed out as I motioned to my display board. At home, peeling the paper strips and sticking the pads in my shirt had seemed ingenious. Why had no one thought of this before? But as soon as I started to speak, I could feel the right one loosen and slip with every small gesture. I tried to keep my arm clutched tight to my side, soldier-like. *Just because an organism is one-celled, doesn't mean it is dull and uninteresting.* Finally, I had no choice but to flip the page of my board, and down the minipad shot like a toboggan on an icy slope, landing on the floor in white, feminine-hygiene victory. The crowds roared.

So I became quiet. This seemed the safe thing to do when embarrassments hunted me like a stalker hunts a former lover. Again my mother tried her wisdom on me— *Laugh it off*, she said. *Everyone else is too busy trying to forget their own humiliations to remember yours. You're no different than anyone else. Why do you think that years later we still have dreams that we went to school and forgot to get dressed?* And again, this might be true. Still, it seems to me that if I get a pimple it will be in the middle of my forehead like an Indian bindi, and if the answer is *spermatozoa*, I'm the one that will be called on. I've just found that it's best to lie low.

Quiet People, I can tell you, usually have friends who play the violin way, way too well, and know that continental drift isn't another way you can get your coffee at Starbucks. My friend Karen Jen won the Youth Math Extravaganza (I noticed that the bold letters on the sweatshirt she got spelled Y ME, but I didn't mention this to her), and Sarah Elliott and I became friends in P.E. because the V-sit was the highlight of our gymnastics ability. Last winter, Sarah made a wild pass of her basketball and whacked Ms. Thronson of Girl's State Volleyball Championship fame on the back of the head. One minute there was Ms. Thronson, her shoulders as big as the back of a dump truck, blowing her whistle—*Threeep!* And the next minute, *bam*, she was down on her knees as if praying for forgiveness for making us do that unit on wrestling. Sometimes you don't know your own strength.

If you are kind, or were one of my friends in the pre-doughnut days, you've cringed for me over the years, sending supportive thoughts with a glance. But maybe, just maybe, when it is my turn to read aloud in English class (because reading aloud means that Mrs. Forrester can grade papers rather than really teach), you also notice that my voice is clearer and stronger than you thought it would be. When I read Fitzgerald, when I read the part about the light at the end of Gatsby's dock, you see that Mrs. Forrester puts down her red pen and pauses with her coffee cup halfway to her lips, her eyebrows knitted slightly in a look of the softest concentration. That's when you wonder if there might be more to me. More than the glimpse of my coat flying out behind me as I escape out the school doors toward home. At least that's what I hope you think. Maybe you're just thinking about what you're going to have for lunch.

Old Anna Bee, one of the Casserole Queens, told me the same thing once, that there was more to me. She took one finger, knobby from years of gardening, and tapped my temple, looking me long in the eyes when she said it so that I would be sure to take in her meaning. I liked the way it sounded—as if I lead a life of passion and adventure, the stuff of a good book of fiction, just no one knows it. It sounded like I have secret depths.

And I guess for one summer, just one summer, maybe it was true. I did have passion and adventure in my life, the stuff of the books at the Nine Mile Falls Library where my mother works. Summer, after all, is a time when wonderful things can happen to quiet people. For those few months you're not required to be who everyone thinks you are, and that cut-grass smell in the air and the chance to dive into the deep end of a pool give you a courage you don't have the rest of the year. You can be graceful and easy, with no eyes on you, and no past. Summer just opens the door and lets you out.

It was nearly summer, though school wasn't let out yet, when I got that brief glimpse of Travis Becker's motorcycle on the long lawn of the Becker estate. I had walked home by myself that day, instead of with my friend Sydney, as I usually do. Sydney has lived next door to me forever; we both have movies of us when we were babies, sitting in one of those blow-up wading pools, screaming our heads off.

"We're only screaming because of those bathing suits you guys had us in. They look like the kind you see at the community pool on the old ladies recovering from heart surgery. They've got skirts, for God's sake," Sydney said one night as we all watched the movies at her house.

"You were *babies*. The old ladies, by the way, only require heart surgery after seeing what girls wear to the beach these days," my mother said.

"Personally, I think Sydney started screaming then and just never stopped," her mother, Lizbeth, said, dodging a few popcorn pieces Sydney threw her way.

Lizbeth was probably right. Sydney was one of those people who weren't afraid to express themselves, through words, through clothes, through honking a horn at another car during her Driver's Ed test. She once got grounded for grabbing the family goldfish out of the bowl and threatening to throw it at her brother during an argument. Sydney and her whole family, really, were the kind of people who made you feel that power was possible if you could only get to the point where you didn't care what anyone thought. Sydney was a year older than I was, and my only friend who didn't know more about algorithms than was actually good for the health. She was more like family, though.

"You are a cool and beautiful person," she had said to me after the minipad incident. "Just remember that high school is a big game where the blond, perfect ones sit on the sideline while everyone else crosses a mine field trying not to look stupid. In the real world, this all reverses." She sounded a bit like my mother. "Being blond and perfect prepares you for nothing in life but being married to a brain-damaged former football jock named Chuck and having a license plate holder that says FOXY CHICK." Next year when Sydney went off to college, I would miss her more than I could say.

But that day, fate sent Sydney to the dentist, and I walked home on my own. I got to go the way I liked: the long way. After you get out of school and pass the Front Street Market and the used bookstore and the community theater where they put on plays that usually star Clive Weaver, our postman, you can go home two ways. Sydney's way, the quickest on foot, is down a side street, cutting through Olsen's Llama Farm and the property of Johnson's Nursery. But I like to take the main road, Cummings Road, the same one we take in the mornings when Mom drives my brother and me to school on her way to work. Nine Mile Falls sits in the center of three mountains, and Cummings Road weaves through the valley of the largest one, Mount Solitude.

When you walk, you can look at it all more closely—the winding streets named after trees that lead to snug neighborhoods; the small houses that sit right on the road near town, with their lattice arbors and gardens packed tight with old roses. If you go far enough, you walk past the sprawling lawn of George Washington's house, at least that's our name for it, the huge colonial that is odd and unexpected in our Northwest town, as odd and unexpected as finding a decent car at Ron's Auto, the place you pass next. Ron's Auto is in a dilapidated building with old junkers parked in front and RON's spelled out in hubcaps on the fence. If you're looking for a car that actually starts, I'd probably look somewhere else.

You get a little of everything on Cummings Road. Mom says it's like a living bookshelf, each piece of property a separate, distinct story. If that's true, then it's a shelf organized by wacky Bernice Rawlins, mom's co-worker. When she puts away the books at the Nine Mile Falls Library, you never know what will end up where. She once put *How to Be Lovers for the Rest of Your Lives* in the children's section next to *Horton Hears A Who*.

The best part of Cummings Road, though, is Moon Point, a part of Mount Solitude. Paragliders leap from Moon Point in numbers that are almost mystical—thirty-five at one count, soaring like brilliant butterflies and floating so close to the road before they land that if you ever drive past in a convertible, you worry that a sudden, unexpected passenger might drop in. There is something special about the winds there, how they whip down from Mount Solitude and swirl back up again. I don't know how it works; I only know that people come from all over to paraglide off Moon Point. There's even a school on the grounds, the Seattle Paragliding Club, housed in an old barn. The club's logo, wings carrying a heart aloft, is painted on the side of the barn, huge and colorful.

You get all kinds at Moon Point—the professionals with their gliders all rolled up into neon cocoons and strapped to their backpacks with precision, and the people who don't have a clue what they're doing and get stuck in the trees. Chip Jr., my younger brother, saw one once as we drove past. "There's a paraglider in that tree," he said, his face tilted up toward the window. I didn't believe him—Chip Jr.'s favorite joke, after all, is telling you that he saw the governor in the men's bathroom on his field trip to the state capitol. But sure enough, there was a guy stuck high in a fir, his legs dangling down and his glider tangled hopelessly in the branches.

I love to see those paragliders weaving softly around Moon Point, their legs floating above you in the air. When they drift in for a landing, their feet touch the ground and they trot forward from the continued motion of the glider, which billows down like a setting sun. I never get tired of watching them and I've seen them thousands of times. I always wondered what that kind of freedom would feel like.

That day, I stopped at Moon Point for a while. I walked past the row of cars that were always parked in front of the school—active, mud-splattered cars and trucks. I looked for my favorite one—the van with a whale painted on the side and an I LOVE POTHOLES bumper sticker, and was happy when I saw it there. A car with a sense of humor. I sat on the ground with my chin pointing upward and counted an even twenty paragliders soaring against the wooded backdrop of Mount Solitude. I stayed a long while, sat on the grass, and listened for the flapping sound of tight nylon wings against the wind. I had some things to think about. That morning, even before my alarm clock went off, I could hear my mother running the vacuum. It was a bad sign, a sure start to at least three days of hurricane cleaning, endless whiffs of lemon Pledge, odd colored liquids in the toilet bowls, the *seeek, seeek* sound of paper towels wiping down ammonia-squirted mirrors. This cleaning—it meant that my father was coming. It meant that my mother would once again lose her heart to a man who was no longer even her husband, but whose ring she still wore on a chain around her neck. And it meant that my brother and I would be walking around the broken pieces of that heart for days after he left.

I watched the paragliders until the sun snuck behind Mount Solitude. The shadow it cast quickly stole all of the summer heat, and so I decided to head home. Past Moon Point, right after the tiny Foothills Church with its white steeple, that's where the Becker estate is. Construction men worked on that house for nearly two years. The only thing that was on the property before then was an old remnant of an earlier building, broken segments of brick and stone, a single fireplace, something that once was, only no one remembered what that something was. Then one day a bulldozer suddenly arrived, followed shortly after by men in orange vests directing traffic around all of the equipment that was coming and going. Traffic backed up badly on Cummings Road for three straight months. First there was the smell of fresh tumbled earth, and then the smell of mud, and finally of cement and asphalt, new wood. The day the driveway was poured and work began on a pool, my mother, a terrible driver, knocked down a record of five orange traffic cones as we wove through a narrow channel. The lawn was laid out using the same method as does Poe, our dog, when he snitches one end of the toilet paper and trots off—it was unrolled that same way. Instant lawn. Green as money, Sydney's father said, but it wasn't really true. It was brighter than that, bright as cartoon grass. Sydney's dad just had lawn envy.

The stone wall, that's what took the longest. After the wall itself went up, masons with cement-splattered overalls came day after day to add small tiles of intricate designs. The disappointing thing about the wall, and the iron gates that were added last, was that after they went up you could no longer see what was going on behind them. So we filled in the details on our own. The house inspired gossip all around Nine Mile Falls. First the owner was a movie mogul, then a chain-store tycoon, then the owner of a hotel; he came from southern California, Florida,

Boston. Everyone agreed that the piece of property had been too long overlooked as one of our best, set against the firs and evergreens of Mount Solitude, a segment of Fifteen Mile River running through the back of the property.

The truth about the Beckers was not nearly as interesting as the stories. John Becker was from Seattle and made his money as an early stockholder in Microsoft; he and his wife, Betsy, had two sons, Evan and Travis. After we had all of the facts, stories continued to circulate. It was as if we had a need to make this house and the people in it more than they were; maybe the size of the place required a story big enough to fill it. Evan and Travis went to private schools; Evan had supposedly been kicked out. Travis had been arrested. Girls were always claiming that they were dating one or the other, or both at the same time. Every four or five months, John and Betsy were said to be getting a divorce, with plans to put the house up for sale, but no sign ever went up.

That day, after I watched the paragliders, something relatively rare happened—the gates were left open. Not to say that this never occurred; just usually, to your bad luck, you only noticed it too late, when you were zipping past in the car and what you saw was only from looking back over your shoulder. This time they were open, and I was on foot and alone. It was like something out of *The Secret Garden*. A hidden place that compelled you to go forward to a mystery that lay beyond. I pictured myself at that point in the old movie, when it goes from black and white to color as she steps through the gates. All right, let's be honest. I trespassed.

I stopped when the house was finally in view. I let my eyes take in that beautiful yard and the oak tree picturesquely just left of center that the construction workers managed to leave in the ground. I saw it there, then. This motorcycle. All gleaming chrome, parked there so boldly, so wrongly, right on the lawn. Think of a defiant act—think of a boy in black leather talking back to a policeman, think of a stone thrown through a plate of glass—that's what that motorcycle looked like. Stepping too close to the edge, saying no, or yes, and not caring about the consequences.

Right then one of the garage doors went up, giving me the fright of my life. I felt frozen in place, and I wasn't sure if I would seem more guilty staying where I was or walking on after I'd already surely been spotted. I don't even know why I felt so bad when it was really only a glimpse I had been stealing. My feet, by default, made the decision whether we were staying or going—they wouldn't move. So as the door went up, same as a curtain when a play is starting, revealing Travis Becker on that almost stage, I was still standing there, staring.

I didn't know it was Travis then, of course. I only saw this boy, good-looking, oh, God, with a helmet under one arm, looking at me with this bemused smile. Right away I got that Something About To Happen feeling. Right away I knew he was bad, and that it didn't matter.

Chapter 2

In spite of all of its odd wonders, Cummings Road can be a dangerous place, at least for animals. We've got a lot of wildlife here. Nine Mile Falls is across Lake Washington from Seattle, in the thick of the Northwest. Some people, at least my assigned fourth-grade pen pal, think this means we live in log cabins and shoot bear for breakfast. Please. It's Safeway and Lucky Charms for us, just like for the rest of you, but it is true that we've got plenty of animals—deer, raccoons, rabbits, the salmon in Fifteen-Mile River that runs through town. We also have coyotes and wolves and countless other things. My school was shut down last year because a cougar was spotted on the grounds, and a brown bear once wandered around the shopping mall nearest to us, probably looking for a good sale on bear items. A full-grown buck with huge antlers ran down Main Street one time, as if fleeing from a bad domestic situation.

People drive too fast on Cummings Road. Regular cars whip down it in the darkness; semi-trucks on occasion, too, come so fast in the other direction that your windows rattle, and on rainy days you are sprayed with blinding splats of water. People have lost their lives on that road, but of course it is worse for animals. Almost every morning you'll see a dead animal or two, a deflated lump of fur, the thick side of a deer. You get so used to seeing something like that out there that your heart sinks automatically and you end up sending compassionate feeling to a clump of carpet that fell out of the back of someone's truck.

Sometimes you feel very sorry for those animals, and other times you run out of pity and become impatient with their stupidity. You wonder why, with all of the lulls in traffic, they will choose that moment to dart out across the road. I mean, an animal's instinct for survival is supposed to be so keen, right? Yet here is the rattling of a semi, coming closer and louder with every second, and the wind starts rumbling, the street shaking, beams of headlights blaring from the darkness, and *boom!* That's when the animal shoots out from its safe haven and meets his end. *You know how when people die, they are supposed to see a single brilliant light?* my mother once said. *These animals see a* pair *of them.* I can't help but think that sometimes it's opossum/raccoon/deer suicide. Like this poor opossum has simply had enough of rooting around for food, fighting the troubles of daily existence, tired of being just *so ugly*, and says to himself, *Now!* If so, there are a lot of depressed animals out there, and more depressed opossums than any other species.

"Seventeen," my brother, Chip Jr., said from the back-seat of the car the day after I had first seen Travis Becker. Chip Jr. unzipped his backpack, fished around inside, and took out a small spiral notepad. I heard the *tick-a* as he pressed the end of his pen into working position with his thumb. He entered the new number into his book, then clicked the pen closed again. This was Chip Jr.'s roadkill tally. Seventeen was the number of days the two rac-coons, whom we named Romeo and Juliet for their joint jaunt into death, had been lying in their spot on the side of the street.

"I wonder if I should call someone," my mother said. "I never know who to call." It was a mystery who picked the animals up—they would be there and then they'd be gone. I'd never once seen it happen. What a job.

"It beats the record of that opossum. Fourteen days," Chip Jr. reported.

"Love is rough," I said. I knew nothing about this per-sonally. The only person I'd dated thus far was Sydney's cousin, who visited one summer from Montana. He was allergic to bees. He jumped around like a tribesman dur-ing a rain dance whenever he heard anything that buzzed even slightly—a fly, Sydney's electric toothbrush.

My mother started singing some song. "Romeo and Jul-i-et," she sang. She rolled down her window a bit and stuck her nose out to smell the nearly summer air. "Ahh," she said.

She was in a good mood. I knew why. "You're messing up my hair," I said to her.

"It's a mess already," Chip Jr. said.

I looked over my shoulder and glared at him.

"It looks like the dog's."

"Quit kicking the bottom of my seat."

"I wouldn't put my foot near your butt for a million dollars," Chip Jr. said.

"Guys," my mother said. But she wasn't really paying attention. I think we both wanted her to. We wanted her to keep being our mother and not be transformed into this other woman that we knew was coming. We were throwing bombs in the road, trying to divert her attention, trying to make her remember who she really was. One thing was for sure—my mother would have been a lot better off had Chip Jr. and I been in charge of her heart.

We passed the spot of empty land by the roadside where something different was sold nearly every day—peaches, lawn ornaments, fresh fish, wagon wheels. That day it was bird feeders, to which I gave a passing glance, and then we went by the Becker house. Sometimes it is like your mind has a plan that it hasn't even told to the rest of you yet. My heart thudded, bouncing around like Chip Jr. when Sydney's family got a trampoline for their backyard. The gate was closed.

"Look," my mother said. She did this little snort

through her nose. Poor Joe Davis, minister of the tiny Foothills Church, had a problem on his hands. A few years ago the church had bought a signboard, one of those kind that sits on the ground and has stick-on letters. Ugly, my mother says, for a church that has a steeple and looks like it belongs on a Christmas card. The sign is sometimes used for church news, CHRISTMAS EVE SERV-ICES, that kind of thing, but more often for a simple quote that Joe Davis, or maybe Renny Powell, the young guy who takes care of the grounds, thinks is something we could all ponder until they decide to change the sign. The problem is, someone always swaps the letter G for the letter *D*. Today the sign said DOG IS LOVE.

"Dog be with you," I said.

"And also with you," my mother answered. She was not what you would call traditionally religious.

We arrived at my brother's school first, but instead of dropping off Chip Jr. in front like she always did, my mother parked.

"What are we doing?" I asked.

"I just . . . I've got something to tell you guys," she said. Her open window had loosened some of the hair from the braid she wore, giving her that frazzled look of someone who's just pulled a sweater over her head.

"Look." I pointed. "You're frizzy."

She gave herself a distracted glance in the rearview mirror. She smoothed her hair down with her hand, tried to get one especially flyaway piece to stick down with one finger and spit. "It's your dad," she said.

"If this is a news flash that he's coming, we already know," I said. "At least *I* already know."

"I know he's coming," Chip Jr. said.

My mother stopped fussing with her hair, whirled around to look at Chip Jr. and then at me. "How do you know he's coming?"

"You can tell," I said.

"It's obvious," Chip Jr. said.

My mother did something then that made me feel strangely unsettled. She blushed. It was one of those glimpses into your parents' own humanness that you could do without. "Oh," she said. She rubbed her forehead with two fingers like she had a headache starting. "Well, at least you guys could be excited about it."

"Yipee," I said.

"Yipee eye oh kay yay," my brother said.

"Git along lil' doggie," I said. It was a dog-theme morning.

"Ride 'em up, move 'em out," Chip Jr. said. These were the times I liked him a lot.

"Stop being mean," she said.

We were all silent. She was right. We were being mean. After a while I said what I could.

"Of course we're excited, Mom," I said. "He's our dad, isn't he?"

My father is a performer in a roller coaster amusement park with a Western motif. He's good at what he does. He's a singer. They have this saloon there where he performs, with swinging doors and a long shiny bar, and the tables have playing cards shellacked onto the tops. The only things that aren't too accurate, in my opinion, are the waitresses. No one wore skirts that short then. For that matter, you couldn't get surgical boobs either. There are more huge round things in the Palace Saloon than in a bowling alley.

The Gold Nugget Roller Coaster Amusement Park is a state away from us, in Oregon. I went there once. The amusement park is supposed to resemble a miniature gold-mining town, with fake buildings that house things like the Iron Horse Shooting Gallery and the General Store. An old steam train circles the place and gets robbed by bandanna-masked villains on the way. The best roller coaster is an old wooden one that goes through a mineshaft. I guess part of the reason it is so scary is that it looks like a lawsuit waiting to happen. The time I rode it, the woman in the car ahead of me lost her hair ribbon on one of the descents. It fluttered down and away, probably landing somewhere on the Buckaroo Bumper Boats that were below us. Next to the Red River Theater, where they play John Wayne movies for the old people and roller coaster phobics, is the Palace Saloon, with shows at noon, two, and four.

All of the shows are supposed to be different—"Singin' Round the Campfire," say, versus "The Wild Ride Rock-'n-Roll Show"—but my father does them all. His music comes from a boom box hidden behind a bale of hay, or he plays his own guitar, and he changes his clothes from outlaw black to sincere cowboy with a red scarf and fringe vest.

As I said, he's good. It is, after all, what he left for— to make it in show business, though I know he had a different kind of show business in mind. He still does, actually. He always has that next big maybe—a producer who wants to find him a record deal, a country singer who is considering recording the song he wrote. His voice is beautiful, it really is. When I was there, the people who had straggled in, and who sat fanning themselves from the heat with a menu and drinking Cherry Cokes and eating curly fries, applauded loudly and even whistled when he was done. The women did, anyway. He told each show's audience about his next big maybe. Handed out photos of himself where he looked like a Ken doll in a Stetson. But I never went to see him there again. There was something about those curly fries that made me sad.

My father was a musician when he met my mother. He was singing part-time for a group called the Wailin' Five that performed at high school dances and at a bar or two. During the day he worked loading trucks for a frozen-fish factory, where my mother was a secretary while she went to college to become a librarian. My mother was dating the president of the frozen-fish factory, who was twice her age and who asked her to take out her spiral writing pad during dates to jot things down that came to his mind. Today he'd be one of those people with the cell phones permanently attached to his ear, answering its ring during his kid's school play or talking on it as he walked hand in hand with his date. I've seen that happen. Once we saw a guy talking on his phone while he was ice skating on Marcy Lake, which is one of the most perfect spots you would ever see during the winter, surrounded by snowy hills that look lush and soft as a doughnut rolled in powdered sugar. If you could interrupt that to be on your phone, the pair of you ought to be joined in wedded bliss, if you ask me. Anyway, according to my mother, Mr. Albert Raabe was that kind of guy.

Mr. Albert Raabe, though, made a mistake one day when he trusted Chip McQueen, factory worker, to drive my mother home from work. Chip was asked to do this favor by Mr. Raabe himself, who had a sudden important meeting. Word of this task spread fast among my father's friends at the factory; the boss' girlfriend, after all. They decided to demonstrate their support—they plastered a huge JUST MARRIED sign on the back of my father's car.

Neither of my parents knew the sign was there right then, since the car was backed into one of the tight spaces of the factory lot. My father couldn't understand why everyone was honking at him. He made sure his lights were on, his brights off, his turn signal in the neutral position, even that the belt of his raincoat was not hanging out the door. His confusion rapidly turned to annoyance. He even swore under his breath at a bakery truck, whose driver laid down on the horn long and loud. He almost flipped off a car of kids who were beeping madly and swerving around them in what was supposed to be a jovial fashion.

After he dropped off Ann Jorgensen at her doorstep,

Chip McQueen went home, where he still lived with his parents. His mother, my grandmother Ellen, woke him in the night. She had gone outside to scare off two fighting cats and had seen the car in the driveway. Was there something he needed to tell them, she asked?

My father did not laugh or get angry. Instead, in some sort of optimistic need, he saw what happened as a sign from the Fates, even if it was a sign drawn with a Mr. Sketch by a couple of guys named Bill and Larry. He decided to pursue Ann Jorgensen, and was obviously successful or I wouldn't be here telling you this story. She said his charm was like the wind when it blows you so strong from behind that you almost feel as if you can sit down on it. It just took her away. She was his, she said, when she first heard him swear under his breath at the bakery truck driver. That intensity promised things, and although she wasn't sure what those things were, they were sure to be exciting. He lost his job at the fish factory and so did she.

My father was like that about signs. Seven years later, on April Fool's Day, my father turned on his car radio at the precise moment a Chip someone-or-other started singing a song called "Follow a Dream and You'll Never Get Lost." He told my mother that he'd had it with babies and bills and the mortgage, and the next day he quit his job at Blaine and Erie Accountants and dug out his old guitar from the back of their closet. When he left, the stuff that he'd removed from the closet to reach the guitar—his old baseball trophy, my mother's wedding shoes, various winter boots, and a nightgown that had slipped from its hanger—still lay on the floor in front of the closet. He didn't bother to put anything back. My mother left that stuff lying there for a long time. She just kept stepping over it until she barely noticed it was there.

My mother was sure my father would be coming back home, only because she couldn't imagine living without him. He had brought only a few clothes with him, an unopened package of Oreos my mother had just bought, and an enormous silver tea service that his parents had given them as a wedding gift. This indicated to her, in the logic of the recently left, that he'd certainly be returning soon, at least to get more things. This gave her hope. Ten years later she still had it.

The only thing that she seemed truly angry about was those Oreos. She went out and bought six more packages of them and stacked them on the kitchen table. She would glare at them, then cry in their direction. Finally she started eating them, just one a day. She was halfway through the fifth package when my father showed up. It was the first of his many unpredictable visits. I heard him singing in the shower. He'd joined some band. He sounded happy. When he left again, he took the sixth package of Oreos with him, and nothing else.

Here is something that Peach, one of the Casserole Queens, says about men and women and love. You know that scene in *Romeo and Juliet*, where Romeo is standing on the ground looking longingly at Juliet on the balcony above him? One of the most romantic moments in all of literary history? Peach says there's no way that Romeo was standing down there to profess his undying devotion. The truth, Peach says, is that Romeo was just trying to look up Juliet's skirt.

All day I was just waiting until it was time to walk home. That vague feeling of possibility had formed into a plan. I would lie to Sydney, tell her that I had to stay after school for help on my math, so that she would go ahead alone. I knew it would be unlikely I would even see Travis Becker again, but life had suddenly turned out to be one of those moving walkways at the airport. You stepped on, stumbled a bit, then just headed where it was taking you. That *maybe* felt like energy inside, as if I just ate one of those Power Bars that are supposed to make athletes leap higher and run faster, although the only time I ever ate one of those things, none of that ever happened. Two bites and I was having all kinds of weird images about what it was made of and if it was safe to eat something that looked and tasted suspiciously like gerbil-cage chips.

I needed that energy to first get me through the school day. After all, the highlights of it were when Shannon Potts stood by her locker and yelled "Fuck" as a teacher passed; having a sub in math; and listening to Adam Vores try to slosh liquid in his stomach after downing three cans of Diet Sprite. Sometimes you wonder.

"Thirty-nine grams of sugar, thirteen spoons of it, in this Sprite," Mr. Sims, the math substitute, said.

"That's why I drink diet," Adam Vores said.

"Do you think this is a joke? This is no joke. Sugar can whack out your brain. It can whack out your veins. Brains and veins."

"This guy's a poet," Miles Nelson whispered. I smiled his way. He was a Quiet Boy. He wore very tall shoes to compensate for a malfunctioning adolescent growth spurt. We had a toaster like that once. Wouldn't pop up.

"What did you say?" Mr. Sims squawked. He looked Miles' way. "I heard you. You think I couldn't hear you? I got excellent hearing." Miles blushed fiercely. "You think I'm wasting time here? I'm not wasting time. I'm teaching you about life. This lesson is my gift to the world."

"We're supposed to be correcting our math home-work," Cindy Lee said. Cindy Lee lived in fear that if she breathed through the wrong nostril she might ruin her perfect grade point average.

"I'm not just a teacher, you know," Mr. Sims said. He glared at us a little. I wondered if he could be someone we might read about in the news one day when he finally 'snapped'. "I got my own window-cleaning business. You don't know what I see."

"Glass?" Adam Vores said.

Mr. Sims ignored him. "I clean windows in this old people's home. Every day I wonder, how many more people might be alive to be in that place if it weren't for poison like this?" He shook the Sprite can around.

"Don't open it after shaking it like that," Cindy Lee said. I was thinking the same thing.

Mr. Sims sighed. He opened up the math book. He

licked his finger as he turned the pages. "Three forty-five," he said.

Kim Todd decided that the ramblings of this maniac were preferable to real learning. "What happened to your teeth?" she asked him. It was like putting more quarters into the machine.

Mr. Sims went on to tell us about getting punched in the mouth during an argument, and how the tooth's root later died, which certainly meant the hitter had performed a kind of homicide, which meant the guy became his arch enemy until he realized that Whoever Angers You Controls You. He hoped we'd remember that.

I guess it was no wonder, looking back, that I felt I needed Travis Becker in my life.

"What do you mean you have to stay after school for help on math?" Sydney said. "I thought you guys had a sub."

"How did you know about that?"

"Someone said the guy still had a shackle dangling from one ankle. He was supposedly the most bizarre sub since that woman who taught art all day with a parakeet on each shoulder and said Picasso cut off his ear because he heard people whispering in it."

"Picasso didn't cut off his ear."

"No kidding. What do you think I am, stupid? You're not getting help from that sub is what I'm saying. I won't let you alone with him."

"I meant science. Not math. Science. Chemistry. Test tomorrow."

"I want you to make me a promise," Sydney said. My stomach lurched. I thought she was on to me. I'm a terrible liar. If you want to lie, your whole body has to be in on it, and I never could get all of me to fully cooperate. "If you ever, and I mean *ever* use anything you learned in chemistry in your real adult life, I want you to call me. From wherever you are. Even if you're eighty, I want that call. 'Sydney, I actually used something I learned in chemistry class.' Promise me."

"Okay," I said.

She whacked my arm with the back of her hand and headed off toward home. After a safe while, I began walking in the other direction. I stopped at Moon Point, but I spent more time looking at my watch than at the paragliders. I left just as the sun ducked behind what suddenly became the dark shoulder of Mount Solitude.

The gates of the Becker estate were open again. It was just how I saw it in my mind when I was making it all up. There, guarding the gates, sat the question—yes or no? But my feet answered before I did. Travis Becker was rolling his bike by the handlebars over to the driveway. It looked heavy. He saw me standing there, watching him. He waved me inside, and I went. I was like one of the paragliders hiking up Mount Solitude to Moon Point. Instead of reaching the top and soaring down, though, I was one of the few who every year fell off the cliffside, unbalanced by the weight they carried on their backs. I went down just as fast.

"Want a ride?" Travis Becker asked.

Chapter 3

I always thought the greatest thing would be to be able to fly, on some rich Oriental carpet, maybe, *Arabian Nights*–style, above a foreign, turreted city, or just with my own wings, swooping, antigravity, seeing things from a rare perspective. Riding on the back of Travis Becker's motorcycle was the closest thing to flying I'd ever experienced.

He put his helmet on me. My head felt enormous and heavy in it, wobbly, like a newborn baby trying to keep its head up. He yanked the strap tight under my chin, too tight, cutting into the tender skin there. I tried to slip a few fingers underneath to loosen it.

"It needs to be secure," he said. He knocked on the top of the helmet with his knuckles and smiled. For a moment I thought he was going to lean in and kiss me, just like that. It was strange to be seeing the real him, there on the lawn of his own house, when previously I'd only heard him spoken of in the halls at school, or once in the grocery store line. He had blond hair that was parted on one side and swooped over to the other, cut-marble cheekbones and a mouth that could almost be called feminine. His eyes were beautiful in an old-fashioned way; he could have easily been a coddled, sickly prince from years ago, a doomed artist from the thirties, or *Anna Karenina*'s Vronsky, dashing, the kind of guy a woman throws herself under a train for. He seemed to know that about himself; sometimes he would wear clothes that made you think of another time—a long navy wool coat with two rows of buttons, a beret and scarf, a Nehru jacket—but I didn't know that then. I only noticed that he looked at you with the smugness of someone who has a secret, who knows something you don't. The secret was probably money.

Travis straddled the bike, held one hand out to me so that I could swing my leg over. "Hold on," he said. I did. I put my arms around Travis Becker. I had my arms around his waist, which was solid and definite under the soft cotton of his T-shirt. I could smell his cologne—a clean musk, a smell that made you want to free your hair from a ponytail. *Maybe,* I thought then, *I won't always have to be me after all.* Still, I was nervous on that lawn, by that house. I could see a grandfather clock just past the parted draperies, but averted my eyes quickly so I wouldn't be caught looking. I was happy to be leaving; at any moment I pictured his mother appearing, wearing slacks and some shirt that would have cost as much as my mother made in a week at the library, telling me to put my arms back where they belonged.

The bike roared to life, cruised down the driveway, and arced out of the gates. That arc felt wonderful, like turning on your side on one of the roller coasters at the Gold Nugget Amusement Park, the squealing feeling of maybe going over but being mostly sure you wouldn't. We sped down Cummings Road and passed my neighborhood, where no one knew I was speeding by on Travis Becker's motorcycle. I mean, *there I was with my arms around Travis Becker, riding his motorcycle!* The arms of his T-shirt were flapping in the wind. I was riding past my own street, away. It felt great. It felt terrifying.

And then Travis Becker accelerated. Just after my neighborhood, where Cummings Road goes on for a long, straight stretch and all that is out there are the U-Cut Christmas Tree farms, Travis Becker hit the gas. There was a sudden, huge jolt backward as he changed gears. I leaned forward, held myself tight against Travis Becker, fighting the force that made me feel that if I loosened my grip, I'd fly off the back. I'd never been on a motorcycle before, but I knew this wasn't just regular speed, this was fast. Way, way too fast.

I hung on tight. My heart thumped madly; I was sure he could feel it. I was struck solidly with the knowledge that I was somewhere I shouldn't be, way beyond my depths, in a very wrong place. I wanted off. I wanted out of there, and my own earlier planning and plotting to pass that house when he might be there seemed foolish and embarrassing beyond belief. God, I didn't belong there.

Travis Becker laughed loudly over the wind. "Whooee!" he shouted. His hair was whipping around wildly. He didn't even have a helmet on.

A shout, *Slow down!* stuck in my throat. I didn't, couldn't, let it out. Here it is—I was afraid of looking stupid, which is, of course, when you do the most stupid things of all.

I thought about the possibility of hitting a piece of gravel. I thought about the way you lunge forward when you stub your toe. I thought about the way your skin would be peeled off if your body flew across the asphalt at this speed.

I shut my eyes against Travis Becker's back, and when I thought I couldn't take any more, he went faster. Up a notch of speed, and I closed my eyes, squinched them tight and prayed simply to get out of there safely, though I wouldn't blame God or anyone else for not listening to someone who had gotten herself into such a mess. *I'm not here,* I begged my mind to believe. *I'm somewhere else.* I could feel sweat dripping down my arms in rivulets. If I got out of there alive, I'd be embarrassed about my wet shirt.

He slowed down again, turned in to one of the Christmas tree farms, and stopped, turned the engine off. Already some of the trees in the rows were taller than Travis Becker, though some barely reached my knee. I got off his bike; my legs were shaking. He put his kickstand down and got off too. His face was red, his eyes bright and exhilarated, ice blue flashes of electricity. I unsnapped that helmet from my chin, took it off.

"You know how fast we were going?" he said.

"No," I said.

"Over a hundred. Over a hundred, and you didn't even scream."

"Why would I scream?" I said. To tell the truth, I felt like throwing up. Right on top of his expensive athletic shoes.

"Oh, shit," he laughed. "You're fearless." *Fearless*. A single word can hold such power. I could be that, if that's what he thought I was. I could be a lot of things I never considered before.

Travis Becker took off running. "Catch me," he yelled. He disappeared into the rows of tall trees. I could see flashes of his yellow T-shirt between the deep green of the tree branches. It's possible that Travis Becker was a little crazy.

I ran after him. "I see you!" I called. I hate P.E., as you know. I think it qualifies as one of those cruel and unusual punishments we are supposed to be protected from in our constitution. But I'm a good runner. I'm fast.

I darted around one tree, quick enough to see him take a fast turn down another row. I dashed after him.

"I see you again," I called.

"Impossible," he yelled and took off running.

"You're wearing yellow, you idiot," I said.

I wove my way to the row he was in. His back was

against a tree and he was huffing and puffing pretty hard. "I give up," he said. He was bent over, his hands were on his knees. "What did you call me?" he panted.

"I called you an idiot, you idiot," I said. I don't know why I said it. For a minute, running between the trees in that yellow shirt, he made me think of my brother, making a snow fort and hiding behind it, not knowing that the round ball on top of his woolen hat was cruising along over the top, a perfect little moving target.

Travis Becker looked over at me and laughed. "You know what? I like you," he said. "Come on. I got to get back." He pretended to stagger forward from the exhaustion of his spree.

"Just another pathetic rich boy," I said and sighed. I learned my role fast.

"Shit," he smiled and laughed again. "Piranha. Maneater."

That was me, all right. Ruby McQueen, Man-Eater. I could have a T-shirt made.

We got back on his motorcycle. When I held on, I could feel that his shirt was damp and sweaty from running. We drove back at a normal-fast speed. There were no more tests—then at least.

He drove up his driveway and parked on the lawn. I got off, unstrapped my helmet again. I'm sure my hair looked just marvelous.

"Why do you park on the grass?" I asked. "You could fit six cars in that garage."

"Because I can," Travis Becker said. "And I like the

way it looks there." He held up his fingers as if to make a frame around what he was seeing, the way film directors do in the movies. "You know what we did today?"

"Is this a trick question?" I said.

"We did a ton. That's what it's called, doing a hundred on a bike."

"What's doing a hundred and twenty called?" I said. I didn't know this person who was talking. I wasn't even sure I liked her. Maybe I read about her in a book once or something. She was fearless, all right. But to tell you the truth, she was making me nervous.

"Man, you are something," Travis Becker said. He took a bit of my hair, tucked it behind my ear. He looked at me for a while, as if, amazingly, he liked what he saw. "Wait. Wait here. I want to give you something." He turned and jogged toward the house. I hoped he'd hurry. I kept worrying that Mrs. Becker would appear and think I was a trespasser or one of the help she didn't recognize. Maybe she'd ask me to wash the windows.

Travis Becker trotted happily back out. From underneath his shirt he pulled out a black velvet box. He handed it to me. I thought it was a joke. I mean, I knew they were rich, but giving anything in a velvet box to some stranger who you just met a few hours ago seemed ridiculous. Most people wouldn't even give their phone number.

I opened it. It was one of those soft black boxes with the springy lids that come down like the jaws of a snapping turtle. A gold necklace lay inside, held flat by two white elastic hooks. Travis Becker released the necklace, then took the box back from me and let it drop on the grass. "Lift up your hair so I can put it on," he said.

"I can't take this," I said.

"Sure you can," he said.

"This is nuts. I don't even know your name. You don't even know mine."

"You don't know who I am?" he laughed.

"Well, it says Becker on the mailbox." Of course, there was no mailbox. They probably had their mail delivered to their doorstep on the back of some endangered animal or something.

"Travis," he said.

"Ruby McQueen," I said. I've always hated my name. It made you think of a rodeo cowgirl in some porn movie or, maybe worse, a Texas beauty queen runner-up. My parents had agreed on it for their own reasons. Before I was born, my mother was reading a lot of Southern literature, and my father, who was already dreaming of Nashville stardom, thought it would make a great stage name someday.

"Ruby, like the jewel," Travis Becker said.

"Like the slippers. 'There's no place like home.' I still can't take this. Where did you get it, anyway? You just keep these around for girls you give rides to?"

"I was going to give it to someone. I changed my mind," he said. "So shut up and lift up your hair. No, wait. A better idea. Close your eyes." He took hold of my arm and bent it in front of me, then did the same with the other. I felt the cool slither of the gold chain drawing my wrists together and I opened my eyes to see the necklace looped twice around both of them, handcuff-style.

"Hey, it looks great," he said.

"Very funny. Get it off."

"You're my prisoner."

"Off," I said.

"Give me a kiss first to say thank you." He lurched forward and I turned my head; his mouth hit the side of mine. I changed my mind and let him kiss me. I'd been kissed before, just once by Sydney's cousin, and by Ned Barrett in the seventh grade, behind the gym after the school holiday music concert. Ned Barrett had a locker next to mine for two years in a row and played the bass in the orchestra. He was lugging it back to the music room when, suddenly overcome with holiday cheer, I guess, he called me over. I thought he needed help with his bass, but he kissed me instead, the bass standing there like a nosy third person. But Travis Becker's kiss was different. He knew what he was doing, that was for sure.

The kiss left me dazed, forgetting about Mrs. Becker or anything else, for that matter. "*Now* I'll take it off," Travis Becker said. He unfastened the necklace, slid it into the pocket of my jeans. "Don't say no. Or we might not be friends anymore," he said. "Anyway, it's your prize for not screaming."

"I don't know what to say."

"Say thank you."

"Thank you. For the ride too."

I kept it right there in the pocket of my jeans as I walked home. I would reach my hand toward it, rub it between my fingers. To be honest, it did not have a nice feel. It was that flat kind of gold, so slithery and cold that it almost felt wet. It felt wrong in my pocket. I knew it didn't belong there any more than I had belonged on Travis Becker's motorcycle. But I reached my fingers down into my pocket and felt the slick links anyway. Touching it was my only proof that the afternoon had been real.

I like to assign human personalities to different dogs I see. Sydney's dog is a tall, lanky golden retriever. He would be one of those amiable athletes, good at the hurdles but not too bright. My friend Sarah Elliott has an Airedale. He's got this little beard and kind, knowing eyes. King Arthur, in *The Once and Future King*. Fowler, one of the librarians my mom works with, has this poodle that acts like some of the blond girls at school who are always putting on makeup behind their math books and who have apparently become mentally damaged by all that hair swinging, because they now think being called *spoiled* is a compliment. Fowler's not the poodle type, but it followed him home one day after getting lost and wouldn't leave, which shows that even poodles have their moments of humility.

My dog, Poe, though, he's another thing altogether. He's a Jack Russell terrier, but more than that, he's a kindergarten boy with a hyperactivity disorder. Once he ate through my mother's bedroom door, leaving a hole the size of a man's head. Another time he knocked himself unconscious by tripping and falling down the porch steps after he ran full speed out the back door with a mouthful of my brother's dirty socks. He thinks the vacuum cleaner is an intruder, which, admittedly, he has successfully wrestled to submission a few times. The handle has been chewed to a rough and gnarled state, and you've got to wrap a kitchen towel around it if you want to use it without hurting your hands. Last winter he went to get a drink from his water bowl that had frozen during the night and got his tongue stuck there. We are sure that Poe assumes his name is You Dumb-Ass Dog, as that's what my mother is always calling him. He probably thinks it's German for Dog of Great Intelligence.

When I arrived home, Poe was even more keyed up than usual. He was walking along the back of the couch like a circus performer, minus the tutu. He leaped down when he saw me and jumped up, his toenails scratching my legs. His excitement must have had something to do with the car that was in our driveway, the Ford Windstar with the Oregon plates.

"Where's Dad?" I asked Chip Jr. He was sitting on the couch, his knees pulled up to his chin. He was watching TV. Chip Jr. hardly ever watched TV. He was usually in his room building something—card houses, the Taj Mahal out of LEGOs. I'm not kidding.

"In the kitchen."

"Why aren't you in there too?"

"I have to watch this." I looked at the television.

There was a lizard burying something. Close-up to a disgusting pile of what must have been its oblong, yellowish eggs. Of course, that might have been our TV. Our TV was old and decrepit and prone to turning everything to custard shades. It could fill the Winter Olympics with more yellow snow than any sicko eight-year-old boy could even imagine. Librarians, at least the one I lived with, did not put a premium on the latest technological equipment. Or appliances, for that matter. A pair of socks can get our washing machine off balance, making it shake so hard and loud you think it's going to shimmy on down the hall.

"Why do you have to watch this?"

"Because it's about *lizards*," he said, as if that explained something. "Shit." He was acting up, too.

"Shit shit," I said.

"Shit-shit. A Chinese noodle dish. Shit-shit with chicken or pork," Chip Jr. said to his knees.

"Slippers on a kitchen floor. An old lady's. Shiiit, shiiit."

He thought for a while. "Someone with a lisp asking you to take a seat," he said. "Please do shit down."

"Okay. I'm going in the kitchen," I said. I pretended to put on protective gear, snapped on a helmet, knee pads. I saw a little smile start at the corner of Chip Jr.'s mouth, disappearing into a crinkle of his jeans, where his chin was tucked.

My father looked the same, only his hair was longer than usual. He's the kind of man women fall all over, even if you don't like to think of your father that way. That's how handsome he is, and it's the truth, like it or not. He has dark brown hair, long enough so that he occasionally has to comb it dramatically from his face with his fingers, permanent stubble, a strong nose, dark eyes that look like he just woke up or is lost in thought. Everyone says I look just like him (except for the stubble, I hope), and it's true that I have his nearly black hair, worn long and straight, and his dark eyes. But I also have my mother's lines and angles—too-pointy chin, long thin legs, wrists like a bird's, if a bird had wrists. It was hot that day, nearly eighty, and my father wore a T-shirt, denim vest, and cowboy boots, which tells you right there that his vanity was greater than his need for comfort.

My mother was cooking something with wine and mushrooms. The smell rose full and lush from the stove and when she turned to me I could see that she had her lipstick on and that she'd been laughing. Her face was flushed from happiness and cooking steam, and she was wearing something I'd never seen before—a sundress with cherries on it, which fit snug enough to make her seem curvy. Irritation snuck up along my insides. When it came to my father, my mother went from capable librarian who could find you the population of Uruguay in less than a minute to 1950's housewife with apron and pot holder. It was a sci-fi transformation. *Just tell him to get lost*, I said to her once. *That is your father you are talking about, Ruby*, she had snapped. *There are things you cannot understand. We have a history together. It's not something you can just make go away.* Said like she was throwing a bunch of unrelated items into a pot of soup. A carrot, a grapefruit, a kitchen sponge. Finally, she sighed. She resorted to the same old comeback she used whenever we questioned her authority. *Remember, I'm the mother here, and I'm driving.* The metaphorical Car of Life. The only problem is, my mother can't drive in reverse to save her life. She once killed a juniper plant in our yard after backing up in a hurry. And as far as my father went, it seemed like she was always going in reverse.

"What's with the minivan?" I said to him.

"A friend lent it to me. How about 'hello'? Jesus, look at you. You're beautiful. Give me a hug."

His bristles scratched my cheek. When I was little he used to do that on purpose: rub his prickly cheek against mine until I squealed for him to stop. He smelled of some strong, woodsy men's cologne. It was strange to be there in the kitchen with the real him. When you lived with someone in your mind, they became all sorts of things— villain, hero, taking different shapes like a ghost, in ways they could never do in real life. The real him just looked so much smaller, deflated by his humanness. The imagined him could move through doors and appear out of nowhere; the real him was someone who put on deodorant every morning and clipped his toenails.

My mother didn't seem to find him diminished, though. Judging by the light that had suddenly filled her, his absence only made her imagine him with a strength that reality would not alter. She'd sketched in the details, applied the personal vision, same as reading a good book of fiction. She liked the version she'd created. No doubt if she saw the movie, she'd have hated it and claimed it not to be anywhere near what the author intended.

"The minivan. It's got a baby seat in the back," I said into his shoulder. "That can't do much for your image."

He ignored me. He reached down into the pocket of his jeans. It reminded me of what was inside my own pocket, the necklace there, and the thought of it gave me a surge of feeling, a jolt of something like power. "Look what I have for you," he said.

He pulled his hand out, opened his closed palm as if revealing a treasure. In his hand lay six crystals, pointed at the ends like stubby pencils, but a beautiful color, a milky pink, translucent and delicate, a color you could feel a longing to possess. "They're so pretty."

"Rose quartz. Raw and unfinished, from the earth. Sleep with them under your pillow. They're supposed to bring you harmony. Take them." I was reluctant to reach out my palm to his so that he could spill the crystals into it. It was a bit like the White Witch in the Narnia books, with her Turkish Delight. One amazing, buttery bite and you would have no choice but to keep coming back for more. With my father, there always seemed to be two choices—only the extremes. You could be drawn in, climb inside his boat and ride a dream river while looking into the sun, the glare in your eyes keeping you from seeing the waterfall you were about to drop over; or you could stand at the side and watch other people get in, holding a map of the terrain in one hand and your protected heart in the other.

I took the crystals and thanked him. He told me he'd made a special trade with someone for them, someone who had found them in Brazil. I tried to keep one foot on the riverbank and pictured the crystals in a bin in the Gold Nugget Amusement Park General Store, next to the giant jawbreakers and fake arrowheads and pennies the size of a baby's fingernail.

My father came up behind my mother, snitched a mushroom from the pan, and popped it in his mouth. She elbowed him. He took another, made moaning sounds of deliciousness, then put his hands on the curved waist of her cherry dress. "You shouldn't be cooking. Let's go out."

"I've got everything right here," she said.

"I want to treat you. I want to take out my family. I know a great Indian place. Downtown."

"No, Chip, that's okay," my mother said. I could tell she meant it. I could tell she probably got off work early just to shop for all of the ingredients of the recipe, which had been researched with care in the cookbook aisle of the library earlier that day. She'd spent more than she could afford, too, judging by the array of unusual ingredients spread out on the counter, the bags from Renaud's Gourmet, the bottle of wine.

He pretended to bite her neck. It was getting embarrassing in there. "Sweetheart, don't tell me you lost the ability to be spontaneous," he said.

She flinched at the remark. Then she turned off the

stove. She grasped the handle of the pan and gave the mushrooms a firm shake. "We'll have these for appetizers, then," she said. She opened a cupboard door and got out a bowl, a pretty one, not the plastic one with the Froot Loops toucan on it, and tumbled the mushrooms into it. She was being sincere, even if she had to fake it. She was so far down the river that even if I held my hand up to block the glare of the sun, I would only see the tiny dot of her in the distance.

"Hey, C. J.!" my father yelled. Chip Jr. did not like to be called C. J. He was smart enough to associate people who use initials for names with owners of National Rifle Association bumper stickers. "Get your shoes on! We're going out to dinner."

My father went into the living room. He got this in reverse order, talking to Chip Jr. and then going into the living room. This was one of my father's biggest problems: loving the drama of the illogical, the chaos of the spur of the moment. He didn't seem to care that irresponsibility is spontaneity's kid sister. Poe ran over with renewed glee, jumped on my father's knees.

"Baby, yes. Oh, sweet baby," my father crooned to him. I had the ugly thought that this was how he probably sounded when he talked to his girlfriends.

"Change of plan," my mother said to Chip Jr. "Come on, we're going out."

"You went to Renaud's," Chip Jr. said. There was something close to accusation in his voice.

"So? It'll keep. Get your shoes on." Boy, she was

cheery. Boy, we ate well when my father came around.

After a few minutes of bustling, we were at the door and ready to leave. Poe was still following Dad around as closely as dryer lint on black socks. My mother bent down and scooped him up, aiming for the back door.

"He's coming, isn't he?" my father said.

"Poe? In the car?" I said.

"We better leave him here," my mother said, and she put him back down.

"Aw, no. He wants to come. I love this dog." My father scratched Poe under the chin. "I gave you guys this dog."

"And life hasn't been the same since," my mother said. *Dumped the dog on us and left again*, she should have said.

"I came to see all of you. Even my dog." He picked Poe up. The dog had not had this many ups and downs since that glorious and devastating day on the back porch steps. "Come on, Poe, let's go for a ride."

"Chip," my mother warned. But he was already heading outside.

"You'll be sorry," Chip Jr. said.

There was more yellow food in the Indian restaurant than on our television during the fast-food commercials. I admit, though, it was delicious, steamy and spicy and full of inexact flavors. The hypnotic snake charmer music was soothing in a weird way, and better yet, wasn't something my father could sing along to. We had taken my mother's car at Dad's request since his was running low on gas, and it had been an easy trip. Poe had been a perfect gentleman on the ride, sitting upright between my parents as if he were on his way to Sunday church services. We all started to relax. My mother's eyes were glowy in the red candlelight. My father took her hand, rubbed her arm, put his hand under her chin. Chip Jr. read the wine list out loud.

My father was singing something to us all when we went outside; my mother's arm was hooked under my father's and she was smiling. When we got to the car she dropped his arm, reached for the door handle. Then she screamed.

"Uh oh," Chip Jr. said in brilliant understatement.

It looked like there'd been a blizzard inside that car. Poe had chewed a hole in both the front seat and back, and the interior was filled with drifts and mounds of yellowish fluff. It was everywhere; on the floor, the seats, the dashboard. Some had stuck to the roof, as if he'd somehow managed to toss merry handfuls of the stuff in the air. The scream didn't wake Poe, who was curled up in a snug ball on top of a mound of foam, snoozing peaceful dog dreams of mayhem and devastation.

"You dumb-ass dog!" my mother yelled at him when she opened the door.

"Bad dog," my father said without much conviction. "Well, I guess he is a puppy after all."

"He'll be two in a few months!" my mother said. She looked like she was about to cry.

"Time flies," my father said.

"I told you you'd be sorry," Chip Jr. said.

"Look at him," my father said. Poe lifted his head at all the commotion and looked around sleepily. He had bits of yellow fluff in the hair under his chin. "Hey, nice beard, Bud." For my mother's benefit, I tried not to laugh, but it did look pretty funny. She was swooping foam off of the seats with wide arcs, human-snow-shovel-style.

My mother, in the passenger's seat, bit her lip the whole ride home. Repairing the upholstery would later prove to be too expensive, so she would instead drape woven Indian blankets over the holes in the seats. This covered up the surface problem but didn't do a thing to help the bigger issue of the exposed springs, which occasionally rose up to jab you painfully when you least expected it.

"What's this?" my father said, feeling around the seat beside him, one hand on the wheel as he drove. He held up a small black object. "Dog even chewed off the radio dial!" He shook his head in disbelief, then he tossed the knob up in the air and caught it in his palm again, as if it were a lucky penny.

"Shit," Chip Jr. said.

"Chip Jr.," I said.

"No, I mean shit." He lifted up his shoe and showed me the bottom.

I swear that dog was smiling.

At home later that night, I saw my parents in the doorway of my mother's bedroom. My father was holding the ring that she wore on a chain around her neck; I imagined that he'd slipped it out from under the collar of her dress, knowing it would still be there. He took her hand, and slipped the ring on her finger. She just held it there, attached to the chain, until she noticed me. They both jumped back, startled. She released her finger from the ring.

"Ruby," she said.

"Just heading for bed," I said.

I ducked into my room, fast. My own hand reached down into the pocket of my jeans. I took out my own necklace and I held it, coiled up in my palm.

It occurred to me then, just briefly, that our hearts had been bought much too cheaply.

Chapter 4

WALK WITH DOG AND YOU'LL NEVER WALK ALONE, *the* Foothills Church sign read. From a good distance down Cummings Road I could see Minister Joe Davis sitting on the lawn, elbows on his knees, chin in his palm, just looking at that sign. Something about this reminded me of my brother the night before, watching those lizards. It was early morning, too early for much traffic, and I imagine Joe Davis figured not too many people would witness this demonstration of his baffled hopelessness. The unknown sign changer had struck again.

I was sent on a morning mission for my father, who, when he woke up, had a sudden craving for Something With Raspberries. This time I was hoping I would not see Travis Becker outside his house, or rather, that he would not see me. I was driving Mom's car, which still looked like the scene of a brutal cushion massacre.

Joe Davis turned when he heard the car coming. He stood and waved, which told me that Joe Davis probably had bad eyesight but didn't wear his glasses. He thought I was my mother, I was sure, and this became a certainty when he started waving even more heartily, gesturing me to pull over. Even my mother had the feeling that Joe Davis's frequent trips to the library were not just about bringing home more of the murder mysteries he liked. Poor Joe, though, had to pick this day to finally get up his nerve and speak to my mother when she wasn't tucked safely behind the circulation desk. His technique of frantic arm waving could use a little work in the subtlety department.

I didn't want to be rude, so I turned the car to the side of the road and rolled down my window. Joe Davis trotted over happily until he was a few feet from the car and his vision finally kicked in. His face fell.

"Oh, hi, Ruby," he said.

"Is there a fire?"

"What?"

"A fire." I waved my arms around, just teasing him a little, and regretted it immediately. Joe blushed all the way to the tips of his ears.

"I thought you were Ann. I just wanted to show her what the culprit has done now."

"Do you have any suspects?" I knew he liked murder mysteries. I was hoping suspect-talk would redeem me from my earlier remark.

"Colonel Mustard in the conservatory with the candle-stick," he said. "You know what the strange thing is? I'm actually beginning to enjoy this. Can you picture that dog, big and comforting? A loyal friend at your side, making a winter night feel cozy with the way he sleeps curled up in a ball?"

I nodded and smiled. I decided I liked Joe Davis. He was a cozy person himself, the kind of man you picture walking around in socks with a hole in one toe. He wore khaki shorts with lots of pockets and a Wilderness Society T-shirt, and his watch had stopped at ten past four. When it wasn't summer, he was usually wearing a rag wool sweater and jeans, clothes that looked like they knew him as well as he knew himself. The Foothills Church was small, and although Joe Davis lived in a little house on the property, he apparently didn't make much as a minister, as he also worked part time as a carpenter. You often saw his truck, with the ladder hanging on the side, parked around town, in the library parking lot, at the Java Jive, or in someone's driveway, the truck's back doors open to reveal a messy array of tools and extension cords.

"Well, I'll tell Mom you said hi," I said.

"Please do. I'll see her on Monday. I've got overdue fines to pay."

"Not you, a minister."

"Unfortunately, talking about God doesn't make me exempt from overdue fines, speeding tickets, overflowing toilets, or arguments with my brother-in-law, and that's just in the last week."

"Maybe God's on vacation," I suggested.

"Maybe I've got my head in the clouds," Joe Davis said.

I waved good-bye. The funny thing was, Joe Davis never even mentioned the wrecked state of my mother's car. He was either really polite or really blind. Maybe you have as much chance of seeing clearly when you are in love as an opossum has of getting across Cummings Road.

I passed the bald spot on the corner where the goofy things were sold—that day shiny blankets decorated with peacocks and lion heads—and Moon Point. The paragliders had already parked their cars and begun the hike to the top of the mountain. The whale van with the I LOVE POTHOLES bumper sticker was there too, sitting empty. I got the carton of raspberries and some scones at the Front Street Market and headed home. When I got there, I could hear my parents' voices through the screen door.

"It's only going to be a few hours. I can't see how the neighbors will mind, if that's what you're thinking," my father said.

"It's not just the neighbors." My mother sounded tired. I'm sure it was much easier to love my father in her imagination.

"Well, what then? I didn't think you'd mind. So what, I should have asked first? You used to love hearing my band."

"It's just . . . I don't know. I thought you came to spend time with us."

"I did!" his voice was rising a little. "Okay? I did. Look, Seattle has a bigger pool of singers, and I don't want to settle for just anyone. I want to hear as many as I can. What's wrong with that? What's wrong with wanting quality?"

"Nothing's wrong with it. I want quality too."

"I have to be honest with you. You really are becoming uptight."

I hate that, I really do, when people use honesty as a cover for cruelty. You take a moral word like *honest*, stick it next to something mean, and you can almost make an insult sound righteous. And if we're sensitive, we believe those insults. We forget that just because something is honest it is not necessarily the truth.

"Uptight? You tell me you're here to see me and the kids. But you just came to use my house for an audition again. That's not exactly *uptight*."

"Here I'm thinking you're not going to mind, because, frankly, I don't see what the big problem is. I thought you'd be glad to help out a friend."

God. You could almost hear him insert the knife into her heart and twist. "A friend. Jesus."

"Shit, Ann, don't start. Ann." Silence, and then footsteps. I turned around and bolted down the porch steps and down the sidewalk to the car, then came back again as if I'd just arrived. Mom opened the screen door, then let it close behind her with a rattle. It wasn't quite a slam, but it would do.

She wore her tank top and shorts, and her hair was in

a ponytail to help with the heat, which in a few hours would be cranked high. She was barefoot, too, and it all made her seem younger and more vulnerable than she usually did, say, when she was paying bills, with her fingers tapping the calculator buttons, or ironing her work clothes as if she could do it in her sleep.

"Raspberries," I said. I shook the grocery bag in the air.

I'm not even sure she saw me at first. Her attention was caught by a van driving slowly down our street. The driver passed our house, paused, then backed up. "Just great. Terrific," she said. "It's starting already."

"What?"

"Auditions. A singer for your father's new band. Here. Today. Female vocalist. His bass player and drummer will be here any minute. That's probably them now."

"The invasion begins," I said. "Remember what happened last time? They wiped out the contents of the refrigerator. All that was left was that French mustard with the brown dots in it."

"God. I forgot about that part." She rubbed her temples with her fingertips. "This is insane."

The van that had been driving backward stopped, and a guy with a goatee and a long braid popped his head out the window. "Is this Chip's place?" My mother didn't bother to correct him, only hooked her thumb toward the house. A minute later the goatee guy and his friend in a tie-dyed Grateful Dead T-shirt were unloading equipment, sweating and banging up the front steps into the living room. Poe was barking crazily from inside the house. The high point of his life is when we take the vacuum cleaner from the closet, so imagine his thrill and anxiety. He managed an escape through the screen door as an amplifier went in. He trotted over to us for an explanation. My mother picked him up, set her cheek against his fur.

We sat down on the porch steps. Chip Jr. came outside and sat with us. "The guy with the braid's name is Mambo," he said. "Cha-cha-cha."

We watched Poe sniff around the lawn and rediscover pieces of the garden hose he'd chewed up a few weeks before. The hollow thuds and cymbal crashes of the drummer warming up acted as Poe's background music. I took the raspberries out of the bag and ran them under the outside faucet. We ate them out of the carton, and red juice dripped from the slats in the bottom and landed on our bare knees. Chip Jr. stuck one on every finger and did a puppet show where every character was eventually devoured in a grisly fashion.

Cars started to arrive, emptying women of all varieties onto our driveway. Some came in pairs, some with a boyfriend, and one came with her mother. You should have seen some of these outfits—leather minis, a leopard elastic top. And the hair. You'd have seen less hair at a sheepdog convention. Voices of all kinds squeezed through the tiny holes in the window screens and blasted out into the hot day, competing for dominance with the strained volume of the other instruments, and that show-off drummer, whose solos sounded like those times when you pull out one pot lid and everything topples out of the pots and pans cupboard. Mr. Baxter, the neighbor across the street, came out to wash the car, but it was no doubt an excuse to glare at us for the noise and gawk at all the spandex. Chip Jr. went inside to spy, and came back with a report.

"That Mambo was drinking your wine from Renaud's," he said. "Right from the bottle."

My mother sighed. She had vacated her body; she was like some shirt you'd worn all day and then dropped to the floor.

"Do you want to get out of here?" I said. I thought of Joe Davis, sitting on the grass by the WALK WITH DOG sign. I thought of the quiet there. I thought of how good it would be for Mom to ride around somewhere with all of the windows rolled down, which is a good cure for most things, in my opinion. "I'll drive."

"Then I'm wearing my bike helmet," Chip Jr. said.

"No," my mother said. "I can't."

"Wait, what am I thinking?" I said. "It's Saturday. You've got the Casserole Queens." Every Saturday my mother leads a book discussion group for a club of old people. They called themselves the Casserole Queens, my mother told us, because ladies their age always brought casseroles to a fresh widower's home in hopes of snagging themselves a husband. They called themselves this even though the only one of them that would ever do such a thing was Mrs. Wilson (now Mrs. Thrumond), who ditched the group right after her wedding at the senior center, and in spite of the fact that one of the members of the group was male. According to Mom, they let Harold in because he was a former chef and made great brownies and because they could boss him around.

"I'm not going to the Casserole Queens today. I canceled to spend time with Dad. Fowler's taking my place."

"Fowler? They'll eat him alive." I'd only met them once before, but I heard they could get pretty rowdy when they were unhappy. I was thinking of the time Harold rebelled, claiming that from that moment on, he would not be the only one to bring food for the group. Apparently this started a mini-riot, with Peach and Mrs. Wong throwing things at him—little wrapped candies, a Kleenex packet—from their purses.

"Fowler's bringing his poodle. No problem. He won't even need to talk about the book. I can pick up next week right where we left off."

"They need you, though."

"Ha. I think it works the other way around."

"Then let's get out of here." I stood. I could see Sydney next door, hauling the sprinkler to the center of the lawn. She waved, then turned on the faucet until the sprinkler was fountain-high and went back into her house.

"Ruby, thanks. I know you're trying to help. But I've got it handled. Okay? I've got it handled. I need to stay here. One of these people may decide to move in or something."

I sat back down again. The singer finally shut up. You

could hear laughter from inside. "I'd give her a four-point-five," Chip Jr. said.

"Three-point-two," my mother said.

"Would you just lie down," I said to Poe, who was turning endless circles in a spot on the lawn, trying to make sure the view was right from every angle, I guess. He finally plunked down, sighed through his nose.

Sydney came back out, veered around the sprinkler fountain and came into our yard. She tossed us each an orange Popsicle. "Party food. I'm hurt you didn't invite me." She sat cross-legged on the grass.

"Dad's having an audition."

"I figured it out. At first I thought Mom put her tennis shoes in the dryer again. *Ba-bamp, ba-bamp, ba-bamp.* Then she yelled for me to get a look at the bimbo parade." She stuck her chest out and patted her hair. "So what, do they measure cleavage as part of the interview?"

"I don't want cleavage talk," Chip Jr. said. His lips were already orange from the Popsicle after one bite.

"Sounding like a dying animal shouldn't be a problem as long as your clothes are tight enough," my mother said. She opened the Popsicle wrapper with her teeth. Sydney caught my eye, an acknowledgment of my mother's misery. The drummer, for whom, apparently, silence was not golden, started banging again. Another car crawled down our street, the driver looking at house numbers, as if the noise wasn't information enough. It was one of those low-slung pickups, the kind of car that looks like the getaway vehicle of a pawn shop burglary.

We watched the girl park, one tire on the curb. Her hair was done up like a three-year-old's; she wore a shirt that said QT PIE in glitter script.

"Hey, Pigtails," Sydney called. "Sorry for the trouble. The audition's over. They found the one they wanted."

"Goddamn it," the girl said. She got back in her car, slammed the door, and bumped back down the curb. She gunned the engine and screeched down the street.

"Wow. Anger issues," Sydney said.

"Hooray for Sydney, champion bimbo chaser," Chip Jr. said. He stuck his Popsicle in his mouth and started to clap. My mother joined in, hitting her free hand against the fist that clutched her Popsicle. Sydney took a bow. It was a joyful second until Mom's Popsicle split and the chunk of orange ice fell to the ground. A sticky rivulet rolled down her arm. She looked down at it as if it was a mere representation of all that was wrong in the world. I thought she might cry. I thought I might cry for her.

Poe trotted over and began licking what was quickly turning into a pool of sweet liquid. His beard would be stiff and sticky the rest of the afternoon. It was his lucky day. Which only goes to show that often enough, we owe our good fortune to someone else's loss.

By evening my mother had forgiven my father. It made me wonder how many times we forgive just because we don't want to lose someone, even if they don't deserve our forgiveness. The next day we all went to Marcy Lake and swam. It was a near perfect day, and the air smelled like both the sweetness of sun and of the coolness of deep lake water at the same time. We jumped off the dock, and Chip Jr. did cannonballs, and Mom sat on Dad's shoulders and he tossed her in. We ate a picnic lunch sitting on our beach towels, and you could feel the warm wood of the dock through the terry cloth. Dad's hair dried funny, and Mom got sunburned near the elastic of her bathing suit where it had shifted around, showing white skin. We went home with that satisfied exhaustion a day of swimming and sun brings. Mom was really happy. Later that night, before my father left again, the sky suddenly got dark, as it will in a Northwest summer, and there was a rumble of thunder and a burst of rainfall. The rain is bratty here. It can't stay away too long without coming back and throwing a tantrum.

Chip Jr. and I said our good-byes to Dad as pellets of water bounced hard on the ground. I went to my room with a weird feeling in my stomach. It was hollow, with a knot of something that felt like sadness and guilt, though I have no idea what I felt guilty about. My mother had walked my father out to the car. They stood out there for a long time. I listened to the rain falling on the roof and the tree branches and the garbage can lids. We should blame the neighbor, Mr. Baxter, for the rain—he was the one that washed his car the day before.

Mom was out there so long that I was getting worried. I turned off my bedroom light and peeked out my curtains; the window was open in spite of the rain, as it had been a hot day. The rain had that smell of steamy, damp earth and wet asphalt, and I breathed it in. I crouched way down and peered over the windowsill. I could see them in the driveway. My father had my mother's chin in his hand, and then he leaned in to kiss her. I looked away, and when I looked back, he was smoothing her wet hair from her forehead. That hollow feeling, loss, I guess, was gutting my insides, same as a spoon clearing the inside of a pumpkin before it is carved.

It wasn't until he had gotten inside the van, until the headlights shone into my window and cast their glow onto my wall, that he rolled down the window and called to her. The car was in reverse and his foot was on the brake when he told her that the baby seat in the back of the van was his after all. His and his girlfriend's and their new baby's. A few minutes after that he was gone.

For the last three summers I've worked at Johnson's Nursery. Libby Wilson, who bought the nursery from the retired Johnson couple about five years ago, was an old friend of my mom's. Libby's father and Mom's father both worked at the same accounting firm when they were growing up, and Libby was one of the few people around who could contribute her own memories of my mother's parents, one of whom died when I was a baby, the other when I was two. Libby wore leather sandals and dresses with beads sewn on and had those kind of eyes that looked at you long and hard and made you feel like she knew things. She was one of my favorite people. If you saw the way she examined the underside of a leaf with her strong, kindly hands, you would understand why.

I really liked working at Johnson's Nursery. I liked transporting the seedlings from the steamy greenhouse to the big world. There were the flowers with their tender shoots, newly brave, as well as the vegetable starts, which seemed small and hardy and sure as little kids showing you their muscles. I liked unloading the shipments of phlox and impatiens, stinky geraniums and Chinese lanterns. I liked the heavy, floppy bags of peat moss and the sneezy smell of bark; losing myself in the rows of fruit trees and garden trellises; and turning the squeaky faucet handles of the overhead sprinklers, a complicated maze of thin iron pipe. I liked the customers with dirt under their fingernails and serious, satisfied expressions and humble questions of where to find the bonsai, the prickly pear cacti, the gourd seeds, the cure for an ailing magnolia.

That summer when school finally let out, I also liked being a two-minute walk from Travis Becker's house.

The next time I saw him after our first motorcycle ride, he was there on the lawn in the same place, as if he were waiting for me, as if he knew I would be coming back to him.

"Hello again," he said

"Hey. My favorite pathetic rich boy." I didn't even know who was talking. I was like one of those annoying kid toys that spoke when you pulled a string.

"I've been thinking about you," he said.

A feeling rose up, beginning from my toes. Thrill. "I

haven't thought of you at all," I said. Then I pulled the necklace out from my shirt and showed him. God, I felt powerful. I never felt that kind of power before. I understood why people liked it so much.

Travis stepped toward me. He combed his fingers through my hair, stopped his hand at the back of my neck and pulled me to him. He kissed me, hard. He sure was good at that.

"Let's ride," he said. His mouth was shiny from the kiss.

I got on behind him. When he accelerated this time, I put my cheek to his back and closed my eyes. I breathed deeply, imagined waves going in and out. The roar of the ocean was what I heard, I told myself. It was not wind that could send me flying, my body scraping to pieces along the asphalt, not the mechanical ugliness of an engine recklessly pushed to its limits. When we slowed, Travis reached behind him, rubbed his hand up and down my leg. It was a gentle touch. It felt like care and tenderness. But I might have been wrong.

I saw him every day after that, when I walked home from my job at Johnson's Nursery. He was usually outside, waiting for me—*waiting for me!*—or working on his motorcycle. We would just go for a ride, lie on that long, rolling grass, and talk. The first time I saw his friends there I started to walk on, but Travis yelled my way.

"What, are you ignoring me now?" he said. When I joined them, Travis whispered into my hair, "You should at least know my friends." He introduced me to Seth, a guy with gaunt smoker's cheeks who was trying to pretend that he didn't care about anything, and a girl named Courtney, blond, big hoop earrings and a shirt so small it could have fit a Barbie.

"Speaking of ignore," Courtney said. She put her hands on her hips.

"Oh, man," Seth muttered.

"Lover's quarrel coming," Travis said to me.

"He's been giving me the cold shoulder ever since I wouldn't kiss him because I had just put my *lip gloss* on."

"Am not," Seth said.

"He has. He's been barely speaking to me. I mean, I just put my *lip gloss* on." She looked at me and rolled her eyes. "God. Can you believe it?" She ran her hand down the length of her hair, fussed at the ends of it with her fingers.

"Uh uh," Seth said. Seth was a real conversationalist.

I shook my head as if Seth, the ghost figure, had just committed first-degree murder.

"I wouldn't have wanted to kiss her with that slimy shit on," Travis Becker said. "Might as well kiss a slab of raw fish."

"Tastes like candle wax," Seth said. To his credit, it was almost a full sentence.

"Right. And then what happens when we don't look good." Courtney gathered up her hair and let it fall again. Then she tucked a bit behind one ear.

"These two never stop fighting," Travis said.

"We do too," Courtney said. "We didn't argue at all

last night. We were trying to decide on *our song*. I was looking on MusicMadness.com. I really wanted 'She's Everything,' but Seth wanted 'Love Doesn't Die.'"

"Like hell," Seth said.

"Or 'Billy Doesn't Walk Here Anymore,' which is just stupid. It's not even a love song. It's about a guy who gets shot, for God's sake."

"Good song," Seth said.

Courtney rolled her eyes. "Do you guys have your song? Go look on MusicMadness.com." I knew this was stupid, looking for a song in the same way you might look for the best buy on car insurance. But I had another feeling, too. A little jolt of happiness that Courtney had assumed we were a couple. A little jolt of happiness that Travis Becker did not correct her.

There was a musical beeping. "My cell," Courtney said. She reached around to her hip pocket, where a little pink holder was attached. She took out this tiny phone, popped it to her ear. "Courtney," she sang. She held her hand over the mouthpiece. "It's Brandon for you," she said to Seth. "Call him on his own line," she said back into the phone. She hung up on Brandon, whoever he was, tucked the phone back into the pink holder on her hip. It had the unintended effect of reminding me of a law enforcement officer finishing up his job at the scene of a crime; notebook back in pocket.

"What did you do that for?" Seth said. Another phone started ringing. This time from the direction of a convertible sports car in the driveway. The license plate said MOMZ TOY.

"Let him call your cell. I hate everyone always calling on my cell."

Seth jogged to the car, swearing. Courtney followed him. "We gotta go meet Brandon anyway," she said.

I was glad they were leaving. I suddenly felt exhausted. When the people I knew spoke of cells, they usually were referring to the microscopic beings.

Travis walked them to the car. Seth started the engine, but I could still hear Courtney, even from where I stood. "Your friend sure is quiet," she said.

Here was the strange thing. I didn't desperately want to disintegrate on the spot, to disappear instantly from the shamed bucket of water thrown over the top of me. For some reason, this time I didn't feel any of those things. Instead I remembered my mother and Fowler talking one night, ranting, really, about a class full of Courtneys that came into the library that day. The lights of the library were dimmed, the doors locked for the night. Mom's purse sat on one chair, looking as if it were patiently waiting to leave. The surrounding quiet made me want to raise my fingers to my lips and shush their raised voices.

"Media monsters with junior platinum credit cards," my mother said.

"With parents who say yes to it all so they don't have to be bothered. Or trying to hang on to their own fleeting coolness through the kid. I saw this guy the other day with a BMW whose cell phone tinkled Pink Floyd's The Wall. *We don't need no ed-u-cation* played in goddamn tinkly bells. It's *over,* man."

"Anyone who spends a lot of time in a shopping mall is out to get someone, that's all I know," Mom said.

"Shallowness," Fowler said, "is a *disease*."

I watched Courtney in the passenger's seat of Momz Toy. She was a cotton-candy person, wearing a cell phone in a pink case on her butt, and earrings a small kid could hula hoop in, and she believed that even love was something you could manufacture and purchase with no money down and no interest for a year. Travis walked back toward me. I started to turn away. I wanted to go home. Too much cotton candy made me sick, and I was hit with the fact that these were not my people, and this was not my place. I didn't belong with a person who could afford gold-plated Jockeys. I like science cells. I had so much wanted to be behind those gates, but now it was like the time we went to Disneyland when I was small and the boat had gotten stuck on the Pirates of the Caribbean ride. They had to turn on the lights. *Zap*, magic gone. If shallowness was a disease, then it was probably contagious and Travis had it too.

Travis came toward me, put his arms around my waist. I pulled back from him. And then Travis Becker said the one thing that could make a difference. "I'm glad you're not like her," he said.

With that, I would have done anything for him. I did do anything for him.

"I've got a special place to take you to today," he said not long after.

I got on the back of his bike and we rode through town, got on the highway until we reached the exit for

Snoqualmie Falls. It was a beautiful day to see the falls, one of those days that shows off the Northwest in the best light, when the greens are so bright they hurt your eyes and everything looks clean and new. The falls, higher than Niagra, thunder down into a pool of misty white, and a lodge sits at their very edge, surrounded by firs and sheer rock. But we weren't going to see the falls themselves. Travis passed by the parking lot for the lookout, took a back road that curved to the other side of the Snoqualmie River. A pair of railroad tracks snaked alongside the river-bank. When Travis shut off his motorcycle you could hear the thunder of the falls, and just see their frothy white top.

"Is this a behind-the-scenes look?" I said.

"Oh, no. Believe me, you'll be right up close." Travis pointed down the empty railroad tracks.

"No trains come here. There haven't been trains here for a thousand years," I said. At least that's what it looked like. Weeds grew all around the tracks. Tall, dry grass grew between the railroad ties.

"Look for the light," Travis said. "Watch for it. And listen. You'll hear it before you see it. Let's walk."

I didn't believe him. I didn't believe any train would come down those old tracks, or maybe it did once every decade. And I didn't believe he'd be walking around here if trains did come regularly. The motorcycle was one thing, but train tracks, with their steep bank on one side and a hill on the other, were another.

We held hands, walked for a while. I balanced on the rails, one arm on Travis' shoulder, the other out straight for balance. Travis described the food at the fancy lodge restaurant. "Lobster bisque," he said. "Oh, God, it's fantastic. You'd love it. I gotta take you sometime. Roasted saddle of fallow venison. Amazing."

"Sounds like something you'd eat only if your emergency rations had been depleted," I said.

He ignored me. "And the breakfast. Of course you know it's world famous."

"Oh, of course, dahling," I said.

"Wait," he said.

"What?"

"Listen."

I stopped.

"It's coming," he said.

"Very funny," I said.

Travis held my waist and smiled.

"What a joker," I said. "Ha ha."

He put his finger to my lips.

"God, Travis!" He was right. A train was coming. I could hear it. The rhythmic, heavy pumping. Louder. Louder still. "Move, Travis!"

He held my waist as I tried to pull away.

"Tell me when you see the light."

"Oh, God, Travis. Oh, God, let me go. Let me go! I see it! Shit!"

He grabbed me, basically threw me to the bank by the side of the tracks. The ground was shaking under me. The noise was thunderous. I've never heard anything so loud. A huge tunnel of wind blew my hair into my mouth; the air clattered and shook and sounded like it was exploding. My fingers dug into the ground, holding on, clutching dirt and gravel.

"Open your eyes," Travis shouted.

"Oh, my God." I breathed.

"Open them!" Travis said. He was half lying on me. I opened my eyes. The train was behind my head. I could see it there, upside-down. The wheels turning so fast, the underneath of the train, the narrow slice of open air that was the hill and ground on the other side of the train. Travis held me against the clatter and rumbling. Rocks were literally jumping under my back. Finally the train passed. I turned my head where I lay, watched the metal railing of the caboose get smaller and smaller. I hoped I was still alive, but I wasn't sure.

Travis looked down at me. "Ruby," he said. I'd never heard anyone say my name like that before. He took my hand, held it against his heart. He put his own hand on mine. "Do you feel that?" he said. "Feel? They're beating together. They're beating in time."

I was fearless, because that's what he wanted me to be. Maybe it was better to be who he thought I was than who I thought I was. Anyway, all I know is that I played my part, which was to get on the back and hold on tight through everything we did. From that day onward, we went too fast, frighteningly fast. Travis Becker may have been a little crazy. But our hearts had beat in time when the ground shook underneath us, and that was what mattered.

Chapter 5

I started wearing that necklace all the time. It still had that bad feeling about it, that wrong feeling, but I wore it anyway. Like I said, I would do anything for Travis Becker. He dared me to stand on the white line in the middle of Cummings Road while he kissed me, and I did it, the long *baarrr!* of a panicked truck driver's horn in my ears for hours after Travis had taken my hand and we had run to the side of the road to safety. The horn in my ears, my heart in my throat. He had lifted me up, and I wrapped my legs around his waist as he twirled me in circles. *Oh, God!* I had screamed. *Ruby!* he had whooped in exhilaration, my name a battle cry.

And then one day Travis Becker came into Johnson's Nursery and challenged me to leave right then and there, to get on his bike and step away from the counter and the customer I was helping. Right as kind Libby Wilson watched with a box of vegetable seed packets in her arms. I did it. I just walked out of there. I decided I must be in love with Travis Becker. Something that horrible and wonderful had to be love, because what else could it be?

I was sure that wearing the necklace would make my mother ask questions, but this didn't happen. I was also sure she would hear from Libby about me abandoning work that day, but this didn't happen either. My mother, to whom I usually told everything and who noticed every-thing, was lost in the blue haze of grief. We avoided any talk of my father and this person now in the world who was related to Chip Jr. and me. I went one step further and avoided any thought of it. My mother seemed to have the opposite problem, the thought having moved in and taken over, same as she worried one of those musi-cians might. She was a figure in a thick fog, recognizable as a human form but fuzzy and appearing more distant than the physical reality.

Mom's lack of concentration was obvious; she put her car keys in the refrigerator and made us strange, haphaz-ard meals she didn't eat herself—a hot dog, a bowl of yogurt, an orange on a plate. Her eyes were red-rimmed, her face raw and bare in the way it gave away what she wouldn't say. Her whole personality seemed to be on that fragile edge of near tears. I would see the light on under her door until late into the night. I didn't want to add to her worries. My mother was one of those rare, truly good people. She still felt guilty about the one time she put her old baseball cap on one of those huge bags of dog food that was in the backseat so that she could drive in the carpool lane.

I was angry at her too. She should have been better at losing him. She'd had enough practice.

If I were Libby Wilson, I would have told on me, but she didn't. She only called me into her office, a small shed piled with books and paper and plant crates used as file storage, and had me sit in the big leather chair that was worn to a soft pale on the arms. Libby herself was a bit like that chair, big and worn with kindly wrinkles. As I sat there, shame crept around my insides and found a comfy spot, settling heavy in my chest.

"His face is too pretty," Libby said.

I folded my hands in my lap. I didn't know what to say to that. Of course she was right.

"And he wears his money like a cologne. Frankly, I don't like the smell." She poked her finger in the white rock of a cactus garden on her desk.

"I'm really sorry about what I did," I said.

"Ruby . . ." She sighed. "How do I say this?" She tilted her chin up, as if the words might be up there on the ceiling. "I once ditched my mother at a chemotherapy session for a man. I've hated myself every day for it since. I know how these things can make you wacky. He liked enchiladas, I liked enchiladas. I *hate* enchiladas. You know what I mean?"

"I promise it won't happen again."

"To tell you the truth, there are a thousand things I

want to say to you right now, but the most important is that, as you know, I never was lucky enough to have kids, but if I had a daughter I'd have wanted one like you," she said. "So, you know. Stay true."

For the first time since we'd met, I went straight home that day and didn't stop to see Travis. It was almost a relief to walk home a different way, behind the nursery, the way I used to go home from school with Sydney. Libby was right. The stuff with Travis was getting bigger than me, overtaking who I was. I felt strong and clear, proud of my stride, of this passing up. I felt like a burden had been lifted. When I got home, though, and was alone for a while again, that restless summer feeling filled me and I let go of Libby's words, sure as the string on a balloon. They drifted, like that released balloon, until they were too far to see. I regretted not stopping and seeing Travis. He gave me something I wanted, that much was clear. What I wasn't entirely sure about was what that something was. I didn't think having something you wanted could make you feel so bad.

That afternoon Chip Jr. came back from his best friend Oscar's house. He went there most summer days when Mom was at work since Oscar's mom was at home. If I used the word *baby-sat* he'd kill me. Chip Jr. met up with me in the kitchen. I was peeling an orange into the sink, staring out the window. I guess I was thinking with both guilt and pleasure about that too-pretty face of Travis's, his fine, silky blond hair. I was thinking about this dark pact we had seemed to make, this ugly and thrilling partnership of going too far. Lately I could think of nothing else. The hidden life I'd been leading took up a place in me, and I wondered what I had done before it was there, what I had thought about, how I filled that time. That no one knew about all of this gave me a delicious feeling of my own separateness. Like a CIA agent, I was creeping around doing huge things and no one even noticed. I wished I'd gone to see him.

"What are you looking at?" Chip Jr. asked.

"All of the holes Poe's dug in the backyard. It looks like the surface of the moon."

"We should stick a flag out there," he said.

I ate my orange. My fingers were covered with those mysterious white scales you get in the process, and I wiggled them at him.

"Mummy fingers," I said.

"I like apples better. No squirting." Talking about apples apparently inspired him to have one. He opened the refrigerator, tumbled the apples around in the bin until he found the one he wanted. He took a loud, crunching bite.

"You're supposed to wash it."

"I love pesticides. Yum, yum," he said.

He chomped on his apple, appeared to think awhile. We sat in silence, eating, until he finally spoke again. "What's the heaviest thing in the world?" Chip Jr. asked me, his cheeks puffed with apple.

"A blue whale." I slid in a slice of orange. I thought it was a science question.

"Nope. The *heaviest* thing."

"A skyscraper."

"Nope."

"A mountain."

"Uh uh."

"A mountain *range*."

"Nope."

I was getting tired of this game. "I give up."

He looked at me a real long time. He saw me, that I could tell. He saw me, and he wanted me to see me too. "A secret," he said. "A secret is the heaviest thing in the world."

That Chip Jr. was too smart for his own good.

"I like you with your hair wet. It looks brave," Travis Becker said.

"Brave?" We'd just gone for a swim in Marcy Lake. It had been my idea. We were sitting on the dock, at the same place we'd come when my father had been in town, that one right day.

"Sleek." He pulled my neck toward him and kissed me. "Mmm, baby," he said. I had my hand around his shoulder. It was wet and cool, though the sun was quickly trying to change that. His mouth was cold from the lake.

He moved his fingers over, tried to feel around my bikini top. I grabbed his hand and yanked it away. Then I put my shoulder into him and gave a shove, sending him crashing off the dock and into the water. He created quite a splash; a couple of boys about Chip Jr.'s age on the other end of the dock started to laugh. A minute later Travis's head bobbed up.

"Ha," I said to him. "That's what you get."

"You bad little girl," he shouted. He swam to the dock's edge and pulled himself up. Water dripped off him; his swimsuit, fifties surfer shorts with pineapples and palm trees, clung to him as if they'd had a sudden fright and were too scared to let go.

"Served you right," I said.

He grabbed me in revenge and I shrieked and then went flying. I held my nose just in time so I didn't get water in it, and a moment later saw an infusion of bubbles underwater next to me where Travis had jumped back in. I was trying to rise, swimming broad strokes upward, and I could see Travis swimming toward me, a flash of pineapple brightness in the murky water, his hair floating out all seaweed-like.

He took hold of my arm, held me down. His face was whitish underwater, bloated with air, and his hair was still doing a witch-doctor dance. I struggled to be free. I never liked those kinds of water games.

There was a tangle of limbs as I thrashed against him. This wasn't fun anymore. I wanted him to let go. I fought for the surface. I whacked his arm, hard, but he held fast.

He smiled at me, a crooked smile, and I kicked at him so he could know that I wasn't playing anymore. I needed air. I began to panic. I grabbed his fingers and tried to peel them off me, but he just swam there very calmly and waited. Three seconds, five, ten, as I flung and fought, and then he finally released his hand and I shot to the surface, gasping.

"Travis!" I was ready to . . . I don't know what. Scream, leave him, never see him again. God damn it, he scared me. He really scared me, holding me down against my will.

"You didn't know I was on swim team," he said cheerfully.

"Don't you ever . . ." I breathed.

"Don't you ever what?" He treaded water, smiling. "You're beautiful when you're mad, did you know that?"

I swam to the edge of the dock. As my fingers grasped the edge, I decided to forgive him. It wasn't just the compliment, though it's true that compliments can give something far and beyond what the giver intended. They can have the strength of a medieval tonic, a transforming magic that can take on a life of its own. All you need is the right combination of ingredients—need, uncertainty, a hole to fill and a believable wizard to hand over the bubbling liquid. But it wasn't just the compliment. If I let the feelings I had under the water rise to the surface and stay there, if I had *listened*, I'd be making a choice about what was going to happen next. I decided that Travis Becker had just been playing. He hadn't realized what he was doing when he held my head under that long. I made a little edit of him, turning him to fiction. It was easier than you'd think.

After we dried off, we left the dock and sat for a while on the grass in the shade of the trees—firs, evergreens, one stray maple with leaves big as the hand of a giant. My fear was retreating, though a piece of it sat in my stomach, like the rude party guest who stays long after everyone else has gone home. The lake spread before us, twinkly in the late afternoon sun. A cluster of gnats gathered in one spot for a gnat conference, and several ducks snoozed on the shore, their bills tucked snug into their sides. We kissed for a while. Maybe it was the setting, that water with its darts of bright light, looking so hopeful and expectant that made me want to give Travis Becker another chance to be what I hoped he could be. I stopped kissing him, told him about my family, my father, the way I felt watching the paragliders soar around Moon Point. I wanted him to know me, to see my thoughts. He listened with patience or interest, I wasn't quite sure. He leaned back on his elbows and ran his fingers across the lawn.

I plucked a dandelion from the grass, blew the puff of white seeds in the air. I watched them drift, slow and beautiful in their randomness. Several arced and swirled and were drawn to Travis Becker, landing gently in his hair, which was made even more light and golden by the sun and water. He had a radiance that even nature noticed and wanted to be close to.

Travis put his hand to his head. "I got that shit all in my hair," he said.

"My God," my mother said. "What next?" I had expected her to scream and swear, but all she did was stare at the hole with something like amazement. And it really was amazing that a dog that small could cause so much damage.

"It was my fault, too," she said, in the way that good people do. In her distracted state, my mother had forgotten to let Poe out of the kitchen, where he slept at night, to the backyard, where he spent the day. I realized something was wrong right when I got home that afternoon. I heard Poe scratching at the sliding door of the kitchen and the jingling of his tags, and then, of course, there was the smell, too huge and overwhelming not to be disastrous.

I flung open the door, already knowing to expect the worst. Maybe my imagination is not very good, because even though I thought I was expecting the worst, the truth shocked me. There was a long hole in the wall, a gash so deep it had exposed pipe. Scratch marks on the wallpaper indicated that Poe had dug at the wall with his nails until a hole began. After that, it had probably been easy to chew and scrape the blocks of drywall away. The floor was littered with plaster chunks and dust, shreds and bits of wallpaper. He had apparently had some fun with a pair of Chip Jr.'s socks that had been left in the kitchen as well; I could see part of an athletic stripe under the refrigerator; another bit of sock toe had dropped in his water bowl and was floating like a wonton in soup.

Plaster dust was everywhere; small guilty dog prints were set around in it. Poe himself bounded on my legs with the sheer joy of a released prison inmate. From the look of it, he had already tried to dig himself out of his cell with his spoon. Maybe he had been like a claustrophobic in a stuck elevator, panicked for space and air and freedom. Then again, maybe he had just had the best day in his destructive little life.

Poe stopped jumping at my legs. He walked around the rubble and sniffed at things as if the whole thing was a surprise to him too.

"Man, are you in trouble," I said to him.

Chip Jr. and I decided it would be best to call Mom ahead of time to warn her. We cleaned up. Let me tell you, that plaster dust gets everywhere. There was even some in the coffeepot on the counter. By the time Mom came home, we had fixed everything except that gash, of course. The hole traveled halfway down the kitchen wall, ankle level.

I held Poe in my arms as my mother surveyed the damage. I thought for sure his physical safety would be in danger. I put my nose into his fur. He smelled of his own dog smell; a mixture of hay and wet carpet. "I'm just . . . I'm not thinking lately," Mom said. She rubbed her forehead with one hand. Wisps of her hair were held back in a barrette, which looked inappropriately cheerful as she bent her head down.

I wanted her to yell. I wanted her face to turn red with fury. I wanted to hear her shriek *Youdumbassdog!*, her eyes flashing and her voice rising to embarrassing volumes. But instead she did the worst thing. She started to cry. She sat down at the kitchen table, put her head down on one arm and sobbed. Her shoulders rocked up and down. Chip Jr. had left the Lucky Charms out from breakfast; they sat in the middle of the table, bright and unscathed from Poe's rampage. Chip Jr., at a loss at what to do, put them back in the cupboard. I set Poe down, held my arm around my mother's shoulders, which heaved under my hand.

Poe trotted over to the hole, stuck his head in. From behind, in spite of everything, he managed to look both proud and curious.

I told my mother I was going out that night to a late movie with Sydney. It was a stupid, reckless lie. Sydney might appear at any time, dropping by to see me, or driving up alone to her own house. Sometimes lies, especially the bad ones, are like flares thrown out onto the street; meant as a warning of the accident that is up ahead.

We had never gone out in the evening before, Travis and I. He offered to come pick me up but I said no. We met at the Yellow Submarine and shared a sandwich. "So when are you going to tell me what we're doing tonight?" I asked. He had told me that he had a surprise for me. In fact, he'd been wearing a smug, pleased expression since we arrived; he wore it right that moment as he licked the bit of mustard from the corner of his mouth. That night, his clothes were very fifties tennis club. He wore madras shorts and had his hair combed to one side.

"Okay. A clue. Let's just say we're going to the house of some old friends of mine."

"So, what, are they having a party?"

"No. Let's just say it will be a surprise for them. Trust me."

I didn't like the sound of this or the way Travis said it. Satisfaction with an edge. He had taken too many napkins from the dispenser, and when we left they sat there in a big, guilty clump on the table.

We rode into Seattle, across the Lake Washington Floating Bridge, on Travis's motorcycle. The floating bridge separates Seattle and its patchwork quilt of suburbs, Nine Mile Falls being one of them. The bridge is flat, like a single long air mattress lying somehow still on choppy water. There was a sudden coldness as we crossed over; I could feel it through my clothes, and the lamppost light made the lake look black and stern. I tucked my hands into the pockets of Travis's jacket and was glad for my own coat. By the time we got there to meet Travis's friends, my hair was going to look like a chick's just out of the egg.

Travis exited, and I was grateful for the warmth that the slowed speed brought. A few turns landed us in an obviously expensive area of the city, with a view of the lake and the glittering lights of the east side, where we'd just come from. The houses were large and the kind of old that meant money; columned and eaved, with windows of antique etched glass, entryways guarded by pairs of stone lions, gardens that would make Libby drool, tucked behind hedges trimmed sharply as an old man's crew cut. You wanted to run your hand along them.

As we passed a three-story white Georgian-style house on a wide corner, Travis slowed, stopped, and cut the engine. He lifted the faceplate of his helmet. "That's where we're going," he said. I unstrapped my helmet. Steps led to a porch with two huge columns and enormous flowerpots of cone-shaped juniper topiary on either side of the door. The porch light was on, but the house looked dark. You could hear the *breep-breep* of crickets in the night.

"It doesn't look like anyone is home," I said. Which was a relief, to tell you the truth. I was wearing jeans, a tank top, and my denim jacket, and it suddenly seemed hugely lacking. People had worn ball gowns in that house, I was sure. The only one who ever wore a ball gown in our house was this doll my grandmother McQueen had given me when I was three. I named the doll Lieutenant, because I heard the word somewhere and thought it was beautiful. Lieutenant was in the back of the closet somewhere, still overdressed but now shoeless and wild-haired, as if the party had been a rough one.

Travis didn't answer. "I used to live on this street," he said. "The brick one."

"Over there?" Jeez, it was huge and serious as a school for wayward boys. Ivy crept up the walls. "So what's it have, a hundred rooms?"

"Well, the first story is mostly all living room."

"Oh," I said. "Wow." That house had turned me into the monosyllabled Seth.

"My room was up top. Second and third windows. They thought I wouldn't sneak out that way."

"Why did you move?"

"Dangerous neighborhood." Travis grinned. "People were always getting robbed."

"Oh, it looks real dangerous," I said. The only sound beside the crickets was the buzz of the streetlights, and the only one who looked capable of harm was this orange cat across the street, his shoulders hunched up in tough-guy fashion, walking the loose, leisured walk of one looking for trouble.

"And my mother wanted a pool. You know, seeing that it rains here ten months of the year."

Travis balanced the bike, held one hand out to me to help me off. He rolled the bike up onto its stand. I looked again at the dark house. It was late and there didn't seem to be any movement inside.

"Travis, I really don't think anyone is home."

"Shhh, will you? You'll ruin the surprise." Travis strapped our helmets to the bike. I had no desire to wake these people by ringing the doorbell, let alone force a visit on them at this hour. They would have to run around looking for their smoking jackets and feathered slippers, unlike Mom, who once answered the door for the FedEx guy in her flannel pajama pants and her I ESCAPED ALCATRAZ T-shirt that Fowler brought back from his trip to San Francisco.

"Where are you going?"

"Just follow me. And, Jesus, keep it down."

"Why don't you just go to the door?"

"Come *on*."

Instead of going up the steps to the house, Travis was headed around the corner of the street. He reached his hand up to the top of the fence at the property's edge, felt around with his fingers, and then shoved a gate open with one shoulder.

"Travis." That seed of nerves, that ugly dread, was knocking around my insides again.

"I said it's okay. Now would you hurry up? Shit. They're expecting us." I followed him inside the gate, and he shut it behind us. My toe caught on a stepping-stone; we were standing on a garden walkway. It was hard to see in the darkness; the streetlight was blocked by a huge lilac tree, making it glow with a giant halo. I could see the outlines of its drooping blooms, and then as my eyes adjusted I also saw wide stone steps surrounded by a lay-ered garden. I could see the spindly outlines of roses, and I could smell lavender bushes and the heavy grandma-perfume sweetness of hyacinth.

We stepped around a white iron table and chairs, round-backed with intricate cut designs that looked as if actually sitting on them for any length of time would be a third world torture. Travis approached a set of French doors, put his hand around the knob.

"What are you doing? Travis!"

"Ruby! I know these people. You'd think I was *break-ing in*." He stuck his hand in one pocket, pulled out a key ring. "Would I have a key to the place if I didn't know them real well? Is it breaking in if you have a key?"

Travis held up the key ring to the small amount of

available light from the street and looked through the keys. There were a lot of them, labeled with tiny squares of masking tape. I looked down; a pair of women's tennis shoes sat outside the door. I was beginning to be scared out there in the dark, in this strange place that belonged to the woman with the tennis shoes and not me. "How many people give you their keys?" I asked.

"Here it is." He held up the key, stuck it in the knob and turned. Cold air hit my face. These people were not home. These people hadn't been home for a while. Travis took off his shoes. "Will you get in here?"

"Travis, no. I don't know what you're doing, but these people are not home." The ugly seed was building to panic. I felt the way I did that day in the water, when he held me under. I needed air. I heard the crickets chirping and nothing else; there was only silence and that cold, empty air. Suddenly my stomach felt sick with the fluttery wings of fear.

"I'm not going in there."

"Shit, I didn't think you of all people would be this skittish." His voice softened. "Ruby, relax." He held his hand out to me, and I took it. He pulled me gently inside. "I know they aren't here. They're on vacation, all right? I'm feeding their cats, for Christ's sake."

Cats. My heart was still pounding, questioning whether it was safe to slow down or not. "You said we were going to see your friends."

"I did not. I said we were going to their house. Can we talk about this inside, please?" I took off my shoes, same as Travis, and went in.

I started to feel foolish. I actually did. And relieved, too. "I'm sorry, Travis," I said. The tile floor was cold on my feet. The whole place felt refrigerated. It smelled unfamiliar—floral, old wood, some kind of lemony furniture polish. I followed him through the kitchen to an antique-filled living room dominated by a marble fireplace. The streetlights shining through the filmy drapes made everything glow an eerie yellow. There was a large Oriental rug, botanical prints hung by wide, satiny bows, dishes held face-out on display on the mantel.

"Maybe you'd better wait here," he said. "Have a seat. Unless you want to try out one of the beds." He passed his hand over the butt of my jeans.

"I'm sure they would really appreciate that," I said. I sat down on the flowered couch strewn with embroidered pillows, looked over my shoulder as Travis climbed the staircase, with its wide, curved banister polished to a high shine. I kept my mouth shut, looked at the candy dish on the coffee table, which was filled with candies wrapped in pink and purple and gold foil, twisted on the ends. A tall statue of a heron was pointed toward the window, his view temporarily impaired by the closed drapes. You wondered where people who lived in houses like this kept their junk mail and spare shoelaces and batteries they were mostly sure worked.

Framed photos sat on a desk with thin, curved legs at the side of the room. I squinted at them in the dim yellow light—the studio shot with posed formal smiles, the woman who must have owned the tennis shoes, with her gray-blond hair and long skirt, her silver-headed husband, two stick-thin boys that looked close enough alike to be twins, and a little girl in a fancy dress that looked scratchy, all set against a velvety drape. There were several others too: the boys with their father and someone else, in ski attire, goggles on their heads; an elderly couple, the man stooped and frail, the woman sitting on a garden bench and holding a baby. I sat in these nice people's house, these nice people with their candy dishes and ski vacations and tennis shoes dirty from the garden, wondering how they would feel knowing a stranger was sitting on their couch. And then something else occurred to me. That dimness that made it hard to see the pictures clearly . . . Travis had not turned on a light when he had come in.

I couldn't hear Travis upstairs. Unlike my own house, where you could hear someone clearing their throat in the next room (actually, you could probably even hear someone *thinking* about clearing their throat), this house was so huge and solid that I could not hear his footsteps above me. The only thing I could hear was the ticking of the clock that sat on the mantle in front of me, a sound that made me uneasy in the silence and dark. *Tock, tock, tock.*

What had Travis said about coming here? My mind replayed bits of conversation, stopped at a memory. He had said something about surprising these people. If they knew he was coming, how would this be possible? I felt sick again, and I stood. I didn't want to be sitting on these people's couch, leaning my back against embroidered pillows that maybe the lady on the garden bench had lovingly stitched.

"Travis?" I called up the stairs. In the silence my voice sounded as if it could break something. I paced around in my socks, rubbed my hands together against the cold. Through the etched glass panes on either side of the front door, I could see the lights of the east side across the lake, though the glass had split the beams into fuzzy, abstract prisms. Five minutes later, according to the mantle clock—hours and hours, according to the feeling in my chest—Travis came downstairs.

"How are the cats?" I asked. Travis took my face in his hands and kissed me. He pulled me down until I was on top of him on the stairs.

"Did I ever tell you how beautiful you are?" he said. I wasn't going to kiss him there, in that empty house with the creepy ticking clock. I struggled to stand. I wanted out of there.

"The cats," I said.

"You know there are no cats."

"God damn it, Travis." Panic and fear, thundering now. "What are you talking about? What are you saying?"

Travis rose from his place on the stairs. He stood in the entryway, touched the top of a music box that was on a table. He turned it upside-down, twisted the tiny bar that turned it on. "Don't touch that. What are you doing here? What are we doing here, Travis?"

Some song I didn't know played sweetly from the

music box. "You know what we're doing here." He stuck a hand into one of his jacket pockets and pulled out a clump of jewelry—gold, silver, pendants, and watches.

"Shit, Travis. Oh, shit."

I couldn't breathe. I knew what I was seeing, but my brain couldn't even wrap itself around it. And then, an arc of headlights through the curtains filled the living room.

"Oh, God," I said. I grabbed his arm. I had the urge to run, but my body had frozen. The music box was still playing.

"Just stay there," Travis said calmly. "It's probably just someone turning around." But his face looked afraid. For the first time I saw the tight line of fear across his jawline.

We waited. No doorbell or footsteps. "See?" Travis said. "Just someone turning around. No big deal."

I ran to the back door, the way we came, tried to put my shoes back on but my hands were shaking too badly. Travis went to the refrigerator, modern black and chrome, shiny. He opened the door. The light shined on his satisfied face; he took a can of Diet Coke, cracked the top, and took a drink.

I shivered the whole way back over the bridge. I trembled as if I were in the throes of a fever. All the way there I'd had to hold on to Travis Becker on that motorcycle. My hands felt guilty and disgusted, certainly not like my regular hands. These hands were too small to handle what had just happened.

I got in my mother's car where I'd left it. Travis Becker

walked to my window, knocked on the glass. I rolled it down and he ducked his head into the car. "I like the pissed-off act," he said. Which was a good thing, because right then I started to roll up my window with his head still in it. He made a little squeak of surprise, then turned his head sideways and released himself before my furious rolling marred his beautiful, sleek neck. My own neck still wore that necklace he had given me; I was suddenly aware of its ugly weight. I grabbed it and yanked, and the gold cut across my skin but I didn't care. I pulled it until it lay limp in my hand, and I drove off still clutching it. In the rearview mirror I could see Travis Becker standing in streetlight. His expression was so satisfied we might have just become lovers.

There is nothing that can make you feel quite as guilty as walking into a quiet house full of sleeping people, people who are dreaming gentle dreams and who don't know enough to suspect you of wrongdoing. Even the buzz of the refrigerator was innocent enough to make me hate myself. I took off my shoes by the door, walked in bare feet across the floor. Maybe I was getting good at creeping around still houses.

On the way home I had stopped by the side of Cummings Road on a weedy patch thick with blackberry brambles and thistles and wide, furry dandelion leaves. The necklace was limp as a dead body in my hands, and I looked around to make sure no one saw as I flung it deep into the prickly branches. It might have been a

Valentine's Day gift bought by a man who'd gotten off early from work one day and looked carefully through glass shelves, and a sick knot of disgust filled me at the thought that it would lie there in the dirt, eventually covered by rotted blackberries and dry leaves, snow, and mud. I was glad it was gone, though.

There was still a light on, shining under the door of my mother's bedroom. I set my ear against the door, but there was no sound. I turned the knob slowly so as not to make any noise, and opened the door. My mother lay asleep on top of the bed, her glasses askew, giving one side of her forehead twenty-twenty vision. Her hand rested on the top of a book, which was facedown on her lap. It must have been a good one—it was open not quite halfway, and I knew that in the last few weeks she hadn't been able to read anything, to me a more frightening sign of her depression than almost anything else. I turned my head sideways to read the title: *Life Times Two* by Charles Whitney. I eased it from her hand. My eyes caught on the words.

> *I saw her twice that day, the woman I will call Rose, because that's what she was to me. Beautiful, perfect, eventually brutal in protecting her gentle self against my own destructive tendencies. It was on August 14, 1945, V.J. Day, amidst riotous celebration on the streets of New York City that I saw that flash of the crimson skirt that caught my eye in the crowd. It was a cinema moment—I saw the flash of*

the skirt, looked up. She turned and looked over her shoulder at me. With that look, something had been decided. My whole life, though I didn't know it then. I dropped my cigarette, ground it into the street with the toe of my shoe. A definite action was called for, some final punctuation, and that was the most definite action I could think of. Then she turned and disappeared into the crowd.

I saved Mom's place by folding in the book jacket flap inside the cover. I carefully removed her glasses from her head. If she woke right then, her eyes would only see the me she thought she knew, not the me I was.

My mother stirred. "Ruby?" she said sleepily.

"Shhh," I said.

I pulled the quilt over my mother and then I turned out the light.

Chapter 6

"Ruby, we don't do that here," Joe Davis said. He was wearing his shorts with all of the pockets again, and a Sea World T-shirt with a leaping whale on the front.

"What do you mean you don't do that here? You don't have one of those little boxes you go in and we can talk through the window?"

"Catholics do that."

"Oh." We sat in Joe Davis's office, where I'd gone the next day after I'd finished work at Johnson's Nursery. I'd never been there before. I'd expected his office to look, I don't know, more churchlike. He had a desk that appeared to be used only to stack things on, as well as two worn chairs and a coffee table, an ugly gray filing cabinet with a fishbowl on top, with one fish swimming around a fake castle in water that should be changed. The place was full of books, not only stacked on the desk but also in shelves along the wall. All kinds of books, too. Not just religious-looking ones, but books on baseball and oceans and sea kayaking, slim books of poetry, mysteries. A mug of tea sat on the coffee table, with the tea bag still inside and the string draped over the edge, and there was a pencil cup with only one pencil and a large chunk of coral, white and wavy. The only evidence that I was in a minister's office was the crucifix over the door and a picture of a sad-faced Jesus in a flowing white robe and sandals. Even this was hung with a picture of a desert and one of the Golden Gate Bridge at sunset. Why there were never any cheerier pictures of Jesus I'll never know. I realize he had a rough life, but it didn't send the rest of us a very good message about the joys of living, if you ask me.

"I'm sorry to disappoint you," Joe Davis said. He really did look sorry, too. "You don't have to confess, though. You could just tell me what's on your mind."

"I liked the idea of the box," I said.

"I could hide behind my desk." Joe Davis leaped up. He went behind his desk, ducked behind a particularly large stack of books. "How's that?" His voice was a little muffled.

I laughed. "You're going to knock those over."

I saw a hand rise up, slap down on top of the books to hold them down. "Okay, shoot," he said.

I laughed again. His head poked up over the books. "I'm wai-ting," he sang in a pretend-annoyed fashion. "Actually, is it all right if I come back and sit down? My knees hurt with that crouching."

"I suppose so," I said. Joe Davis sat down again. He folded his hands over his chest as if he'd just eaten a good meal and was now waiting for the movie to start. It looked like he would wait there a long time, so I told him about Travis. I told him what had happened the night before. I told him that there were big pieces of me that thought I was in love with Travis Becker. Those pieces of me didn't want to give up Travis. I avoided the eyes of the sad-faced Jesus. He looked very disappointed in me. I wished he had a Sea World T-shirt on too.

"Wow," Joe Davis said when I finished. "That's a lot to deal with, all right. I can see you are feeling pretty bad about it."

His sympathy made a lump rise in my throat and my eyes grow hot with tears. "Aren't you supposed to make me do something, like say a bunch of prayers?"

"I'm sorry, Ruby," he said.

"Don't tell me. Catholics again?"

"Yep. Anyways, I'm thinking the thing you should do is talk to your mom about this."

"I can't."

"Why not?"

I knew he was in love with my mother. I didn't want to betray her by giving him negative information. Explaining why I couldn't talk to her right now would be like telling him that she laughed at the religious channels and couldn't make a fried egg to save her life and always left it to someone else to put a new roll of toilet paper on. Something he should have to find out at least after a few dates.

I thought for a while. I remembered something I once heard about minister-patient confidentiality, or something like that.

"This stays between us, right?" I asked.

"Absolutely."

"She's broken right now," I said. "Everything is in pieces. Even the kitchen is in pieces. Our dog chewed a big hole in the wall."

Joe Davis winced in empathy. He crossed one leg over the other. He wore sandals, too. Maybe good men could be found in sandal-like shoes.

"I can't give her anything else in pieces," I said.

"Things come apart before they can be put back together again."

"What do you think I should do?"

Joe Davis leaned forward, elbow on one knee, and scratched his neck. "You know what I've learned in this job? The people who ask for advice are the ones who already know what they should do."

"I should go to Sea World," I said. He looked at me like I was crazy, so I pointed to his T-shirt. I was suddenly in the mood for a little humor after dropping that package at Joe Davis's feet.

Joe lifted one fist in the air. "Shamu power," he said.

"I'd have a whale of a good time," I said.

Joe Davis groaned, threw his head back as if in pain. "I love Sea World," he said. "But the one thing that bothers me is that they sell fish and chips there."

"Eek," I said.

Then Joe Davis got serious again. He looked at me. "Ruby? Here's the thing. About this guy. Sometimes we are so convinced someone is throwing us a life preserver that we don't notice that what they are actually doing is drowning us."

I remembered that day at Marcy Lake, Travis's hand clutching my wrist, my tight lungs, his crooked smile under that green, murky water. Joe Davis was more accurate than he even realized.

I tossed him some brave words. I owed him something, I guess, for being kind to me. "It's a good thing I'm a strong swimmer," I said. I didn't believe it; I doubt he did either. You know when your own mind means business, and when it is only saying what it thinks it should.

When I left the church office I noticed the sign. DOG IS MAN'S BEST FRIEND. It looked like Joe Davis was having a little fun with the unknown sign changer.

On the way home, I stopped to watch the paragliders. I wanted to see their bravery and their rightness. And that day was a whale-themed day, because to my surprise, for the first time ever, I saw him. The *I Love Potholes* guy with the whale van. He wore shorts and sandals, a T-shirt emblazoned with a heart with wings, the logo of the paragliding club. He wasn't much older than I was, and had rough, tumbled, curly hair, the start of a beard. He was taking his backpack from the van and caught me looking his way.

"You going up?" he asked.

"Just watching," I said. I figured I owed him an explanation for my staring. "I've always liked your van."

"Yeah?" He smiled. "Then you've got to see this." He set his pack down, leaned inside the driver's seat. "Keep watching," he called.

I watched the whale. A spurt of water came from its spout. More like a dribble really. A drool, dripping down the side. The whale-van guy emerged again. "Isn't that lame?" he said, his eyes happy.

"Oh, jeez. Pathetic," I said. "That is so bad."

"I know it. You ever been up?" He nodded his chin toward the mountain.

"No," I said.

"Oh, you've got to. See that spot up there? The landing?" I nodded. "From up above it looks like the mountain has a bald spot."

"Hair Club for Men," I said.

"Exactly," he said.

He picked up his pack and waved, and after a while I headed off. My mom was home early that day; when I got home she was already in the kitchen making dinner. She was walking around in her bare feet and cutoffs, with an open book in one hand that she was reading as she stirred a pot of spaghetti sauce. Chip Jr. had already come home from Oscar's house. He was creating what looked like the Empire State Building on the kitchen table with sticks of spaghetti. Poe didn't even say hello. His focus was on Mom and anything she might drop as she cooked; his eyes were glued to her hands as if he were under a hypnotic spell.

I barely got a hello from Mom either. "Good book, huh?" I asked. It was the same one I had seen in her room a few days before—*Life Times Two*, by Charles Whitney, thick enough to have her engrossed and to cause her fingers to splay like duck feet with the effort of holding it open.

"Mmm hmm." She stopped stirring the sauce, moved to the counter where she'd begun making the salad. Poe trotted after her, his eyes still never leaving her hands and their amazing possibilities. My mother took some torn lettuce leaves from the salad spinner and dropped them into the salad bowl, still reading. Her aim gradually wavered until she was missing the bowl completely and a little pyramid of lettuce greens was rising on the kitchen counter. This was better than TV.

"Mom," Chip Jr. said.

She looked up. "What? Oh, shit." She grabbed the leaves and shoved them in the bowl with irritation, as if they had willfully misbehaved. One fell on the floor, to Poe's great delight; he jumped up and trotted over to sniff it. Then he sat back down and looked up again in wait. The lettuce leaf looked limp and rejected. It should have. That dog would eat underwear, for God's sake.

"Let me help you," I said to Mom. I could see the spaghetti sauce rising slowly to the edge of the pan, bubbling all lavalike. I caught its handle just in time. It was one of my mother's biggest problems, the way she immersed herself in something to the exclusion of everything else. She could move from world to world, and it was tough trying to find the secret door to wherever she was.

"Time to put this down," she said, stating the obvious. It was too bad in a way. I was looking forward to actually eating and seeing how she was going to manage reading while spaghetti slapped all over her chin. "You," she said to me, as if she only now noticed I was there. "I need to talk to you." She put the cover flap inside the book and set it down, away from the possible splatterings from the stove. My stomach flipped. Oh, God. Nerves tightened my throat.

"Oh, jeez, Poe," Chip Jr. said. He waved his hand back and forth, fanning the air. Poe continued to stare up at Mom as if nothing had happened.

"Dog, you were not named for the poet and short story writer and forefather of the modern mystery," my mother said down to him. "You were actually named for Sir Potent Fart, king of the exiled canines."

It was the first joke I'd heard her make since my father's last visit. Jokes, a regular dinner, reading—my mother was returning to us again.

She strained the spaghetti, steam rising in a sudden gust, and slid some onto our plates. She ladled the sauce on, dropped the heel of bread pretend-accidentally to Poe, who brought his prize to the living room, where he could spread the crumbs all over the carpet. I waited. I was making brave efforts to remind the sick feeling that there were lots of things she could want to talk to me about. Maybe I'd forgotten to do something she asked.

Water the garden? Get gas in the car? Not break into someone's house in the middle of the night while Travis Becker took their jewelry?

Mom ate for a while, looking down at her plate. As the silence grew, I was sure she would not be struggling with words if I had left the gas tank empty or didn't water the garden. Outside, someone was mowing their lawn. Chip Jr. was doing an apparent pasta science experiment. On the first mouthful, he rolled up the spaghetti as high as he could around the fork and up the handle. On his second bite, he took a single strand between his lips and inhaled, until the end of it finally whipped past his lips like the back car of the Tornado Train Roller Coaster at the Gold Nugget Amusement Park.

"Ruby," my mother said finally. "About the other night."

"Uh oh," Chip Jr. said.

"What night?" I said. I was giving her every opportunity to let this be about something else. Even I could tell that my voice was too cheery.

The lawn mower sound stopped right then. The room was suddenly too quiet. I studied my tangle of spaghetti. Poe was back. He sat by my chair and panted, *Heh heh heh*. I didn't know what he thought was so funny.

"The night you went to the movies with Sydney."

"Oh, right," I said.

"She called over here after you left, saying they ordered a pizza. They asked if you wanted to come over."

I didn't say anything. I just kept looking at that

spaghetti, hoping it might do something to save the day. It was one of those times where you just don't understand yourself and how you got into such a mess. I was having a lot of those moments lately. The real me had gone off on vacation somewhere and I was being house-sat by someone who had wild parties and smoked in bed.

"Is this about a boy?" my mother said. I guess she thought that most troubles had love at the heart of them. She was probably right.

"Yes," I said.

"I knew it," Chip Jr. said.

"Oh, Ruby," my mother sighed. "You know when you start to lie about something that you are in territory where someone is going to get hurt. If you need that lie, you've stepped over the line onto dangerous ground."

"I know," I said. I did know, too.

"Who is he?"

"That rich guy that lives in the castle," Chip Jr. said.

"One of the Becker boys?" my mother said.

"How do you know?" I glared at Chip Jr.

"Oscar's brother saw you throw him in Marcy Lake."

"Spy," I said. Did everyone have to know your business?

"Yeah, right," Chip Jr. said. "This is actually a hidden camera." He held up his bread roll.

"Shut up," I said.

"And this is a miniature microphone." He held up a cherry tomato from the salad. He spoke into it. "Yep, she's here," he said.

I shoved back my chair. I shoved a little too hard; it fell over with a crack and Poe did a little sideways scurry from the fright. I don't know why I was so angry. I went to my room. I slammed the door. I could hear the framed pictures on the other side of the wall—overly large school photos of Chip Jr. and me, caught at our height of ugliness, with teeth that looked too big for our faces and glazed expressions of goofiness—slide off-kilter. I sat with my back to the door. My mother knocked a second later, as I knew she would. All of this was familiar from those Disney movies where a Teenager Makes a Scene. I guess that's where I learned what to do.

Mom rattled the doorknob. Then she gave up. I could hear her slide her back down the door, and I knew she was there, sitting on the other side of it. She was quiet for a long time, and then her muffled voice came through the door, right at my own ear level.

"Is he a nice boy?" she asked.

"No," I answered truthfully.

"So I guess you're trying not to see him anymore," she said. "At least I hope."

"Right," I said.

She didn't talk for a long time after that, so long that I thought maybe she'd gotten up and left. I stayed where I was. My thoughts had to catch up to the rest of me. I was almost getting sleepy when I heard the soft *flip flip flip* of playing cards being snapped down.

"Hit me," I heard Chip Jr. say.

I got up and looked into the hall. My mother and

Chip Jr. were both outside my door, holding a fan of cards. My mother lay on her side, her head propped up with one hand and her legs stretched out, and Chip Jr. sat cross-legged. Poe was lying sphinxlike, chewing someone's sock.

"He can see your cards from there," I warned Mom.

"Cannot. Wanna play?" Chip Jr. asked.

I sat down in their circle. They reshuffled for me and started again. This was not supposed to be how the Teenager Makes a Scene was supposed to go. Then again, my mother never watched much television.

"Man, this hand stinks," she said.

"I've been doing some thinking," my mother said in the car as she drove me to work. Since she asked me about Travis Becker, she'd been treating me like a sick child, studying my face as if looking for signs of fever and hovering in my orbit as if her presence was the one thing that was keeping me well.

"If it's about Travis Becker, I don't really want to talk about it," I said.

She sneaked a quick look at me; as I've said, you've got to keep your eyes on Cummings Road when you're driving it. Her look was easy to read—she couldn't understand, we'd always been able to talk, she was hurt. Mothers can give all of that to you in one brief look. There wasn't much to understand, really. I didn't want to talk because I had things to hide. Secrets are the ultimate hiding place.

We passed the open corner where different merchants brought their products. That day, it was fresh-picked cherries, set out in baskets on a card table. A woman in a sun hat and a tank top and shorts sat on a folding chair. She read a book, head down, as those cherries baked in the already warm sun. Her white, jiggly arms would turn bright red by noon if she wasn't careful. When we passed the Becker estate, I forced myself not to look.

"Listen," Mom said. "I know these things are hard. If you really don't want to see this boy anymore, then it's best to keep busy, is all I was going to say. When you get time on your hands, that's when your mind takes advantage. Give it an inch, it takes a mile. Then the phone's in your hands and you don't know how it got there." Mom was in top mother form, driving the Car of Life. "Take it from me, I've been there a thousand times. It's this weird, powerful battle."

"It's been a week," I said. She was right, too. It *was* a weird, powerful battle. My thoughts were drawn to Travis in a way I didn't even seem to have control of, like an overfed mouth to chocolate, a drunk to another drink. It was a compulsion. I was in love with him, I thought. I didn't even like him. I hated what he had done, and wanted to see his hair, made golden by the sun, again. It was as if he had taken up residence in my body, an unwelcome visitor bringing longing and intrigue and dread.

"If you can get through the worst, you won't even count anymore. Tonight we'll have Sydney and Lizbeth for a sleepover—how's that? Saturday you can come with me to the Casserole Queens."

"No, Mom. Please. I don't want to hear about hip operations."

"It's not like that. What were you, fourteen, when you went last?"

"I don't know," I moaned. Thirteen or fourteen, and all I could remember was that when we got out of there my cheeks hurt from smiling and from using my Old People Voice.

"I want you to come. And what about Libby? Can she give you extra hours?"

"This sounds like strategic military planning," I said.

"It has to be," she said. "It *has* to be," she said again, as if she hadn't really heard herself the first time. "Listen. I personally have had enough of being pathetic in the name of love. Your father had a baby. A baby! Enough is enough."

"I could have told you that a long time ago."

"Watch it, girl. I'm digging up roots twenty years deep. You think it's easy? You've got a couple of months' worth, and it's no picnic. Give me my bag," she said. She wiggled her fingers in the direction of the floor where her Nine Mile Falls Library canvas tote, sold at last year's book fair, sat. I heaved it up onto the seat beside her. It was always full of books and magazines and mail and maybe a bowling ball, by the weight of it. I swear it was a hundred pounds.

She fished around inside with one hand, taking quick looks down and swerving the car unnervingly.

"Let me do it," I said. "What are you looking for?"

"A postcard. In that stack of mail near the front. A beach."

I flipped through and found the postcard, in between her bank statement and the garbage bill. A beach during sunset, with a palm tree in the corner. "This it?"

"Give it to me. Don't *look*."

I handed it over, but not before I saw the writing on the back, my father's writing. *Missing you*, it said.

She rolled down her window and tossed it outside. It fluttered in the speeding air; in the side mirror, I could see it land on one of its corners and travel end to end in a spry fashion, like those funny birds in the nature shows that appear to run on water. Finally it lost its burst of enthusiasm and landed flat. The tire of a pickup truck behind us rolled over it and made it shudder. I couldn't see it any more. I imagined it lying there, beach side up, giving some animal a last, tempting view of life on earth before becoming roadkill.

My mother rolled up her window. "This is war," she said.

My mother had apparently already gotten to Libby before I'd even arrived at work that day. I was in the stockroom at Johnson's Nursery, tying my apron behind my back, when Libby came in. She was wearing her big batik dress and had a handkerchief tied around her head, and her eyes were even bluer than usual, set against her face, which was getting more tan by the day. She took a swig from a water bottle, then held the bottle against her forehead.

"All year we complain about the rain, but then it gets nice and we can't take it," she said. "If it gets as hot as yesterday, I'm turning on all the sprinklers and standing underneath. Damn the customers."

"I second that," I said.

"Ruby, I meant to ask you," she said. "I know it's summer and all, but I could really use you a little longer for the next few weeks. Say, until five thirty? These longer summer hours and all these shipments, I just can't get caught up." Libby spun the water in her bottle in a slow circle.

"There's no particular other reason you're asking this?" I said. Five thirty was when Mom got off work.

"Well, like I said . . ." Libby shook her head and laughed. "Damn, Ruby, I'm a terrible liar."

"Your voice gets too high," I agreed.

She looked at me for the first time since coming in the stockroom. "I know it. I've been that way since I was a kid. The lie just gets stuck in my throat, and the other words can't squeeze through."

"My mom called you."

She took hold of my shoulder and shook it. "It's just because she loves you, right?"

"I know it."

"I really do need you, though. I've got perennials up the kazoo."

"I've seen them."

"Rich and Allen can bench-press six bags of beauty bark but they can't make change to save their lives. If you tell them that, I'll kill you." She took another swig of water. "If you want to stay late tonight, I'll take us all out for Coke and onion rings after. Does Smelly's have onion rings? I saw some onion rings on a commercial and can't stop thinking about them."

"I think so. But I'm going to have to pass. Mom's got the evening shift covered. We're having a sleepover."

"Oh, jeez. I can just see her inviting those old ladies she does the book club for, in their sleeping bags and curlers."

"The old people are tomorrow," I said.

Libby started to laugh. "Man. When I hear the helicopters, I'll know she called the National Guard. SWAT team on your roof with machine guns."

"Ha," I said.

"Guys in jackets with big letters, FBI, on the back."

"You're hilarious."

"Oh, Ruby," she said. She tried to look serious, but her smile was still peeking out the sides of her mouth. She plunked a kiss on my forehead and ruffled my hair before she left. It was the same thing she used to do when I was three. It was one of those moments when you get that snug, solid feeling. When you realize there are people in the world that really care about you.

I took that feeling around with me for the rest of the day as I rang up orders of dahlia tubers and hanging fuschia baskets, sweet alyssum and tomato plants, weed killer and bone meal and wheel barrows of peach trees and chinaberry. I hardly thought of Travis Becker. After lunch I went outside and unloaded flats of perennials and deadheaded the geraniums, helped load magnolias and beeches and bags of manure into the sagging trunks of cars, and transplanted a few cramped root-bound rose trees.

Libby was right—it was too hot, and when it came time to have a break I went out near the sample waterfalls and garden sculptures, to the plot of land where we keep the larger trees in the ground, and where they need to be watered with thick hoses as the sprinklers don't reach out that far. There's a pond out there too, where we keep several koi, and it is shady and pleasant there, the burbling of the waterfalls giving you the very sound of coolness. No one else was around, and I turned on one of the hoses and let it run into the roots of the beech and Purple Robe locusts, waiting for the cold water to come before I took a long, sweet drink. I wanted to pour it right over my head—I was tempted by that delicious possibility—but instead tossed a handful of water on the back of my neck, and another on my face and breathed it in.

"There you are," Travis Becker said, as if he'd been looking for me from the moment I drove away from him in the Yellow Submarine parking lot. He startled me; I hadn't seen him come around the shady bend toward the tree plot, and hadn't heard his soft steps over the sound of hose water spilling to the ground. I jolted at his voice, jerking the hose, causing it to make an embarrassing splash across the front of my shorts.

"You scared me," I said.

"Uh oh," he said, and pointed to my shorts. "Accident."

I blushed, though with my face already red from heat, he might not have noticed. It was just great that he found me right then, with my tank top stained with sweat and my apron dirty and my bangs now pointy-wet.

He didn't seem to mind. He leaned in and kissed me, just like that. His mouth was warm against my cold one.

"Mmmm," he said. "Just like taking a drink. I've missed you."

He wore a beret, dark shorts, and a dark shirt. You'd think this would look ridiculous. It didn't. You pictured him walking the Pont Neuf in Paris, smoking a Gauloise, one of the crowd from *A Moveable Feast*. As I said, he had that kind of face—timeless. It was the surroundings that looked wrong, not him. That face was more welcome to my eyes than it should have been. He looked good to me.

"Where've you been?" Travis asked. "My fearless girl gone chickenshit?"

A curl of anger rose up in me. I wanted to snatch his beret and throw it in with the koi. I made a lunge for it, but Travis stepped back neatly, as if he were anticipating my move.

"That's the Ruby I love," he said. "I miss the way you wear your hair pulled back in that clip. I miss the way your eyes get wide when you're afraid."

I turned away from him. There was a robin on the ground, under the cedars. It was trying to drag a huge twig in its mouth, but the twig was entirely too big for it. The robin hauled it a few steps, rested, and tried again. It reminded me of Mom lugging our Christmas trees into the house.

"I miss your wrists. They're so small they're breakable. I miss the way you look at me like you couldn't care less."

"How's this?" I gave him a blank expression. But it was a lie, and he knew it.

"You're special, Ruby. I've never met anyone like you before. We were becoming so close." He stepped toward me again, and I let him. He ran his hand down my back, untied my apron, pulled my hips to his. I heard voices; Allen's, one of the nursery workers, and someone else's, a customer.

"The water pump's got to be enough to circulate the whole thing at least once, say, every two hours," I heard Allen say.

I felt myself slipping back to him. I didn't even have the decency to clutch at branches, try to hold on with my fingernails as I slid, slid down the mountainside, heading for a valley vivid with color and dangers I knew little about.

"Follow me," Travis Becker said. He strolled off up the dirt pathway, gazing at the garden statues and waterfalls as if he were a browsing customer. I know what I should have done. I should have tied my apron and gone the other way, back down the path from the tree plot and inside the building. I should have found a shopper looking for something that would kill aphids and cutworms.

Instead I saw that Travis had gone off the path meant

for patrons and was walking fast toward the greenhouses, and I followed him. There are several greenhouses out there; one large hothouse and one small, cool greenhouse that Libby uses for her personal prizes—her orchids. That's where Travis was heading, his hand already reaching out for the knob on the glass door, disregarding the EMPLOYEES ONLY sign. I was nearly running—I could feel the loose ties of my apron flap against the back of my legs. I needed Travis out of there, and in some way I felt down, down, deep, I just plain needed Travis. He had left the door open a crack, and I pushed it open and walked into the coolness. Those orchids in there, that's what I felt like. Hidden and growing quietly, secretly unfurled, waiting for that glass door to be pushed open so that they could be seen, be discovered.

Travis, in his black clothes, stood in a corner, glass rising around him, leaning on the shelves that held the fragile orchids and looking my way. "Come here," he said.

"Be careful behind you," I said. "You don't belong in here."

"This place smells like armpit." Travis did not turn to look at the flowers behind him. I liked the smell in there—wet earth mixed with sweetness. The sweetness of pink, if pink had a smell. Those flowers were so difficult to grow that it took three to five years for them to even get a bloom. I had to get him out of there before Libby saw us. Outside the glass panes I could see Allen and the customer down the pathway, the customer a big bearded guy with one boot up on the rock ledge of the fish pond.

"This is one of the coolest spots in this town on a hot day," he said. "That and the freezer storage of the Front Street Market."

Goose bumps rose along my arms at the mention of the cold and his clear message that he'd been places he shouldn't have. "How do you know about this greenhouse?" I said. "This is private."

"I like to know about the places around me," he said. "Would you come over here?"

"Travis, you've got to get out."

"Come here first."

"I mean it."

"One kiss."

"Shit, Travis." I had one eye on Allen and the customer.

"One kiss and we'll leave. Baby, come *here*."

I went over to him. He rubbed his hands up my arms to warm them. He kissed me, his tongue taking its time in my mouth. He pulled my body to his. I was worried he would lean back into the orchids and crush them. Our lips made such a messy slurping sound that I was somehow embarrassed for the orchids, so open and gentle, to hear.

"Now," he said. He was holding my wrist. He took a pen from my apron pocket, a felt-tipped marker, took the cap off with his teeth. He turned my wrist around. "Hold still." He wrote on the inside of my arm and then recapped the pen. "There. My phone number. Now there's no excuse not to call me. I don't give it to just anyone."

His presence, the black of his clothes, was so wrong in there amid the glass panels of light and the tender colors of the flowers. It was the same black that was now on the thin inside skin of my arm. I had that same feeling with him there in Libby's special place, among her trowels and her gloves formed to the shape of her hands, that I did seeing the woman's tennis shoes outside on the porch of the house Travis had stolen from. It was the invasion of something innocent.

Travis hooked his arm around my neck and pulled me close again. He moved his mouth across the skin of my shoulder up to my ear. I closed my eyes. "We could do it right here on the floor," he whispered.

I opened my eyes. Outside the glass panes a flash of color caught my attention. A batik dress, a blue bandanna. "Travis! We've got to get out of here!"

He turned around slowly, followed my gaze. "Look who's coming."

"Goddamn it, Travis. Goddamn it."

I could see Libby walk up the path and stop at the pond with Allen and the customer. She put her hands on her hips. She gestured toward the waterfall, made motions with her hands in description. Cottonwood fluff snowed down upon the scene outside the glass, drifting, I was certain, into the pools of water. I remembered the solid, contented feeling I'd had earlier of being cared for. One look up and I was certain her kind, know-all eyes would see Travis' black figure in the glass.

"Get down," I hissed.

"So you liked my idea," Travis laughed.

I was beginning to panic. I felt hot tears of desperation spring up. I tugged on the leg of Travis' shorts. "Down!"

Travis didn't move, but Libby did. She crouched down beside one of the waterfalls and stuck one arm inside the pool. The customer was nodding. Libby's back, thank God, was to us.

"Get out! Go now!"

Travis looked through the glass with the casualness of someone checking his watch when he had all the time in the world. Panic wrung my stomach. I wanted to scream at him. He walked toward the door with infuriating, horrible calm and left. I waited a moment and left behind him, following him onto the patron walkway that led away from the waterfalls, toward the hedge trees and rows of standing junipers. He spoke to me over one shoulder.

"Don't forget to call," he said.

I went into the bathroom right after I'd gotten inside the Johnson's Nursery building after Travis had left, and tried to scrub that marker off my arm. The shadow of the number was still there, though, as was Travis' own shadow— every time I looked toward the greenhouses, I thought I saw him there. Whether he really was there or whether my fear had imagined him, I don't know; all I know is that I saw flashes of black behind the glass panes where the orchids lay. I felt nauseous at my own weakness that let him come back in my life.

Sydney and Lizbeth came over that night. We all rolled our sleeping bags onto the floor of the living room. My mother and Lizbeth sat cross-legged on the floor and talked about poets and polished their toenails.

"I hate to take the obvious road, no cleverness intended, but I really like Robert Frost," Lizbeth said.

"I think it is so great that his name is Frost and he writes about winter and snow," Sydney said. "How perfect is that? I mean, it's like an ice cream man with the last name of Cone."

"Our lunch lady's name is Candy Sweet," Chip Jr. said.

"No way," I said.

"It is too!" he said with so much sudden indignation that I knew he was probably telling the truth. Either that or the polish fumes were getting to his head.

"I used to know a woman named Anita Hurl," Lizbeth said. "Get it? I need to hurl?"

"She had very cruel or very stupid parents," I said.

"When I was a kid I thought *diarrhea* sounded like the name of a beautiful woman," Sydney said.

"This conversation is getting gross," Mom said.

We watched an old Frankenstein movie Mom had brought home from the library and we made fun of it. It was in black and white—and yellow, thanks to our television—and even though we were laughing at it, it was actually pretty scary. It was enough to make me not think about

Travis Becker for a while, and the fact that I had recently let down my mother in her belief that we were well on our way toward extricating him from my life. Chip Jr. must have thought the movie was scary too, or else he was sick of us, because he made some excuse and went to bed. Poe ate popcorn out of the bowl on the floor when he thought we weren't looking.

Everyone went to sleep, finally. I listened to the rhythms of all of their breathing, and the crickets outside, through the open screen window. The evening coolness that drifted in made me think of the coolness in that greenhouse; the crickets, of that night in someone else's garden. I put my fingers up to my arm. Of course, I had already committed the number to memory. I still know it now.

Chapter 7

"Here," I said to the short woman in the jeans and white work shirt, which was open at the neck to reveal a chunky beaded necklace. "Please. Sit here." I rose from the soft floral chair in the room, which I had taken before all of the old people started to arrive.

The woman dropped her book bag on the floor with a *thunk* and sat in a wooden rocker to my left. "What do you think, because I'm old that if I don't get the softest chair I'm going to have a stroke and die?" she said.

She adjusted her roundness on the chair, reached down into her bag, and opened her glasses case.

"No, I um . . ."

"Don't worry. I won't kick off just yet."

"Don't mind Peach. She thinks Attack the Newcomer is a parlor game. Like charades," Harold Zaminski said.

The last time I had come to the book club I was fourteen, and all I could remember was that Harold pretended to pull a quarter from behind one of my ears. This time when we met, he had taken my hands and told me how lovely I'd become in his smooth, husky voice that sounded the way a soft old leather chair would if it could talk. It was impossible not to love Harold. He had aging-movie-star good looks, with comb marks still in his slicked-back hair and the thoughtful, intelligent face of a longtime reader. He smelled like a fresh splash of Old Spice, and was a practical joker. My mother called this passive-aggressive behavior, since as the resident male Harold was always getting picked on, and his pranks were his small acts of revenge. The week before, he'd taped down the handle of the spray nozzle on Miz June's kitchen faucet so that when Mrs. Wong turned it on, water shot straight out. Harold was always forgiven because of the food he brought. On Miz June's dining room table I already saw the apple tarts, with their bumpy crusts lightly browned and sprinkled with powdered sugar.

"Ann," Harold called toward the kitchen where my mother was pouring coffee with Miz June and Anna Bee. "Peach already has her fangs out and they're pointing Ruby's way." The book club was always held in Miz June's house, a delicate yellow-and-white Victorian on one of Nine Mile Falls' side streets. It had a wide porch with hanging flower baskets that she watered with the raised end of the garden hose, and a carriage house out back, now the garage for her rarely used Lincoln Continental, pale yellow with the license plate MIZ JUNE. It was a gift from one of Miz June's many admirers, Chester Delmore. You could see the car in there if you peered through those dusty windows. If you didn't know better, you'd think those headlights were going to blink at you in some sort of surprised pleasure at being noticed after such patient waiting.

"Tattletale," Peach said.

"Viper," Harold said.

"Children. Enough bickering." Miz June entered through the doorway of the dining room, carrying a silver tray with china cups that trembled like nervous kids during a thunderstorm as she set them down on the marble-topped coffee table. The double strands of pearls Miz June wore swung toward her chin as she leaned over. Miz June made you think of climbing roses on a white trellis. She had a cap of blond hair and fine features, and wore a floral dress that matched her living room, which was raspberry-toned and gracious with its Victorian parlor furniture and fringe lamps, polished mahogany fireplace, and vases of dried hydrangeas. A painting over the fireplace showed a Victorian couple in a boat against a soft green lake; the man in the hat bent toward the woman as if in proposal, while she had her head turned toward the water as if he were more boring than the all-weather channel. According to Mom, Miz June seemed to attract men the same way a summer evening attracts mosquitoes. I got the feeling from that painting that Miz June, in spite of her gentle demeanor, probably liked the *zzzip* sound of a bug light.

Peach had finally gotten her glasses free from the case, plunked them on the end of her nose. "Well, I must say, having Ruby here is actually much nicer than the junior librarian-in-training you sent us last week."

"Fowler is hardly a junior librarian," my mother said as she came out of the kitchen followed by Anna Bee. Anna Bee had arrived at Miz June's on her Schwinn, her poof of white hair tucked under her bike helmet that had a small lightning bolt on the side. She rode her Schwinn everywhere. You could see her around town, her basket filled with a sack of groceries or a waxed white doughnut bag or a package tied with string as she headed to the post office. It made you proud of her.

"His hair was too long," Harold said. "He looked like a hippie."

"Cute dog, though," Peach said.

"Lovely little dog. It escaped and tinkled in the upstairs hallway." Miz June sipped her tea. "Beauty had never seen such bad manners." Beauty was Miz June's cat.

"He was nervous. All these new people," Anna Bee said. Her little white socks had dragonflies on them. You could see them when she sat down, along with a peek of thin, pale leg where the socks stopped.

"I heard about that," my mother said. "Fowler felt terrible." She dived for a change of topic. "I'm going to be bringing Ruby for a while. She's having boy trouble."

"Jeez, Mom," I said.

"Ah." Miz June set her cup down. "It runs in the family, then."

"So what are we, her punishment?" Harold winked at me.

"Punishment, fine. Just don't expect us to do the wise-old-person routine. I hate that," Peach said.

"I don't mind sharing my experience," Anna Bee said. She took a seat on the settee. She sat down very slowly, as if unsure whether her butt would land in the direction she was aiming.

"I find that most old people aren't wise, they're just old," Miz June said.

"We're as screwed up as everyone else," Peach said.

"Speak for yourself," Harold said.

"And sweet. They think you're sweet just because you're old. For Christ's sake."

"I'm sure you don't have that problem," Harold said.

"Keep in mind this," Peach shook her finger at me. "If an old person is sweet, they've probably always been sweet. If they were wise, they were probably always smart. Nobody changes that much."

"Well, every *body* changes quite a lot." Miz June sighed.

"I keep thinking that my neck resembles the skin of a lima bean if you popped the bean out with your finger," Anna Bee said. She lifted her chin so that we could see. She was right.

"You should see the butterfly tattoo I got on my keister years ago. It's now down on the back of my thigh," Peach said. "Like it flew there."

The doorbell interrupted that image, thank God.

Harold went to the windows, peeked out. "It's only Mrs. Wong."

"It's a miracle. She's only fifteen minutes late," Miz June said.

"What this time?" Anna Bee said. "Car trouble?"

"Be nice," Mom said.

"Her arm got stuck in the mailbox. A bunch of sheep were flocked in her driveway and she couldn't back out her Mercedes," Peach said.

"Her nephew came down with mengue fever and was near death on her doorstep," Harold said.

"*Dengue* fever," Anna Bee corrected.

"That's what I said."

I heard a *thunk, thunk, thunk* up the porch steps, and then the doorbell. "Sorry, sorry," Mrs. Wong said as she bustled in. She waved one hand around. She was dressed chicly in black and white, her wrist circled with gold jewelry. Mrs. Wong's accent was still very heavy. "There was a little problem at the Golden Years Rest Home. Grandfather Wong hit his neighbor in the jaw." She slugged the air in demonstration. "He thought the man was stealing his magazines. I had to go calm him down."

"Ninety-year-olds shouldn't be getting *Playboy* anyway." Peach chuckled at her own joke.

"I don't bring him that filth. Let me tell you, he would like a *Playboy*, too," Mrs. Wong said. "I bring him *Reader's Digest*."

"Grandfather Wong should have paid the guy to steal them then," Harold said.

"Good God, take him something with a little substance," Peach said.

"How many amazing recoveries from disease does anyone care to read about?" Harold said.

"You know who has the *Playboy*. Mr. Wong, that's who. He hides it whenever I come home. I am sure of it," Mrs. Wong said. She took off her dress shoes and put on a pair of old red slippers she'd taken out of her bag.

"I hear a car," Miz June said.

Harold scooted back toward the window, peeked out again. "It's them. Delores today."

"Who's Delores?" I asked my mother.

"One of Lillian's daughters. Nadine is the other one." Lillian was a neighbor of Peach's and a recent newcomer to the group. Her daughters brought her, Mom told me later, as a part of a "stimulation program" they had developed to help improve Lillian's condition after her stroke.

"That sports car is ridiculous," Harold reported. "The poor nurse is jammed in the backseat with the wheelchair."

"The nurse is a bimbo," Mrs. Wong said.

"All skull and no brains," Peach said.

Harold sat down quickly, opened the book they were reading on his lap as if he were a character on stage taking his place. "Delores is a bitch," he said.

I wondered how anyone would be able to get a person and a wheelchair up Miz June's porch steps, but it apparently wasn't a problem, and when the trio came into view from Miz June's living room windows, I could see why.

Lillian's hair was as white as the wicker chairs on Miz June's porch, and she probably weighed about as much as one of them too. Delores was short but square and strong, with hair sprayed to attention and a blue-and-white shirt with a faux nautical feel. Ship ahoy! She and Nurse Bimbo had no problem lifting Lillian and setting her bones in the wheelchair. Delores dripped authority—you got the sense that Lillian's stroke had now settled an old score between them, altered the playing field in a way that spelled victory for Delores. There was a slice of glee in the way she situated Lillian's wheelchair in the circle of book club members and placed the Whitney book, *Life Times Two*, onto Lillian's lap. One thing was for sure: Delores would always have the last word now. The stroke had left Lillian speechless except for an occasional sound, and her left arm and leg were dead at her side. She looked as unbearably silent and weary as the trays of pansies at Johnson's Nursery left too long without water—drooped and limp, there not by will but only by nature's thin strings. Lillian was so wispy that my heart wanted to break, the way it does when you see fragile things. Nurse Bimbo waited out on the porch, cracked open a can of Diet Coke that magically appeared in her hand. She must have known that Delores would be busy for a while playing Good Daughter in front of us, so she first slurped at the top of the can, then tipped back her long neck and drank that Diet Coke at leisure.

"It was very kind of you to indulge Mother this way," Delores said. She placed a folded afghan over Lillian's legs. It was too hot for an afghan. Even Lillian's crane fly legs didn't need that blanket, probably made by Delores, in red, white, and blue yarns. A patriotic afghan, which was pretty hilarious, if you asked me.

"You mean the book?" Mom said. "It wasn't just for Lillian. We all wanted to read it. A Charles Whitney is always worth reading. I'd highly recommend it."

Beauty, Miz June's white cat, sauntered in and rubbed herself against Delores' legs. Little white hairs clung to her navy polyester pants.

"Mother is the reader in the family, as you know."

"I remember you said that she met Charles Whitney long ago. That must have made a lasting impression," my mother said.

"I shook Neil Diamond's hand once, and I wouldn't wash it for a week," Delores said.

Delores left and took Nurse Bimbo with her. I could see Delores brushing the cat hair off her pants, her big butt pointing upward, round as the top of a breakfast muffin. Nurse Bimbo crushed her Diet Coke can with one hand with power-lifter strength as they went down the steps.

"Lillian met the author of the book?" I asked.

"Lillian is not an umbrella stand," Peach said. "Ask her. She understands everything perfectly. Don't you, dear?" Lillian's eyes looked out at us without blinking. They were a bit like a baby's eyes, keen and alert and watchful on the other side of that window of nonlanguage. For a second, the baby seat in the back of my father's van flashed in my mind. The baby, a sister, took on a moment of realness. A baby who saw things, reached for things, listened to the rhythm of my father's voice and knew whose voice it was.

I did as Peach said. "Did you meet the author of the book?" Lillian looked at me with those same eyes, then nodded. I started to think about how Lillian had once done all kinds of things—watered plants and fed babies and cooked a holiday meal. I learned later from Mom that Lillian had been bringing Whitney's first book, *The Present Hours*, to every meeting since she first came.

"She more than *met* him, if you get my drift," Peach said. "No one can convince me otherwise."

"Don't let her tease you, Lillian," Anna Bee said.

"She had his picture on her nightstand!" Peach said. She scooted to the edge of her chair, trying to get her point to us more quickly.

"So you said a hundred times," Harold said.

"Maybe it just looked like him," my mother said.

"She had his *picture* on her *nightstand*." Peach settled back on her chair again. "I saw it there, didn't I, Lillian?" Lillian nodded. "She was selling an old television, and I went to look at it. We didn't see each other much, did we? I'm sorry I wasn't a better neighbor. You always seemed to like to keep to yourself."

"What did you need another television for?" Anna Bee asked.

"It wasn't for *me*. Mark and Justine had just gotten married," Peach said. "I was trying to be helpful. They ended up getting a good buy at Costco. Anyway," she said to me. "The next time I was there, to see her after her stroke, it was gone. Poof. Replaced with a photo of Walter on their wedding day."

"Well, Charles Whitney was no doubt a lot nicer to look at," Miz June said. She had put on her reading glasses and was giving the photo on the jacket cover a good look.

"Woo woo," Mrs. Wong fake-whistled her appreciation.

I leaned over and looked at Harold's copy. I didn't know what the fuss over his looks was about, but keep in mind, the guy was eighty. Charles Whitney looked both sweet and wise. His eyes were smile-crinkled though his expression was serious, his white beard was rough and like a sea captain's in a children's story. He was shown standing on a cliff at the edge of the sea, hand toward the brim of his cap, his shirtsleeves rolled up to the elbow.

"The picture she had was in a *frame*," Peach said. "And it *disappeared*. I'm surprised Delores and Nadine let her bring that Whitney book with her every time. I'm surprised it didn't *disappear*. I don't know why no one believes me that there's more to this than meets the eye."

I knew why no one believed her. We'd been hearing the stories for a long time. Once Peach had convinced the group that she saw a dead body in her neighbor's yard. My mom even called the police. The dead body turned out to be a garbage bag full of old lawn chair cushions, and Mom says the policeman she talked to still winks and smiles whenever he sees her. And then there was the time that Peach had the group convinced that Adolph Vonheimer, an old library patron, was a former Nazi. There was his name, for one thing, but more importantly there was the swastika tattoo on his leg, which later turned out to be a particularly bad case of varicose veins, according to Miz June, who saw him in shorts at Tru-Value.

"I saw them try to take that book from her once," Mrs. Wong said. "Nadine took it from her lap. Lillian clawed her arm like a cat with her good hand." Beauty, speaking of cats, had settled on Mrs. Wong's slippers.

"Lillian has strong hands. All those years of playing the piano." Peach moved her fingers along imaginary keys in the air.

"Bravo for you," Anna Bee clapped her hands in Lillian's direction.

"You should have told us about this," Miz June said to Mrs. Wong. "We need to keep our eye on Lillian. We have a responsibility as her friends."

"Damn right. I would have given that Nadine something she'd remember," Harold said. He put a fist in the air.

"Smell that manly power," Peach said. "Bam, boom."

"We should have known this, though," Anna Bee agreed. "It *is* a little suspicious."

My mother let out a little groan. Our eyes met, and she rolled hers at me.

"Sorry, sorry," Mrs. Wong said. "Next time I will let you know. I will watch like a hawk."

"I hope Neil Diamond washed his hand with Lysol after touching that Delores," Harold said.

The Whitney book was a thick one—it seemed right that a life of eighty years should not be easily held in your hand—and my mother and the Casserole Queens had agreed to read it in quarters. That day the group discussed the first section: seeing Charles Whitney through a childhood with a demanding mother who'd turned to bookmaking and husband-hunting to get by; his stint with the merchant marines at the start of World War II; and the big band dances and bouts of drunken fights and women at various ports around the world during the war. All these explosions, of one form or another, and Charles Whitney's discovery that writing was one way of ducking for cover. I wanted to go home and read it right away.

"His central problem seemed to be one of longing," Miz June said.

"Everyone's central problem is longing," Harold shouted from the bathroom over the monsoon sound of his own peeing. Harold drank too much of Miz June's tea.

"There's nothing intrinsically wrong with longing," Anna Bee said. "Longing has led to great things. Every great discovery and accomplishment has its base in longing. It's only when you look to someone else to fill that longing that there are problems."

"She read ahead," Harold shouted from the bathroom again. He had great hearing for an old guy.

"How would you know if you didn't read ahead too?" Peach shouted back.

"Both of you read ahead," Miz June said. She probably did too.

"At any rate, love shouldn't be the answer. It's not even the big question," Anna Bee said. "It's more . . ." Anna Bee's hand trembled gently as she held her teacup, like a blade of grass in a slight breeze.

"Background music," Miz June said. "The perfect background music."

"Setting?" my mother ventured. I heard a flush, then the faucet running, and then Harold appeared.

"The yeast, but not the flour," he said.

"Christ, give me a hankie," Peach said.

"Background music," Miz June insisted. "Benny Goodman." She snapped her fingers.

"Well, I for one know someone who let love take the place of everything else," Harold said.

"Mrs. Wilson-now-Mrs. Thrumond," Anna Bee said quickly. The tag was sticking out of her sweatshirt.

"Ditching us the moment she got married." Mom had made Chip Jr. and me go to the wedding at the Senior Center. Mrs. Wilson-now-Mrs. Thrumond wore a white dress and a veil, and some old guy who looked barely alive played the accordion. The little plastic people on top of the cake had shiny black hair and looked about twenty. Mr. Thrumond had to sit down and rest after their first dance.

"Never trust a man," Mrs. Wong said. "Mr. Wong

cheats on me every chance he gets. Men are trouble." Poor Mr. Wong. According to my mother, he was as faithful as Mrs. Wong's slippers, formed to the very curves of her feet and willing to walk a million miles for her. He'd never had the full love of Mrs. Wong, or of anyone else, for that matter.

"Amen to that," Peach said.

"You were happily married for fifty years," Miz June said. "I'm not sure why you're agreeing."

"He left me," Peach said.

"He *died*," Miz June said.

"Same thing," Peach said.

"I'd like to read one more passage before we end," my mother said. "It marks the transition, the turning point in the book and in Charles Whitney's life. V.J. Day 1942. It's the passage just after Charles sees Rose for the second time that day—imagine the odds? In that chaos of New York City.

> '*There was something about her mouth that made me feel possibilities,*'" my mother read. "' *The way a train ticket holds possibilities, the way a boat docked at sunset does, the way a voice on the radio announcing victory does. A mouth can have that. It can seem brave, and bold. Finite and infinite. After a war, you need both of those things.* "Why don't you kiss me," she said. "Celebrate a new world." *And so I did. I could not forget that kiss. I still cannot. I put my fingertips to her face. Indeed, the world*

changed that day, but the change in my life was no smaller or less significant. That moment took my sorrow and made it swarm the streets in victory, shouting in joy and rightness, and from that I have never quite recovered.'"

We were all quiet for a moment. My mother always did read beautifully.

"Lovely," Anna Bee said.

"Refreshing. Now that's the way it should be. Today everything is sex, sex, sex," Peach said. "Love today is *undulating*. Oh, no."

We followed Peach's eyes. Lillian had begun to cry.

"It was your undulating comment," Harold said.

"It was not, you idiot. It was the book."

Tears rolled down Lillian's wrinkled face; her thin white hair seemed as soft as dandelion fluff that might blow away with a puff of air. She was too fragile for pain. The wristwatch she wore seemed cruel, like a KICK ME sign stuck on someone's back. A lump grew in my throat. I was embarrassed and ashamed to be young and witnessing what should be private.

"Maybe this wasn't such a good idea," my mother said.

"I will get a tissue," Mrs. Wong said, and got up.

"Lillian?" Peach said, and patted Lillian's small shoulder.

Lillian raised her good hand from her lap. It trembled as she moved it toward her face, which she touched with her fingertips. Harold looked down at his lap.

"Didn't I tell you people?" Peach said softly. She kissed the top of Lillian's head, the little white poof. "It's all right, dear."

"Harold!" Mrs. Wong shrieked from the bathroom. *Herro!* it sounded like. She appeared in the doorway, tissues in one hand, her blouse and the front of her pants splotched with water. Apparently Harold had moved on to the second phase of his two-part faucet plan, and had been having some fun with the masking tape again.

"It wasn't me," Harold lied.

It was true that I didn't think about Travis Becker the whole time I was there with the Casserole Queens. It was not just distraction, though, the way it was with the Frankenstein movie. Maybe all of the years in that room just made the world seem bigger. Being with them had been like sleep, the way it steals your mind sure as a thief and takes you to this land you both are and are not fully a part of. And then you wake up, of course, and there is the life you know, which you look at blind and blinking, like you've just come out of the movie theater.

I couldn't sleep that night. The moon was nearly full and it was a hot night, and I stuck various parts of me out of the sheet to see what they would look like in the zebra stripes made by the moonlight coming through the slats of the venetian blinds. I gave my legs zebra stockings and my arms zebra gloves, and my foot a zebra boot. I turned over my pillow to the cool side, a fresh start on a new attempt to sleep, but that didn't work either. Thoughts nagged at me—my father, a baby. Charles Whitney on that crowded New York street. But more than that, one particular thought nagged at me, and it was the image of that phone number written on my arm, that blackness like a vein under my skin, coursing with blood and with a life of its own.

I imagined my finger on those numbers, could see them glowing green on the phone in the night, a loud buzz of the dial tone in my ear. I could imagine the ringing in Travis' dark house, breaking his sleep in his turret room. He would know it was me, of course. I did not think about what the Casserole Queens had said about longing. To an untrained eye, need and love were as easily mistaken for each other as the real master's painting and a forgery. All I could do right then was feel this wrenching hole in my stomach and heart and call it love. It felt something like Travis's hand on my head, pushing me down, down under that water.

I rolled over for the hundredth time and realized that there was a sliver of yellow light under my doorway. Someone was up, and after a few minutes I decided to investigate. Before I knocked at her bedroom door, I could hear that my mother had the computer in her bed-room on. It was an old one; it had a loud hum that was annoying and comforting. The thing was heavy enough to anchor a small ship, but she'd gotten it free from the library when they got newer models.

"Come on in," my mother said. "Did I wake you?" Her hair was frazzled and looked confused and cranky to be awake at that hour. She wore a huge white T-shirt (a pang—I hoped it wasn't an old one of my father's) and her glasses.

"It's just hot," I said. "What are you doing?"

"Something stupid. Ridiculous. A stupid idea."

We McQueens were hard on ourselves.

"What?"

"Don't laugh."

"I won't."

"I'm thinking about Lillian. And Charles Whitney. What Peach said. I'm doing a search on him."

"Uh oh."

"I know it, I know it. They get me every time. I *vowed* I wouldn't let it happen again. I told myself, *Remember the dead body. Remember the dead body.* It's crazy."

"Maybe it's not so crazy."

"Something about that book has really gotten to me too. I feel awake again. For the first time since your father told me about the baby. It makes you remember that this is only one chapter in a long life."

"It would be so great if Lillian really did know Charles."

"Oh, God, you see? That's exactly how I get into these things. Come on, *Charles Whitney?* I'm sure Peach is just concocting a little excitement for her life. Again. She wants to be Miss Marple."

"Why should we think that just because we know Lillian, she shouldn't know someone famous?"

"We don't even know Lillian. She's like an unopened box."

"Who knows? She could have been someone important in his life."

"I had a friend in high school whose mother claimed to have dated Elvis. We all made fun of her."

"Maybe she really did."

"It just seems so improbable. A regular life, a regular person, intersecting with something large. Fiction, right?"

"Let me know if you find anything."

"Ha. You're hooked too."

"Think dead body."

"I don't even know what I'm looking for," she said.

I knew exactly what she meant.

Chapter 8

I called him, of course.

"That didn't take long," Travis Becker said. His voice was like honey over the phone. I wished he were beside me; I wanted to taste that voice in my mouth.

We didn't have much to say to each other. Talking wasn't mostly what we were about. We listened to each other's breath in the phone. Travis told me he wanted to see me. He had something to show me. I told him no more going to other people's houses when they weren't there. I didn't, *couldn't*, use the words *breaking in*. He said okay. He said it wasn't like that—he wanted me to go to his house that coming weekend, Saturday night, after nine. I told him I would think about it. We both knew, I guess, that that meant I would go.

For a few days I was like a chocolate in a box, looking

well behaved and perfectly in place, all the while harboring a secret center. The guilty knowledge I held of a wrongdoing about to occur made me brim with goodwill, as if already trying to atone for what I hadn't even done yet. Might as well get a jump start.

My intentions screamed. I thought they did, anyway. I gave off a thousand clues that I was only going through the motions of living until Saturday night came. I figured that anyone who knew me well would just have to take one look at me to know that an imposter had taken my place. My eyes had a way of wandering off, seeking that figure in black that I felt might be watching me from anywhere. At Johnson's Nursery, I would try to hold my focus, try, try, yet my gaze was pulled from Libby as she spoke to me, moving slowly toward that greenhouse and the glass panes where the orchids sat, tender and open. Libby's mouth was moving, her hands gesturing, the words *Corsican mint* and *weeping larch* and *pink wisteria* flowing to my ears dreamily, like the words of an ancient, unfamiliar language. I had begun to doubt that anyone really knew me, or ever really paid attention. No one noticed a thing.

My mother was also obviously struggling with intentions of her own—for the last three days a letter addressed to my father sat on the table by the front door, stamp affixed in the corner and ready to go. She hadn't yet made any moves to fix the hole in the kitchen. It gaped, open and hurting, and the bad part was I was getting used to the way it looked. Chip Jr., in what I guessed was an action meant to make us see the hole again, put an old G.I. Joe inside, facing out, as if he were a soldier in a bombed-out building in some war-torn country.

That Saturday afternoon my mother brought me to the Casserole Queens again. *Just stick with it,* she had said. *They grow on you in ways I can't explain.* I went, though the guilt of premeditation dripped from me, I was sure, like sweat. I didn't know what I was going to be doing that night—I didn't even want to know, in case knowledge might burst that delicate bubble of anticipation—but I had plotted my escape, had planned my outfit. The bad thing was, I now felt accountable to the group of old folks, as well as to Libby and my Mom and Chip Jr. I guess if other people cared about you, then you ought to too.

"How are you doing, Harold?" I asked that afternoon as everyone gathered.

Harold was dressed smartly in his khaki shorts, with collared shirt tucked in crisply. For the first time I noticed the thick piece of pink plastic behind one ear. Hearing aids seemed such an invasion of dignity. *Old age* was such an invasion of dignity. Harold was holding Beauty, who was tucked up comfortably in his arms. He rubbed her head with one of his thumbs. "Exhausted. I have my son and his family visiting. My three-year-old granddaughter comes into my apartment for the first time. She looks around and says, 'Nice place you got here, Grandpa.'" Harold chuckled.

I smiled. "She sounds cute."

"Cute isn't the half of it. She's a tap dancer. Her

mother's got her in all these classes. She wears the tutu everywhere. Tap, tap tap, in the grocery store, on the kitchen floor, on the sidewalks. I got here two hours early to get some peace."

"Look, Peach got her hair permed," Anna Bee said. She stood behind Peach's chair and patted her curls. "She hates it when I do this."

"Get your damn hand off my head." Peach sat in the cushy chair that I had sat in the last time. This time Peach had gotten there first.

"But it feels so sproingy," Anna Bee said.

"Let me feel," Miz June said. She was wearing a new silk scarf. She said she'd gotten it from a *beau*, a pursed-lipped word that made you think of bowler hats. She went and patted Peach's head. "It is sproingy. Try it, Ruby."

They were right. It was bouncy but soft. It reminded me of the poof on the top of Fowler's poodle's head.

"It feels like that hippie's poodle," Miz June said.

"I was just thinking the same thing," I said.

"Goddamn it," Peach said. But she didn't move away. In fact, she kept her head very still. I think she liked the attention.

Harold came over. "Here, hold the cat," he said to me. He transferred her to my arms. Something about passing a cat makes them seem to grow twice their length. Like passing an accordion or something.

"I want to feel," Harold said.

"Over my dead body," Peach said.

"Yippee," Harold said, but he snuck a quick, mischievous pat before he went to answer the door.

"You're late," he said to Mrs. Wong.

She set down her bag and it landed with a *clunk*. "I had to follow that cheat Mr. Wong. When he goes out, I know what he is up to. Hanky-panky."

"Did you catch him?" I asked. My mother glared in my direction. We weren't supposed to encourage her.

"He went to the store. He bought stamps. *This* time," she said. She took off her shoes, put on her red slippers over her knee-high nylons.

We waited around for Lillian. "I'd hate to start without her," my mother said. We waited a while longer, and then my mother began, summarizing what they'd since read. Charles Whitney had met the love of his life, the woman he would only call Rose. After docking in New York and falling in love with Rose, he became ill with pneumonia, and Rose did a shocking thing for the time— she took him in to live with her at her apartment in Hell's Kitchen, where she lived during the war, writing poetry and supporting herself through her job at a munitions factory. Rose nursed Charles, who wrote the first chapter of *The Present Hours* at that time; it was initially a short story, but sold as a novel a year later. Rose, apparently, was a passionate nurse, and it wasn't just the infection in his lungs that made Charles short of breath and panting during their time together. "*'Everything about her left me breathless,'*" my mother read. "*'Her beauty, her skin, her poetry, the abundance of spices in her bad cooking.'*"

"I'm worried about Lillian," Anna Bee interrupted.

"Me too," Miz June said.

Mom sighed. "Me too."

"We could go over there," Peach said. "It did look quiet this morning."

"I've got binoculars in my purse," Mrs. Wong said.

"We'd better wait awhile," my mother said.

My mother continued the travel through Charles Whitney's life. Charles recuperated and found work on the waterfront. He'd asked Rose to marry him, but she had said no. Charles had drunk heavily during the war, and his habit had continued. Until he stopped she would not, could not, be his wife. He asked again, but she declined. She loved him, she said, more than she had ever known was possible, but she would not recklessly hand him her life. In a fit he would describe as a tantrum, he left Rose. He continued to write, and thought of her. A year later he had stopped drinking entirely. His stubborn, rejected heart did not allow him to call her. By the time he realized he could take it no more, another year had passed. He tracked down Rose through her family. The news devastated him. She had married an Army lieutenant the week before.

The phone rang. Miz June got up to answer it. Harold took advantage of this break and went to the kitchen to make tea. Miz June returned a moment later. "Ann? It's Delores."

My mother left the room to take the call. "Lillian's not coming anymore," Miz June told us.

"What?" Peach said.

"Delores said that last time had been too much for her. They took away her Whitney book. She said it was causing her mother too much upset."

"Taking away the book was what upset her!" Anna Bee said.

"Afterward Lillian had pulled out all of the books on her shelf that she could reach."

"She was angry," Anna Bee said.

"She was looking for something," Mrs. Wong said.

"She's Rose. I know she's Rose," Peach said. "Can't anyone else see what's right in front of our faces? Names changed to protect the innocent."

"Why does she have to be Rose? Charles had lots of lovers," Anna Bee said.

"You read ahead!" Harold shouted from the kitchen.

"*You* read ahead," Peach shouted.

"What? I can't hear you," Harold shouted. He was such a liar.

"Delores says that her mother's mind is obviously going," Miz June said.

My mother came back into the room, sighed. "They're not letting Lillian come anymore."

"We heard," I said.

"She had his *photo* on her *nightstand*," Peach said.

Harold came in with the tea, poured a few cups. I could see the peek of a tattoo under his shirtsleeve. My mother sat down. "I have something to tell you all."

"You're running off with the hippie librarian," Harold said.

My mother ignored him. "I don't even really know whether to say anything. In fact, it's against my better judgment. But I found Lillian's marriage certificate. She married Walter in 1948, the same year Rose wed. They married in New York. Walter was an Army lieutenant. I found him listed in the military records."

"I told you," Peach said.

"It doesn't necessarily mean anything. There were lots of Army lieutenants in New York after the war," Harold said.

"I shouldn't have even said anything," my mother said.

"I'm going over to see her," Peach said.

"Now, wait," Mom said. "I want you to remember the dead body. I want you to remember poor Adolph Vonheimer."

"Certainly, we do still have some reading to cover," Anna Bee said.

"The moral of the story today is that love stinks," Peach said. "Now let's go."

"You're just bitter after the mass murderer," Harold said.

"He wasn't a murderer," Peach said. "At least I don't think so."

"Peach entered into a correspondence with a gentleman through a newspaper advertisement. When he sent a photo, we noticed he was wearing prison coveralls," Miz June explained.

"Car mechanics wear coveralls," Peach said.

"They aren't usually orange with 'Department of Corrections' on the pocket," Harold pointed out.

"Those walks on the beach he mentioned in the ad were going to be a tad difficult to manage," Miz June said.

"Not if he jumped over barbed wire and managed to avoid being shot by the guards," Mrs. Wong said.

"Tea?" Harold said sweetly.

"I blame that asshole Henry for leaving me," Peach said.

"He *died*," Miz June and Mrs. Wong said together.

They sipped their tea. "At least you tried to move on, Peach. Henry's been gone for a long time. Everyone else seems so eager to jump into love," Anna Bee said. "Everyone is looking for themselves in someone else."

"You-know-who was certainly eager," Peach said.

"Mrs. Wilson-now-Mrs. Thrumond," Mrs. Wong said.

"Couldn't even stay in the book club a second after the ring was on her finger," Harold said. "The husband was barely cold."

"I married a cheater. He always goes behind my back for hanky-panky. Here's what I say about love: Two Wongs don't make a wight," Mrs. Wong said.

Everyone groaned. "How many times do we have to hear that one?" Harold said.

"Sorry, sorry," Mrs. Wong said. She still looked pleased with herself.

"Oh, my gracious!" Miz June said. "Your teeth!" she said to Mrs. Wong.

"What?" Mrs Wong said.

"You too!" Anna Bee pointed.

"Anna Bee, yours too."

The ladies bared their teeth at us. They were stained a garish shade of blue. God knows how many soakings with denture cleaner it would take before they got *that* out.

"Harold!" Mrs. Wong shouted.

When we got back home, I had only an hour before I left for the night to meet Travis Becker. A great burst of guilty goodwill sent me outside, where Chip Jr. sat with Poe on the front lawn. He looked lonely. Chip Jr., not Poe. Chip Jr. was tearing off grass and putting it on Poe's back.

"What're you doing?" I asked.

"What do you care?"

"Fine, never mind, then."

We sat in silence for a moment and watched Poe get decorated with grass. Finally Chip Jr. said, "I was just wondering what dogs thought about."

"Oh," I said. "Easy. Food. Pooping in places they shouldn't. What to chew up."

"No, I mean, I wondered what they *see*." He stopped putting grass on Poe. He had quite a nice green cape now.

I crouched down alongside Poe, in his same position. I put my chin low to the ground. The grass smelled good. "He sees his own paws, the fence, and the roof of Sydney's house," I said. "Mom's old tennis racket you left on the lawn."

"That's not what I meant," he said. "What things look

like through their *eyes*. Oh, never mind." Chip Jr. often got frustrated with us mere mortals. I put my head against Poe, listened to his heart beating. It was a solid sound, but a scary one too. It made me remember that we are just a collection of working parts that could stop working at any time. I lifted my head.

"Let's play Things I Hate," I said. Chip Jr. loved that game.

"I don't get it," he said.

"What?" I said.

"Why are you being so nice? You walk around with your eyes all funny for days and now you want to be nice."

"What do you mean, funny?" Of course he had seen, I thought. He always saw when I thought no one did.

"You don't look at anyone when they talk. You're always looking around like those people you used to hate. The ones you always say talk to you but are looking around, hoping someone better will appear."

I had the strongest image come to me then. Chip Jr. and me and Mom at the drive-in movies when there was still a drive-in movie left around here. The metal speaker hung from the edge of the window, and Chip Jr. and I were wearing our pajamas. The voices through the speaker were tinny and faraway. We were young enough that Chip Jr.'s pajamas had rocket ships printed on them and feet attached, the plastic feet that *shish-shished* when he walked. Chip Jr. sat snug right next to me, the three of us crammed into the front seat eating Red Vines and drinking cream soda. His breath was sweet, and he had red between his teeth from the licorice. When I turned around I could see the big looming screen of the movie behind us, not a Disney cartoon like we were watching, but a serious-looking adult one. It was large and mysterious and somehow removed in spite of the size, the lack of sound keeping you out of that world inhabited by the cars facing the other way.

For a moment I missed those rocket ship pajamas something fierce. My heart felt like it could break. Poe got up, shook the grass off his back with something that resembled patience. For his good behavior, I patted his side. Also for my own sake—there was something very comforting and solid about the *thup, thup* sound of patting the side of a dog.

I looked at Chip Jr. for a long time. A good long look, so he knew it was him I saw. "I'm sorry," I said. And then, "Things I Hate. Paper cuts."

"Sore throats."

"Those paper seats in the bathrooms. You get them all positioned and then they whoosh off when you go to sit. Or stick to your legs after you've been swimming."

"We don't use those too much." He thought. "When that elastic on the sheet pops up from the corner of the bed."

"I hate that."

Chip Jr. pointed to his head. "Bang massacres." My mother had given him a bad haircut. You could never trust my mother with the scissors, or hedge clippers, for that matter. It was true; Chip Jr.'s forehead had grown to embarrassingly huge proportions. He was calling it The Bang Massacre of July 27th.

"It's not that bad," I lied.

I looked at him, my brother with the glasses and the bad haircut and the odd way he had of watching out for me. He was always the one who noticed. I had the sudden longing to be back there in that car at the drive-in, jammed into the front seat next to those pajamas with the little balls of lint on them from so many washings, us passing the can of cream soda awkwardly to each other, our elbows maneuvering like people on a crowded dance floor. I wanted to see the movie reflecting in his and my mother's eyes as they stared forward through the windshield. I wanted to look back over my shoulder where the other movie played, where mouths moved wrongly to the cartoon voices playing in our car. But most of all I wanted to turn back around again and face front, to be fully in the world we were immersed in, where the voices matched the moving lips, where everything fit just the way it should.

Chapter 9

That night the air was cool and almost wet, the way it is when the clouds are stuffed with liquid but it hasn't rained yet. Heavy, lethargic clouds had lain around all day, a sudden and surprising interruption of the energetic sunshine we'd had for days before. That's what happens in the Northwest during the summer—manic-depressive weather. Sun and optimism and bathing suits and the confident, playful smell of sun lotion, and then *bam*, you wake up to the sound of the furnace going on and the dusty smell of warm air whooshing through vents that haven't been used in a while. You have to put on socks, and the browning lawn looks relieved. Mrs. Wong and Anna Bee had brought their sweaters to the book club that day; both sweaters had little pearl buttons.

Anyway, it was a bad night for a pool party, which just

goes to show that money can't control everything. Of course, I didn't know it was a pool party that I was going to, or even a party at all. I thought I was meeting Travis alone. I didn't want to ask for the details. On one hand, it was like knowing your birthday present before the day. On the other, I didn't want him to give me any information that my mind would get all parental about.

There was no way I was going to get out of my house without a sound lie, so I took a chance and asked Sydney for her help. She wasn't happy about being an accomplice. She was, after all, a charter member of the Help Ruby Ditch Travis Club ever since the sleepover. *This is not*, she said, *what friends do. Friends don't make excuses for friends to go see Mr. Hollywood who has a little taste for danger.* Did I know that everyone said he was a thief? Did I know that she would have to feel personally responsible if anything happened to me? Did I know that she would crush his nuts if he hurt me in any way?

My mother looked surprised when I told her I was going out with Sydney and her friends that night. I didn't do this very often, mostly because I worried that Sydney was bringing me along to benefit humankind, like some people give away turkeys on Christmas. I could see that my mother was trying to wrestle with her facial expressions when I told her, trying not to let the doubt sneak out through lowered eyebrows. She won, for the most part, though her smile had the frozen, still-trying cheer of a HAVE A NICE DAY bumper sticker on some old, falling-apart Volkswagen.

I escaped fast, waited on Sydney's porch for a while and then ran out to Cummings Road. It wasn't the best idea, walking along there where anyone might see me, but the light was dimming and all that waiting around on Sydney's porch made me late. A car sped past, music bumping from its open windows, and some guy yelled something my way, words that got snatched by the whoosh of air through his open window. The quick blast of bumping music filled me with something like confidence. The adrenaline of possibility made me feel fearless, almost as fearless as Travis thought I was. Why not be open to new experiences? Why be held back by someone like my mother, who for years hadn't taken a chance on anything more extreme than the sweepstakes on the underside of the Pepsi cap? Making my mother into the villain was tougher than I thought, so I went back to the New Experiences theme. I let the things I loved surge into me and grab my heart, sending it soaring upward to an emotional high-dive platform, where it would wait to leap. I took in the calm yellow porch light of George Washington's house, the goofy array of misfit cars at Ron's Auto, waiting for a second chance. I watched the paragliders, fewer in number on that cloudy day, but soaring and drifting, their colors bright against the gray sky.

That's where I was, high as those paragliders, until I saw the long line of cars snaking up Cummings Road and the driveway of the Becker estate. When I saw those cars, I came down, down, fast, as if the wind had abruptly ceased. I felt just as caught as one of those paragliders we occasionally saw stuck in the trees, legs dangling, a fool on display.

I walked up the driveway. Another couple was ahead of me. They were my parents' age—she wore a short Hawaiian dress that sucked to her butt tight as Saran Wrap to a bowl of leftovers and had hair sculpted into a Dairy Queen cone twist; he was packed snug into a polo shirt and shorts, and carried a gift with a perfect bow on top. Clouds of her perfume boldly stalked back my way. It was going to be a loud perfume night. All those perfumes in there would be competing for dominance with prize-fighter determination. I walked behind them dumbly and smelling only of shampoo. Party noises—music, laughter, raised voices—drifted from behind the house and poured out when Hawaiian Dress rang the doorbell and the door opened. They were noises that made me slink back into myself and want to disappear.

Travis Becker's mother answered the door. It was apparently a Hawaiian-themed night, as Mrs. Becker too wore a Hawaiian dress—tasteful, not bold—and a lei of fresh flowers. She had an orchid tucked behind one ear, her hair coiffed around it and flipping up at the ends. I'd never seen her up close before. She was beautiful, it was true—Travis had to get his looks from somewhere—one of those women who maintained her appearance as a part-time job. Travis's mother would be nothing like my own—she would not accidentally suck up socks and drapery hems with the vacuum, and she would not carry a roll of toilet paper in her car for nose-blowing emergencies.

She would have those tiny packets of Kleenex in her purse, and one for the glove compartment.

Mrs. Becker kissed the woman ahead of me, and then the man, and they wished her a happy birthday. I stood on the sidewalk behind them. I felt like those little kids on Halloween night, the reluctant trick-or-treaters that stand on the bottom step looking at you as if you are the monster. The ones who won't come forward no matter what is held out in the bowl in front of them. I thought Mrs. Becker might shut the door. She looked at me quizzically, as if maybe I'd come to ask about my lost cat. For a second it seemed like the perfect escape. *I'm sorry to bother you! I was just wondering if you'd seen Binky? He's a gray Persian.* But then Travis appeared behind his mother.

"Hey, finally," he said. "Come in."

I stepped inside, in the half space Mrs. Becker's body made. "Hello," I said. I forced my voice out. It was that overly polite one that squeaks with misuse and insincerity. "It's your birthday?"

"Don't remind me," she said, although if she wanted to quietly forget it, the loud music and the guy shouting "Your glass is empty, Becker!" probably wasn't the way to go.

"Be sure to get your friend something to drink," Mrs. Becker said.

"Ruby," I said. But Mrs. Becker had already turned around and was heading outside. "I didn't know there was going to be a party. You could have told me. It's her birthday. I would've at least brought a present."

"She's a bitch," he said. "Besides. You like surprises."
That was the thing about Travis Becker, I guess. The new
ways he defined me. I was never one who could be said to
like surprises. Surprises usually meant being caught
unprepared in some embarrassing way, and I was the kind
of person who always carried enough money for a phone
call. I liked the idea that I was someone who could capably handle what was thrown her way. That me would be
a person who would wear scarves and click along capably
in high heels. I decided that meant I would have to dis-
card my urge to beg for us to leave while clinging to the
cuff of Travis Becker's shirt with the surfers on it.

It was the first time I'd been in Travis' house. I caught
glimpses of things as we walked through the house to the
backyard. Marble floors, a staircase with shiny wood
handrails that curved up, a modern living room with pil-
lars and a creamy yellow carpet and paintings that looked
like someone stepped on a mustard bottle. I saw a violin
in a glass case, as if suspended in air. I felt sorry for it—
crafted to make beautiful music and yet as silent and
closed as Lillian. We walked through a huge kitchen,
large enough that if you made a nice cup of steamed milk
with a splash of vanilla before bed, it'd be cold before you
crossed the room. Big trays of food were set about, large
discs of cheeses and hors d'oeuvres of such varying shades
and shapes that they made me think of the pretend food
Chip Jr. and I used to make with our Play-Doh. Smells
drifted in from outside on curls of barbecue smoke; outside the first thing I noticed was a waiter carrying a tray

of salmon fillets, pink and shiny and ready to be singed. I got a tiny bit of pleasure out of the fact that salmon are not exactly Hawaii's state fish.

"Pork is too fattening," Travis said, reading my mind. "You wanna lei?" he shouted over the music and put his hand up the back of my skirt. I swatted him, and then he reached into a huge basket of plastic lei's, choosing a pink one for me, and put it around my neck. The thought crossed my mind that Travis Becker lacked imagination, resorting to the old lei joke. "My brother's in the band. Keyboards. They play their own stuff on the weekends." It was a live band—five guys doing sixties oldies that sounded better than my father's, I realized with equal portions of guilt and shame. I looked around at the pool area. I'd never seen anything so beautiful. It looked like it was out of a movie—small white lights in every tree, a canopy of lights across the patio. Candles in glass holders sat on tables draped in white linen; rose topiaries sat as centerpieces. Candles floated on the pool, and a few people swam among them.

"You know them," Travis said, reading my mind again. Boy, at that rate, he could have his own show in Las Vegas. "My mother is so pissed at the fact they are actually swimming in a swimming pool at a pool party."

I looked more closely, and could see that two of the swimmers were Seth and Courtney, though it was hard to recognize them with their hair wet and slicked back. Courtney was riding around on Seth's shoulders. She leaned over his head, her boobs spilling out of her bathing suit just like the waitresses at the Gold Nugget Roller Coaster Amusement Park, one on each side of Seth's head, a giant pair of wobbly earmuffs. She was shrieking as some other girl on some other guy's shoulders kicked water at her. The floating candles all began to group together like frightened ducklings.

I was glad for a moment I didn't know it was a pool party I was going to. I would have had to think about whether or not to wear a bathing suit. I know I couldn't ride around on someone's neck with my boobs swinging around sure as a pair of water balloons just before they're flung. Really, I don't know how the rules for things get made up. It's not okay to wear your underwear out in public, but it's okay to wear bathing suits, and Courtney's, I could see, appeared to be a piece of yarn that she just sat on and, oops, it got stuck. It looked like it hurt. You kind of wished someone would snap it like a rubber band. I knew I didn't fit in here. Maybe I need therapy, but I get embarrassed undressing in front of my dog.

The guy I didn't know shoved off his hanger-on. She fell into the water with a great splash and came up shrieking. I noticed that these kinds of girls shrieked a lot. The guy heaved himself up off the side of the pool as if he'd just dropped a box he'd had to carry and was now done with the job. He de-clung his bathing suit from his legs, shook his hair, and buried his face in a towel.

"Brandon!" Travis called.

Brandon walked over and we were introduced.

"Ni-iice," he said to Travis. I might as well have been

a new jacket Travis was wearing. "Hot in a girl-next-door way." He grinned. I was no doubt supposed to find the grin irresistible. Calling him an idiot would be an insult to idiots. Jeez, these people you were supposed to want to be like could really be disappointing.

"How 'bout a drink?" Travis asked. "Mai tai? Piña colada?"

"Mai tai," I said. I hadn't a clue what it was. It sounded like something orange juicy and fruity. Maybe it would come with a paper umbrella that would break if you pushed it too far up, like the one I got once in a smoothie.

We walked to the bar. They actually had a real bar outside there, with a bartender in a tuxedo and a bored expression. I felt sorry for him on the other side of that table. He was just a tuxedo with an outstretched hand, when he was actually someone who probably had a favorite color and memories of his first-grade teacher and foods he hated. The mai tai turned out to be red. No umbrella. I took a drink, and the heat of the alcohol stormed down my throat like it had plans to take over my body, which it probably did. I don't know if that's how strong those things usually are, or if the bartender had evil intentions to knock everyone out so that he could go home early.

"Tra-vis," Courtney called from the edge of the pool. She waved her empty glass in the air. She and the other girl stood in the pool with their arms crossed on the pool's edge. Up close, I could see that Courtney wore a little gold cross around her neck that hung between the water balloons. Seth was underwater, obviously trying to see how long he could hold his breath.

"We're empty," the other girl said. You could say that again.

"Get it yourself," Travis said. "I don't do the princess shit."

Courtney pouted. Seth popped up. Spit water out of his cheeks. "Seventy-four!" he announced. He took another gulp of air, ducked back down again.

"Brandon!" the other girl shouted. She held up her empty glass. Brandon came and picked up the glasses. She flattened out her lips in a *see?* smile directed at Travis. "Who is she?" she said, looking at me.

"Ruby," Travis said. "Friend of mine. Tiffany."

"Hi," I said. I kind of wanted to step on her fingers.

Brandon returned with two drinks, squatted down in front of the girls. Seth popped up again. "Seventy-four again. Shit."

I thought I caught Courtney looking into the dark hole of the leg of Brandon's bathing suit. I was right. A second later, she stuck one finger up there, wiggled it around. Seth floated underwater, oblivious to the adventures of his girlfriend's fingers. His arms circled his knees; they rolled up and his toes pointed from the water.

"What is this crap they're playing?" Tiffany said.

"Beatles," Travis said. "She probably hasn't heard of them," he said to me.

"I've heard of them. What do you think I am, stupid?"

Up popped Seth. "Seventy-five!" He beamed. Thank God. Seth was proving himself to be a really determined breath-holder. Like my mother says, it's important to have goals.

"When can we ditch this party?" Courtney said. She'd taken her finger from Brandon's shorts and was now working on her drink like she'd just ran a mile on a scorching day. A few of the adults in Hawaiian outfits were starting to dance. It struck me how the things that we consider normal are often extremely weird.

"You didn't have to come," Travis said.

"My parents brought me," Courtney said.

"Look at my dad," Travis said. "Trying to dance. Looks like a fucking moron." I looked around the patio where everyone was dancing. "Straw hat," Travis directed. The fucking moron who bought Travis the big house and the swimming pool and the motorcycle had his hands in a pair of fists up near his chest, and was bobbing his upper body from side to side without moving his feet. He beamed under his straw hat. He was dancing with a tiny blonde in a sarong who had her arms swaying over her head. Her hips swiveled and her eyes were closed as if she were in some kind of sexual trance. Mr. Becker, on the other hand, reminded me of those shows you see on TV for old people, where they can exercise from their chair.

Seth swam up behind Courtney, put his chin on her shoulder. "You're getting me all *wet*," she said.

"You're in a *pool*," Tiffany said.

"My *shoulder* was *dry*," Courtney said.

"Bitchy," Brandon said.

It was difficult to break into this invigorating conversation, so instead I just stood there, feeling stupid for a thousand reasons. This was one of those events that sounded a lot better beforehand and afterward than it ever was during. I wished I could have some of that Play-Doh food, though.

"We can go to my house," Courtney said. "My parents are *here*."

"Do what you want," Travis said. "We got plans anyway."

"I like this old shit," Brandon said. He danced around a little. "Come on, Tiff." He snapped his fingers.

"Forget it. I'm with Courtney for going to her house."

"We can sneak a bottle of rum from the bar," Courtney said. She heaved herself up from the side of the pool, showing us way more of her butt in that string thing than I ever cared to see. You know, maybe people don't *want* to see your butt. She toweled off; her towel, which had been draped on a chaise lounge, said I'M A BOY SCOUT.

Travis turned to me. "Let's get out of here," he said. "They bore the hell out of me." He grabbed my arm suddenly, wove us through the crowd, and hurried us around the garage, past a trio of guys in Hawaiian shirts and smoking cigars. I was still holding my mai tai, one sip removed, and the jostling made a bit spill out onto the open toe of my sandals. I was sorry only to leave the Play-Doh food and that big white cake, tall and fancy as the one at Mrs. Wilson-now-Mrs. Thrumond's wedding to

Mr. Thrumond. I pictured Mrs. Becker looking around the crowd for her family, spotting her husband in his hat and her eldest at the keyboards, but no Travis. I felt sorry for her then, blowing out her candles, the yellow light in her face, but her son not caring enough to stay around. I felt sorry for her, even if she had those little Kleenex packets.

"Where are we going?" I asked. This time I wanted to know. The person I was trying to be and the person I really was were having a little fight, and the person I really was had won. She'd been around longer.

"Hang on a sec. Stay right here."

Travis trotted back the way we came. I stood alone, holding that stupid mai tai. I sniffed it, and the strong smell shot through my nostrils, a train through a tunnel. I tried to wipe the red splotch of drink off my toe onto the wet grass, and then was suddenly aware that the eyes of one of the cigar smokers were on me. Travis jogged back. He had a napkin full of wonderful Play-Doh food. I had a ridiculous surge of joy at the sight. He held it out to me. I took a round one that looked like a hat the queen of England would wear. Cream cheese with a mystery crunch.

"Let's take the bike."

I followed him to the garage. We went through a side door, happily away from the eyes of the cigar smoker. The Becker garage was quiet; inside, all the sounds of the party had disappeared. The garage was so clean it was eerie. There were no splotches of paint or motor oil on the cement floor, no gatherings of dust or pine needles. It was large enough for three cars in there, but right then there was only a Mercedes convertible with the top down and Travis's motorcycle. I thought of our garage. Here there were no garden tools or hammers or rakes with the clumps of grass still attached; no stacks of newspapers, cans of insect killer, and car wash soap, or badminton rackets and old baby crib frames. Sydney's garage was much the same as ours, packed with grass seed and bags of fertilizer and bikes hanging from the ceiling. Here there was no real evidence of human life. Even Mr. Baxter across the street, whose tools were all hung up on a Peg-Board under labels with their names, still had grocery bags full of cans to recycle and a pouchy bag of golf clubs covered with socks with pom-poms on them. Frankly, that was something else I never understood—why people dressed up their golf clubs in goofy snow hats for what is supposed to be a dignified, nice-weather game.

"Doesn't your dad play golf?" I asked.

"Of course he plays golf," Travis said.

He handed me the napkin of food, which was the best thing that happened all night. I ate another queen's hat and an anthill on a cracker with a suspicious fishy taste. Travis bent down and examined his motorcycle. If he were look-ing for dust or smudges, he'd be looking for a long time.

He straightened, opened the garage door by punching a keypad on the wall. We ate the rest of the stuff on the napkin, and Travis stuffed the napkin in his pocket. "Let's go," he said.

"Come on, Travis. Where are we going?"

"Somewhere you love."

And I was an idiot. I pictured us walking along the lake, hand in hand, with the houses along the shore glowing with warm light and cozy secrets. I pictured us sitting side-by-side at Mount Solitude, staring at its dark shoulder, imagining what it would feel like to leap off.

"What do I do with this?" I held up my glass. He took it from me, and in that moment I realized I might have made a terrible mistake. I had just given him the chance to down it in one gulp like Courtney had, and then get on his motorcycle with me on the back. I pictured a horrible accident; us splayed out on wet pavement. But he didn't do that. Instead he placed it in the middle of that pristine garage.

It looked mean there, that glass. Cruel and deliberate, the red the same color left on a cheek after a slap. It occurred to me then that a lot of life was either about wanting and not having, or having and not wanting.

The arc Travis' motorcycle made out of the Becker drive was delicious. I held tight to his waist. I settled into the feeling, the wind on my bare legs, my head wobbly and heavy from my helmet. It was the coldest ride yet, though, with the clouds full of rain and the sky dark. I was glad for my sweater. We passed Moon Point. The paragliders had a bonfire going, as they did some summer nights, and they were gathered around its warm orange light. By the look of the sky, though, they wouldn't be there long.

I didn't know how long we'd be riding, but I didn't expect to stop after such a short while. No, I didn't expect to stop right then at Johnson's Nursery.

He stopped in a parking space, both feet on the ground. "Hop off," he said.

"Why are we here?" The feathery wings of fear. Just a pulse beat of panic.

"Hop off. Shit, I'm just checking something."

A wave of relief shot through my stomach. He turned the motor off. I got off, hugged my arms around myself. I hoped no one saw me there. It was quiet, and dark except for the round helmets of the landscape lights around the front of the store. I waited for Travis to check whatever he was going to check. He didn't get off, though. Instead, he started walking the bike off the parking strip, toward the section of in-ground trees.

"I thought you were checking something," I said. My relief disappeared as quickly as it came. A thread of fear snaked up my insides and settled in a coil around my heart.

"I am. I'm checking that no one will see my bike."

"Travis," I said. "No. I don't want to be here."

"Yes, you do."

"No, Travis, I don't. I don't want to be here."

I heard the *threep* of crickets. A semi-truck rumbled down Cummings Road and made the air shudder.

He grabbed my wrist. He pulled me toward the path that led to the waterfalls. It was dark there. I thought of the ceramic toads and elves hidden among the plants, watching from the blackness. Libby had set them there, placed them in the ground with her own hands. Travis gripped my shoulders. The moon edged from a bank of clouds and then was hidden again. The light shone on Travis's face and then was gone. "Tell me where they keep the key to the cash register."

"Oh, God, Travis, no."

"Tell me."

"She keeps it with her." I shivered. In fact, I was starting to shake. I saw Libby with that cactus garden on her desk. I saw her fleshy arms and her warm eyes. I saw her looped writing on bills and invoices, the way she sighed and said, *Thank you, another day is done* whenever she locked the door behind her. The plants, her business, her labor of love.

"She doesn't. I've watched her. She always gets it from the storeroom."

"No." Tears were building hot behind my eyes. My throat was thickening. "If you want money, she doesn't have it anyway. She takes it to the bank."

"Not every day. I told you, I've watched her. She leaves it on Saturdays." He waggled his index finger in the air. "Careless, careless."

"Travis, I can't do this." My chest heaved. I started to cry.

"Ruby, Ruby," he said. "Come on, what are you crying for? I'm asking you one small question. Where does she keep the key?"

No! Something shouted inside. But it didn't come

out. I didn't say anything. I only shook my head, a small movement that could barely be said to exist.

"I know what you fear the most. You fear a narrow life more than anything."

I didn't say anything. Just stood there, with tears rolling down my cheeks. I couldn't hurt Libby. Narrow, small. Unknown.

"Isn't that right? A narrow life."

He waited. I knew it was my moment of decision. To belong or not to belong. To be visible or invisible. This voice came from me, from the ugliest part of me. This down-deep blackness. I didn't know I could be so ugly. I whispered. My voice was hoarse. "A hook in the storeroom. Behind the bookshelf with boxes on it."

He took my face between his hands and kissed me. My lips were dry and cold, my mouth gummy from tears and shame.

"Let's go, then," he said.

But I couldn't do that. At least there was something I couldn't do.

"Are you coming?" Travis Becker asked. And then, "Fine. Stay there, then."

His footsteps were soft on the dirt path, and then I heard them crunch on the gravel by the store. I bent in half. Pain bent me in half. I opened my mouth to sob but no sound came out. It was like that time, years and years ago, in elementary school, when I fell off the monkey bars and landed on my back, the wind knocked out of me. I couldn't breathe. The air in my body was held back somewhere, in some greedy place, as my lungs searched desperately for it. It was that same feeling. Gasping. I crouched on the ground. A ceramic frog looked at me with a gentle expression. I heard the crash of glass. Darkness can make a sound very loud. That was the sound of my betrayal—the shattering clatter of a rock thrown into a pane of glass.

I ran then. My feet crunched down the gravel of the Johnson's Nursery parking lot. I ran down Cummings Road, headlights beaming at me, feeling the fear of the opossums and not caring. Running, running, until I saw the sign, lit up by the roadside DOG KNOWS WHO YOU ARE. It hit my heart then, hard. I sank to the ground. I could feel the grass, dewy and cold, soak my skirt.

I sobbed in self-hatred and self-pity and anger. The worst kind of anger, the kind you feel at your own stupidity, the kind that sits and stares at what cannot be undone. I was running from the person back there, the one who could say *a hook in the storeroom* but running, of course, was useless. That dark thing I did—it would sit with me like a stain, a gash, a permanent disfigurement. There are these small things, a few words, a moment in time, a decision yes or no, that are the irretrievable, unforgettable acts. Split-second choices that are as endless in consequence and as powerful as the shifting plates of the earth. One moment. Yes or no?

It started to rain finally. A fine drizzle that covered me like a miserable blanket as I lay down on the hill of grass by the DOG sign. I cried and held my stomach. At that moment, I didn't know that there was someone else out in the rain that night, her heart wrenching in pain.

Lillian had gotten herself out the door and as far as the front lawn before the wheels of her chair got stuck in the wet grass and the hopelessness of her task overpowered her. The police were called after someone reported hearing what was described as *a cry of anguish*. When they got there, they found Lillian with her head thrown back against her wheelchair, her hair and clothing soaked. Her chest racked with silent sobs.

She would not release the book she cradled in her arms. She clung to it, protecting it from the rain with the will of her own small body.

Chapter 10

"Ruby? Is that you?"

I was so cold. My hair streaked down my face. What I had done seemed to fill up every bit of my skin.

"Jesus Christ, it is you! Oh, damn, that's not what I meant. I didn't mean to say that. Forget I said that. Ruby?"

I felt a hand on my back. There was the breath of someone who had just eaten Italian food, warm and garlicky and somehow comforting. He was crouched down beside me. "What's going on? What's happened?"

I shook my head.

"Come on, Ruby," Joe Davis said. "It's okay. It's really okay." His kindness did me in. I started to cry again. "Come on. Whatever it is, it'll be all right. Can I take you home?"

I guess I was rocking. I only noticed it because the arm on my shoulders was rocking, too. "We can at least get out of this rain, can't we?" The arms of the body next to me stretched up, untangled and released a sweatshirt. A moment later, he popped it over my own head. It was warm from body heat. It smelled like cooking smells. I put my arms through the holes.

"Okay, then," Joe Davis said. He clapped his hands together like he had a great plan. He stood above me for a minute, probably trying to figure out what that great plan actually was.

"Well, heave ho, then," he said. His arms went around my back and under my knees and I was lifted up. I rested my head against him as we bounced across the lawn to his car. He was breathing a little heavy. But he was big and old and enough like a father to call it good.

I was wrapped in a quilt on our couch like I was a decent person who was sick, and not like I was the horrible person I was. Someone so horrible should not have her mother sitting beside her and Joe Davis making tea in the kitchen and her brother looking on nervously and her dog trying to jump up on the quilt and being swatted off.

I told the couch pillow what happened as they sat across from me. I heard Joe Davis and my mother in the kitchen discussing the need to call the police. It turned out to be unnecessary. The phone rang a half hour later. The police had called us instead. I heard my mother's concerned tones, questions. She talked for a long time, then was quiet. More questions. Someone had told them we'd been together that night.

"Ruby?" my mother said from the kitchen doorway. Her eyes were worried, but soft. I knew by their softness that something bad had happened. Worse even than I expected. Joe Davis came from behind her. He sat down at the edge of the couch.

"This is a bad night," he said.

"That was the police," my mother said.

I buried my face in the couch pillow.

"They want to arrest me or something," I said.

"It's not about you," my mother said. "It's about Travis."

I breathed. I dared to breathe. "They arrested him. Fine. Good. I want them to arrest him," I said.

"He's been in an accident," Joe Davis said.

"What?" I sat up. "What?" Oh, God.

"His motorcycle. He was driving very fast. You know how bad Cummings Road is anyway. They think he heard the police coming. The road was slick from the rain."

"Is he dead? God, is he dead?" That I couldn't take. That I couldn't handle or understand.

"No, Ruby. He's in the hospital. He's unconscious, but they think he's going to be okay."

It was said later that Ron of Ron's Auto had the acute hearing of a bat—he reported having a restless sleep because he could hear the lyrics of Beatles songs at a party a mile away. Apparently he told police that his old girlfriend's name was Michelle (and if you think it's strange that Ron had a girlfriend at all, batlike in other ways as he was, my mother would be quick to say what she always did about such things—*Every pot has a lid*). The song lyrics of the Beatles ballad had kept him awake and thinking hard. That's when he heard the sound of glass breaking at Johnson's Nursery. He knew it was Johnson's nursery, he had said, because of the slightly *southwestern flow* of the sound. That night, with the call to Lillian's house and the accident on Cummings Road, the police had been busier than they had been since Homecoming night five years ago, when an entire city block was festooned with toilet paper and eggs.

I thought about Travis in some hospital bed. I pictured his chest going up and down to the rhythm of some machine. I pictured the cold beeping sound, and his mother's tears—a birthday gone horribly awry. They were there at his side in their Hawaiian outfits, regretting the cheer of pineapples and palm trees. Mrs. Becker would have thrown a sweater on that didn't match. As I've said, Cummings Road can be a dangerous place.

I felt so much that I didn't feel anything. Numb and dead, as unconscious as Travis himself. I was sure of only one thing; I wanted to be away from Nine Mile Falls for a while, away from what the Beckers must think of me, and what Libby would think of me, and what anyone else would think of me. If I could have wished for anything right then, it would be that.

■■■

I finally slept. I woke up late that morning. I'd been having a dream that I was being hammered into a locked room, a prisoner. My eyes opened and I came back to real life, remembering the shambles I had made of it. The hammering had been real. Someone was hammering in the kitchen. I hoped Mom wasn't trying to fix something, like the kitchen sink. Every time she tries to repair something, it's a disaster. She takes everything apart and puts it back together wrong. She tried to fix the vacuum cleaner once, and now it makes a horrible sound, a machine chewing metal. You've got to wiggle the toilet flushing handle now too. Every time you flush, the pipes hiss louder and louder until it sounds like the toilet is about to lift up off the floor and become the first toilet in space.

I put on my robe and got out of bed. I was surprised to see the crouched figure of Joe Davis in our kitchen, by the hole. Chip Jr.'s G.I. Joe now sat on the kitchen table with his legs hanging off as if it were a thoroughly absorbing show, something military on the History Channel. Poe sat nearby also, prim and still and showing remarkably good manners. He turned and looked at me quickly and turned back to face Joe again. He couldn't bear to miss a second of the proceedings.

Joe Davis looked over one shoulder and smiled. His forehead was sweaty. "Morning," he said. "You won't be able to use the water right now. I had to shut it off. There was a leak in the pipe right here." He knocked at a piece of the exposed metal. "Like I told your mom, you were lucky that Poe destroyed the wall. It could have leaked for years, causing all kinds of damage, and you'd have never known. Now we'll just have to replace a few boards." I swear Poe looked proud at his now important act. His black lips curled in that smile he had.

The coffeepot was on and two cups sat by the sink. The letter my mother had written to my father that had sat on the counter for days was gone. A tool belt hung over one of the chairs. The funny thing was, I didn't even feel embarrassed about Joe Davis seeing me in my robe and morning hair. He was a comfortable person. His hair looked pretty funny itself. Unlike the clichéd butt-crack plumber who came to our house once, who sighed and groaned the whole time like an old pier in a strong wind, Joe Davis was easy and happy in his work. He smiled at the hole like they were friends getting acquainted.

"Okay." Joe Davis got to his feet, opened the back door. I could see some lumber lying on the back lawn. Poe trotted off after him.

Joe turned and looked down at Poe. "Sit," he said. "Stay."

And here was the amazing thing: Poe's little butt shot right to the floor, sure as if it were attached to a piece of string.

"Didn't you hear all of the commotion?" Miz June asked Peach. "It all happened right next door, and you didn't hear a thing?"

Harold cupped his hand to his mouth and shouted, "Must be going deaf." He was one to talk.

"I am not going deaf," Peach said. "I was watching *Miami Vice*."

"Is that show still on? The fellow with the pink shirts must be fairly old to be running around shooting and blowing things up," Anna Bee said.

"Reruns," Peach said. "Back-to-back *Miami Vice* on Saturday nights."

I could picture Peach's television blaring, her sitting in a chair that used to belong to Henry, one with a footrest that popped out, eating out of a bag of microwave popcorn and not even noticing the red, spinning lights of the police car right outside her house, the two police officers bringing Lillian back inside and calling her daughters. I wondered if Lillian, too, had dreams that night of being hammered inside a room, imprisoned.

"That bitch Delores said they found her with another copy of *The Present Hours* in her arms. I guess it was too important to her not to have a second," Peach said.

"She was probably looking for it when she tore the books off the shelf that day," Miz June said.

"I told you. I said she was looking for something," Mrs. Wong said.

"Well, it wasn't on the bookshelf. She must have forgotten where she put it. Delores said that this time Lillian's cookbooks and recipe box were strewn all over the floor." I pictured Lillian hiding her heart's secrets underneath Apple Crumb Cake and Apricot-Glazed Chicken.

"Well, we've got to do something," Harold said.

"Lillian will die in there," Anna Bee said. She looked near tears. Her thin wrists stuck out from beneath a sweatshirt with rows of butterflies on it that was labeled with their names. It continually astounded me how the old ladies always dressed like it was the middle of winter when it was so hot out.

"We will not allow this," Mrs. Wong said. She sounded fierce in spite of her red slippers. "Lillian is not strong like Grandfather Wong. She will die in that place."

We'd heard the news that morning. Four days after our joint night of rain-drenched heartache, Lillian had been taken to the Golden Years Rest Home. Delores and Nadine and their husbands had come to her home and packed up a few of her belongings. Lillian's attempt to run away and her other recent behavior showed she was a danger to herself, they'd said. Mrs. Wong was sure that it really had to have been planned long ago. When her father-in-law, Grandfather Wong, required twenty-four-hour nursing care, they had been on a waiting list for months. Peach said they'd been at Lillian's every day since, packing up and taking boxes from her home. She expected a FOR SALE sign to go up any day now. Peach said she couldn't bear to watch. She'd closed all her drapes, but still couldn't help herself from peeking between the curtains, seeing the sad parade of Lillian's life being packed into the back of Delores' minivan.

We'd had other news since that night too. Travis Becker was miraculously alive and all right, except for a broken pelvis and collarbone. He'd be coming home in a few days, they thought. My mother had also talked to Libby, who would be pressing charges against Travis but not me. I was fired, of course. But worse, she did not want to speak to me.

"So this is why I've called an emergency meeting of the Casserole Queens," my mother said. "I have something very important to tell you."

"The hippie proposed," Harold said.

"Lillian in a rest home isn't enough?" Miz June said. She was ripping off the cellophane from a box of chocolates from one of her admirers. Harold hadn't had time to prepare food. My mother had called them all that morning. She'd come in my room too, and told me we were gathering and I had to be there. I hadn't wanted to go there or anywhere else. I preferred to stay in my bed, wrapped in a quilt cocoon. I was busy imagining myself as Claudia in *From the Mixed-up Files of Mrs. Basil E. Frankweiler*, running away to New York and hiding out in the Metropolitan Museum of Art. I used to love that book. *This is not 'you made your bed, now you have to lie in it' time*, my mother had said. *This is 'you made your bed, now get up and change the sheets.'* I'd wished I'd used the same technique on her in the past.

In the car, she refused to tell me why we were meeting. *Why should I?* she had said. *It's not like you tell me anything before it happens.* This is what I'd been getting over the last few days. She was a balloon full of air, yet her anger would not come out in one explosive pop, but instead through a slow leak. I wished in some ways we'd just have it out in a big fight, but that wasn't what my mother did. She preferred the small, brief jabs, then retreat. Small seeps of hurt that still drew blood. We drove a little further. *You've decided we should have secrets, so secrets it will be*, she said.

Miz June set the box of chocolates on the table.

"That one's the cherry," Harold helpfully pointed it out. He made a face. We all took a piece, avoiding it.

"Orange cream," Peach said. She'd taken a bite, looked at the other half as if it were something she'd found on the bottom of her shoe. "I hate orange cream."

"Caramels are the best," Harold said.

"They are not good for dentures," Mrs. Wong said.

"I spoke with Charles Whitney," my mother said.

This stopped all talk of chocolates and of anything else. The room was silent except for the soft thrum of Beauty's purring from where she sat on Mrs. Wong's slippers. Miz June, who had delicately pinched a chocolate between two fingers and was heading it toward her mouth, stopped in midair and changed her mind, setting it back on the napkin in her lap.

"Well?" Anna Bee finally said.

"Goddamn it, Ann, speak," Peach said.

"I called him. Just like that. I was surprised he was listed. Monterey, California. You would not believe how easy it was to find him. Five minutes on the Internet. I just . . . It seemed crazy, but not crazy. I just couldn't get past my own curiosity. Damn it, you got me again." She shook her finger at Peach.

"She's Rose, I know it," Peach said.

"The first time I called I got a woman."

"Ah, he's a ladies man!" Mrs. Wong said. "Like Mr. Wong."

"No, it was his daughter, I guess. She told me he was at a game."

"Baseball fan!" Harold said. "Good man."

"No, a soccer game. I guess he coaches his grand-daughter's team. Can you picture him, big beard and all, coaching little girls' soccer?"

"A scholar and an athlete," Miz June said.

"Go on, Ann," Anna Bee said.

"Well, as I said, I asked for Charles Whitney. The woman said he wasn't there, and asked if she could take a message. I felt like an idiot. 'Is this his wife?' I asked. I was worried. I didn't want to make her uncomfortable if it was, talking about Lillian/Rose."

"That was very sensitive of you," Miz June said.

"The woman laughed. 'No,' she said. 'His daughter. He's wifeless.' She sounded so friendly. 'Wifeless.' I told her everything. I told her I ran a book club for seniors in Nine Mile Falls and we were trying to unravel a mystery of sorts. We had a feeling that one of our members, silenced by a stroke, might have known him. I just let it all out, foolish or not. She didn't say anything. It was silent on that phone except for a dog who started to bark in the background."

"An animal lover too!" Anna Bee said.

"I thought she'd left me hanging there. I pictured a

phone dangling on its cord in some kitchen. But then I could hear just a small intake of breath. Like a sigh, only in reverse. And then she said something that nearly knocked me over. She said, 'Nine Mile Falls? You don't happen to mean Lillian Hargrove do you?'"

"Holy shit," Harold said. Mrs. Wong munched her second chocolate and reached for another. You could just imagine how she would pound a box of Raisinets in a movie theater at the exciting part.

"You guys were right. I couldn't believe it. After the dead body. After the Nazi. You guys were right."

"I told you!" Peach shouted. She stood up from her chair, did a little dance, her old body a symphony of looseness, chin swag swaying, her chest swinging to and fro. "Lillian is Rose, Lillian is Rose!" I felt it too. A surge of excitement. I wanted to get up and dance too. Lillian, so frail in her chair. A secret life. Possibilities for those who seemed to have run out of them. The quiet people.

"I said, 'Lillian Hargrove, yes,'" my mother said. "'That's right. He does know her, then.'

"'I'm going to call my father right now and have him call you back,' Joelle, his daughter, said. "'He's at a soccer practice. My daughter's. He coaches her team. But trust me, he'll want to be interrupted.'

"I sat by the phone," my mother said. "I just looked at it. It seemed . . ." My mother's voice broke a little, and she swallowed. "It seemed to have the power to make miracles."

Mrs. Wong had her hankie out. She dabbed her eyes. I felt a lump growing in my own throat.

"It rang not three minutes later. 'Is this Ann McQueen of Nine Mile Falls?' he said. Charles Whitney! The real him. I couldn't believe it, I tell you. I mean, the man is a two-time National Book Award winner. He had this deep, rumbly voice, like a ship's engine. My hand was shaking.

"'Yes,' I said.

"'Lillian Hargrove', he said. No, he *breathed*. He told me everything I needed to know when he said that name. I could hear kids in the background. Little girls, a whistle. Another man's voice giving directions.

"'So you do know her,' I said.

"'Indeed I do,' he said. 'Indeed I do.'" My mother's eyes were bright. Tears were rolling down Mrs. Wong's cheeks and Harold had his head down, twisting his wristwatch and clearing his throat a lot.

"I could almost see him," my mother said, "hunched around that phone, soccer bags and balls and water bottles at his feet, girls in little uniforms running on a green field. He told me he and Lillian were lovers during the war. He told me they'd been in contact over the last year or two, since Walter died. They'd been writing letters, calling. They'd been making plans to be together. Secret plans. Lillian had tried to tell her daughters about Charles, but they disapproved. Protective of their father. So they kept their plans to themselves."

"That bitch Delores," Harold said, but his voice was a squeak. Mrs. Wong still clutched her hankie. A bit of black mascara had rolled down her cheek, underneath her eyeglasses.

"But they had an argument," my mother said. "Lillian worried that her daughters needed her. She had second thoughts about leaving them. And then . . ." My mother paused.

"And then Lillian had her stroke," Peach said. "Oh, God."

"Lillian had her stroke. Charles didn't know what happened. He called and called. He wrote, but he never heard back. His calls were not returned. He thought she had left him again.

"'I've been miserable without her,' he told me," my mother said. "'I thought I'd lost her.'"

"I told him what had happened. I told him about Delores and Nadine putting Lillian in the rest home. 'Bring her to me, Ann,' he said. 'I'll take care of her.'

"I explained that Lillian wasn't in good shape. She would require a lot of care. She couldn't take care of herself.

"But he said I didn't understand. 'None of that matters,' Charles Whitney said. 'Lillian is my soul mate.'"

The Casserole Queens ordered pizza. My mother called home and found out that Joe Davis had done the same— he and Chip Jr. were sharing a Canadian bacon with extra cheese and watching a show on nature photography. Harold pretended to be dissatisfied with the quality of the food, but scarfed down four pieces before I stopped counting. He even used his finger to scrape the cheese stuck to the top of the box.

"Delores and Nadine *knew* he was trying to reach her. What about all of the phone calls?" Peach said.

"They saw the letters. No one can tell me they didn't," Mrs. Wong said.

"Children don't like to see you live your own life sometimes," Miz June said. "They chaperone you like you are a wayward teenager."

"They forget you're a woman and not just a mother," Peach said.

"They think they are the sole owners of a sex life," Miz June said.

Yikes. Open brain, remove image. Maybe she was right.

"Someone needs to talk some sense into Delores," Anna Bee said.

"Maybe she'll understand if we explain," Miz June said.

"One thing I've learned," Harold said. In his exuberant pizza eating, he'd dropped a splotch of red sauce on his white polo shirt. "Talking sense to people who are not sensible is as productive as talking into your underwear drawer, and a whole lot less pleasant. Delores and Nadine are the defenders of their dead father's memory and their mother's virtue. Stand aside."

"We've got to do something," I said. The hollowness I'd felt over the last few days was gone. Filled with a sudden urgency. Purpose, I guess. I never knew how powerful purpose is, how large. The way it can find the grooves and furrows.

"If we phrase it in the right way, maybe they'll come around," Anna Bee said.

"If we steal Lillian out of the rest home, we don't have to care whether they come around or not," Mrs. Wong said.

"What are you saying?" my mother said.

"I have connections," Mrs Wong said.

"We could steal her out of there," Harold said, as if it were his idea.

"Drive her down to California," Miz June said.

"We'd have to make sure she really wants to go," my mother said.

"I'll go see her," Peach said.

"We'll both go," Anna Bee said.

"This can't work," my mother said. Harold's face fell. The voice of authority was speaking. I was about to open my mouth, give her a lecture on taking a chance—*soul mate!* when she said something surprising. "My car would never make it."

"I've got a car," Miz June said. "The Lincoln. I've only driven it a few times. It barely has any miles on it, from when it belonged to Chester Delmore's dead wife."

"Gas guzzler," Anna Bee said. She was always environmentally responsible.

"Room for lots of people. Four seat belts in the back. Three in front."

"Well," my mother said. "It's decided. It's a mission for true love, which I, for one, had lost hope in."

Miz June opened a drawer of a side table and

brought out a pen and a page of stationery, decorated around the edges with roses. You could smell a faint whiff of sweetness—it was scented. "I'll have to go, of course, since I'm driving." She wrote her name down. I had an image of her driving twenty miles an hour all the way to California, her nose pressed to the windshield. It would be faster to take Anna Bee's Schwinn. "Ann, as the leader of the group and only sane member. Which means Ruby and Chip Jr. too, I assume. And of course we can't forget Lillian. That leaves two seats." Miz June waited for agreement. Everyone nodded.

"We'll draw straws," Harold said.

"Mrs Wilson-now-Mrs. Thrumond will be sorry she left now," Peach said.

Anna Bee scurried to the kitchen. I'd never seen her move so fast. This was like *Charlie and the Chocolate Factory*, with the golden tickets. "Do you have straws?" She shouted to Miz June. It wasn't like her to shout, either. She had a surprising set of lungs.

"In the pantry. Top shelf. I like them with my lemonade. Scissors in the drawer under the phone."

"Ann will hold the straws," Harold said, though he was the only one we had to worry about as far as cheating went.

Anna Bee came back with the straws. My mother turned her back on the group, put the straws in her fist. Everyone chose. It was solemn as a church service.

"Yippee," Peach said. "I'm in."

"Long straw," Harold said. You could tell he was suppressing his glee.

"Short," Mrs. Wong said.

"We'll still need you to help steal Lillian," Miz June said.

"That's the most important job," I said.

"I'm out too." Anna Bee said. Her face dropped.

"Thank goodness," Miz June said kindly. "Someone's got to stay behind and look after the pets. Beauty and Harold's fish. And, oh, my sweet peas."

"Joe Davis can look after Poe now that they are best friends," I said.

"Joe Davis, the minister?" Miz June asked. One eyebrow shot up.

"Ann, you're blushing," Anna Bee said.

"He's helping us fix a few things," she said. "Poe just has a new leash on life, ha ha."

"Things are looking up!" Peach said.

"As long as I don't have to sit by the viper," Harold said.

"I wouldn't sit by you if I were dead and couldn't tell the difference," Peach said.

"Road trip," Harold said.

Chapter 11

That day, the day we stole Lillian, we were all capable of magic, each and every one of us who had gathered on our front lawn holding a copy of the plan for the human heist that my mother had copied on the library copy machine. You could see it later, that magic, in the pictures Chip Jr. was running around and snapping maniacally with the old camera Joe Davis had given him that morning. The camera was a present after their discussion the night before, when Joe Davis told Chip Jr. that he thought Chip Jr.'s noticing and curiosity were the best kind of compliments to God, like an art lover's appreciation and study of a painting. If so, his new compliments were going to cost Mom a fortune in developing, as Chip Jr. was noticing and capturing everything. *Click*, Harold in an uncharacteristically tacky orange baseball cap, knapsack over one shoulder, posing with one arm around Peach and making rabbit ears with two fingers behind her permed head. *Click*, Joe Davis with his eyes fixed on my mother, a beautiful blur at the outside frame of the photo, as Poe sat upright at his feet in perfect focus, looking up at the minister adoringly, as if he'd just found the Supreme King of Red Meat. *Click*, Miz June's puff of blonde hair in the Lincoln, which sat at the curb all gold and chrome glinting in the sun like a carriage in a modern fairy tale. *Click*, Anna Bee and Mrs. Wong sneaking a look at the *Playboys* that Mrs. Wong brought along for Grandfather Wong, Anna Bee's face red as a geranium and Mrs. Wong's wearing the expression of a lost soul stuck by a roadside trying to read a map upside-down. And *click*, me, a pencil behind my ear, caught by surprise, glancing over one shoulder as my name was called, looking relaxed and happy and, most amazingly, myself. Not small or narrow, but full and alive, and for a moment, not racked with thoughts about Travis and Libby.

You could see the magic we all had that day. The magic that comes with the force of a mission, lit with a fine and rare energy. The magic of purpose and of love in its purest form. Not television love, with its glare and hollow and sequined glint; not sex and allure, all high shoes and high drama, everything both too small and in too much excess, but just love. Love like rain, like the smell of a tangerine, like a surprise found in your pocket. We were all part of that.

Miz June wanted to get going. She kept revving the

accelerator of the Lincoln, urging us to get a move on. My mother went to the bathroom five thousand times like she always does when she gets nervous. Joe Davis kissed her good-bye behind the hydrangea bush. Every time Chip Jr. kneeled to take a picture, Poe would trot over and stick his nose up to the lens, wanting another close-up. Later, we'd have six fine shots of this one segment of Poe's face—huge smeary black nose, slightly wet lips, enormous, slightly deranged-looking eyes.

My mother quizzed us one last time about the plan, which Lillian had agreed to with a nod and tears in her eyes when Peach and Anna Bee had last visited. Finally we loaded into the Lincoln, with Mrs. Wong and Anna Bee in Mrs. Wong's Mercedes behind us. We waved good-bye to Joe Davis. Sydney and her mom drove up the street just then and yelled "Good luck!" through their rolled-down windows.

Even though Miz June stepped on the gas too hard and we all lurched forward as violently as those crash test dummies in the commercials, I had never felt so happy. It was like a party in my heart.

The Golden Years Rest Home was not officially in Nine Mile Falls, but sat on the boundary marker of it and the neighboring town, as if neither wanted to claim it. As those kinds of places go, it really wasn't that bad— hunched, drooling people weren't abandoned in Pine-Sol–smelling halls, like the one place we went to with my seventh-grade choir class. This one had art by the residents up on the walls and a large, attentive staff, which was exactly what our biggest challenge was going to be. That and the fact that Lillian's daughters were there twice a day, as Peach had already found out when she had visited.

Still, the Golden Years was a place we all wanted to forget about, the way we draw a line in our brain between us and things terrible or unjust. The rooms' residents with the small gray heads drooped in sleep while the television blared, were not people who once worried about a math test or first learned to drive or hated mustard or fell madly in love. They were void bodies. I guess we were all hoping that if we ignored old age it might go away, the same way my mom turns up the radio whenever her car starts making bad noises.

Stealing Lillian was Mrs. Wong's show, and for the first time in the group's history, she met them on time. In fact, she was the first to arrive. She'd even drawn us a map of the place. First floor, reception. Second floor, library, recreation, and dining. Third floor, living quarters. Our two major Points of Challenge, as she'd labeled them on the page, were the main reception desk as you walked in, and the nurses' station in the middle of Lillian's floor. We'd divvied up the one receptionist and the three nurses we'd have to get past. It would have been easy if we could have just taken Lillian for a long, long walk, but that wasn't possible; the staff required a relative to sign her out and a nurse chaperone to take the resident out to the yard. The Golden Years people were lawsuit-paranoid—obviously imagining reckless relatives going for a stroll and forgetting to bring Grandma's oxygen stand. The only way of escaping was going to be with a mad dash after all of the nurses had been diverted.

Our plan was this: first, Peach and I would arrive to visit Lillian, get her ready, and stuff her things in a bag. After we were in, Harold would arrive. His job was to go to the room of the nearly comatose (and therefore silent) Mr. Fiorio. A few minutes later, Mrs. Wong would enter with the *Playboys*, Grandfather Wong's payment in exchange for his performance. Grandfather Wong was excited about the plan, so much so that Mrs. Wong had to bribe him with a can of Almond Roca to make sure he didn't spill the beans ahead of time.

After five minutes, Grandfather Wong would begin making a commotion. This would busy at least two of the nurses, Mrs. Wong assured us. Enter Harold. He was to call the third nurse, claiming an emergency in Mr. Fiorio's room. Finally, Mom would arrive in the front, asking the receptionist for information about Golden Years for her mother (who was long dead). She was to do everything she could to get the receptionist to the back room, where the copy machine was, and away from the exit. Miz June was to man the getaway car, and Anna Bee was to keep a lookout for Delores and Nadine in the front parking lot. Chip Jr. would run to help load Lillian's things in the trunk, and act as extra lookout. All of this had to be done as quickly as possible, for although we knew that Delores and Nadine visited daily, we didn't know when they might appear.

"Okay, snap to it," Mrs. Wong said, knocking on the glass of our car window when we reached the parking lot of the rest home. I barely had my seat belt off yet. Anna Bee stood behind Mrs. Wong and peered over her shoulder. I hoped no one was watching us. We already looked pretty suspicious, if you asked me. Anna Bee was rubbing her hands together like a bank robber.

"Good luck, Queens," Miz June said. Too loudly.

"Let's go kick butt," Harold whooped and spun his fist around in circles.

We were doomed.

Peach and I walked up to the automatic doors. I was ridiculously nervous. My stomach was dancing to some music I didn't like. I could feel rings of sweat growing under my armpits. I was glad for the drifts of clouds that periodically covered the sun—I needed any help I could get to lower my body temperature.

"You're my granddaughter," Peach said. I looked over at her. She looked as if she'd dressed up for the occasion of stealing Lillian—her lipstick was a bright pink and she was wearing a sweater with glamorous beads along the collar that she obviously hadn't worn in a while. It had those little hanger bumps on her shoulders.

The doors *shushed* open and suctioned closed behind us. Peach looked straight ahead. I felt like I could get a serious case of nervous giggles. Peach was so serious and walking at such a clip that I flashed on the image of her crossing the floor to the "Mission: Impossible" theme. I wanted to burst out laughing. I wanted a bathroom.

Maybe I'd judged my mom and the bathroom-nerve thing too harshly.

Peach gave a wave to the receptionist. "My grand-daughter," she said to her. Maybe she should have made me hold a sign. But the receptionist just smiled and went back to whatever she was studying on her desk, probably a *People* magazine.

We went up two floors in the elevator. The ride took about five years. Peach gave us each a mint from her purse, which I could hear clicking against her teeth as she rolled it in her mouth. That clicking made me want to scream.

We passed the nurses' desk. "We're here to see Lillian," Peach said. "This is my . . ." She was just about to let loose with the granddaughter thing when one of the nurses said, "Oh, hi, Ruby."

"Friend," Peach said. "My friend, Ruby."

"Hi, Mrs. Connors," I said. Her daughter, Justine, had been in my class during elementary school. In the fifth grade I went to a sleepover at her house, where I stayed awake all night because I worried I might snore or do something else embarrassing when I was asleep. Justine was one of those people who were friendly to you when none of her friends were around.

"How's your summer been?"

"Good, thanks."

"Ruby was kind enough to offer to drive me to see my good friend Lillian. My car is having trouble," Peach said.

"How nice of you," Mrs. Connors said.

"Broke down in the street, which gave me a real

fright, and I don't want to take that chance again," Peach said.

"My brother is a car mechanic," Mrs. Connors said. I could read Peach's mind. *Figures*. "If you'd like his number." Mrs. Connors reached for a pad of paper.

"Oh, that's all right. My nephew offered to have a look. It's at his place now." Peach was gaining new relatives by the minute. "Well, we ought not keep Lillian waiting." Peach's smile looked like it was ready to crack and slide down her face. I could hear footsteps coming down the hall. That was sure to be Harold, heading for Mr. Fiorio's room. He was early.

"She's in good spirits today," Mrs. Connors said.

Again, I read Peach's mind. *I'll bet*. At least that was what I was thinking. Past the desk, Peach took a pinch of her sweater near the chest and waved it in and out. "Whew," she said. "You had to go and know someone. Do you think she suspected anything?"

"Nah," I said. Here's what I've noticed—a guilty conscience is like a pimple. We think people see it way worse than they do.

"I hope we don't have trouble with Lillian's roommate." Peach knocked on the door.

"Lillian has a roommate?"

"Come in," the roommate said.

"Helen," Peach said. "Didn't I mention her? Deaf as a doorknob. Hi, Helen," Peach said loudly.

"More people for Lillian. No one ever comes to see me. This place is like Grand Central Station," Helen said. She lay in bed in a flowered housecoat. Her face was dominated by a huge pair of glasses. It was all you noticed. Her ears may have been suffering, but her eyes were getting military-size help. By her bed was a picture of a cat in a frame. I wondered if she'd had to leave him, a beloved friend, behind somewhere. Lillian was upright at the edge of her bed. She gave us a wide smile. I don't think I'd ever seen her smile before—it was as if she'd suddenly inhabited her body again. Her eyes even twinkled. You could see that she was once beautiful. You could picture her dancing. You could picture her writing poetry, arranging flowers in a vase. She made a fist with her good hand, held it near her chest. *An excited heart*, she seemed to say. *Happiness*.

"Oh, Lillian. I am thrilled for you," Peach said. I wanted to cry. Lillian's little slippers with the elastic all around the top made my heart feel as if it might break. I was also filled with surging energy. We had to make this happen for her. We had to get her out of there.

Peach looked at her watch. "Oh, dear, we're almost late. Going to the doctor," Peach said to Helen.

"I've never liked Walter. Bad breath," Helen said. "Why my sister married him, I'll never know."

"Doctor," Peach shouted. "Ruby, get the wheelchair. We've got to hurry. Grandfather Wong will be erupting at any minute."

"Doctor," Helen said. "She doesn't need a doctor. She's the picture of health. Look at me. My foot's been swollen for three days." She plucked one foot out of the covers and held it up. I was worried her housecoat was going to slide too far up and I was going to see more than I wanted to. Her foot did look kind of swollen. "No one will listen to me."

"That's because she talks without stopping," Peach said. Lillian gave a patient nod. *You got that right*, she seemed to say.

I'd already checked the closet, but no wheelchair. I looked in the adjacent bathroom and under the bed.

"Come on, Ruby, get on with it," Peach said.

"I think we've got a problem," I said.

"We can't have a problem. We don't have time for a problem."

I looked behind the door, any space big enough. "Do you have a wheelchair?" I asked Helen.

"No one is allowed to leave without the nurse. She brings it," Helen said. It made her feel good to know the rules, you could tell. Her voice was sitting up straight.

"Shit," Peach said.

"Don't panic," I said. I felt like panicking.

"Find one!" Peach said. She had her back to Helen. She was stuffing a few of Lillian's things in her bag.

"What are you doing over there?" Helen said. She narrowed her eyes. Those glasses were like two telescopes.

"Do something, Ruby! We can't get her out of here without a wheelchair!"

"Don't worry." Something people say when they are worried as hell. "I'll go look in another room."

"Just hurry."

I peered out in the hall. I could hear Mrs. Wong talking to the nurses.

He's been very excitable today.

And then Mrs. Wong: *Oh dear. One of Grandfather's bad days.* She clucked her tongue in concern.

He keeps saying someone's getting kidnapped.

Shit, shit!

Last week it was the F.B.I. Mrs Wong said. She was good at this. Well, no Almond Roca for Grandfather Wong.

Wheelchair. I sped into a neighboring room, two owl-like faces giving me surprised looks. The room was identical to Lillian's except for a few personal items. There would be no wheelchair here, either. I knew there were some behind the nurses' station, but that would be way, way too dangerous. Supply closet? I crept down the hall. *Please,* I begged. *Please, just a little bit of luck.*

Mrs. Wong stopped talking. I heard her heels clip down the hall and the nurses start to talk about her behind her back.

I wish I had a chunk of her change.

Car salesmen wear less jewelry, Mrs. Connors said.

I was filled with anger. I would have defended Mrs. Wong if I could right then. Mrs. Wong had guts. Mrs. Wong had spirit. It struck me how much I cared about her, about all of them.

And then there it was. The wheelchair, thank God. Sitting and facing the bed of a man in a plaid robe with matching plaid slippers, two rooms down from the owl faces. The man wore a sweater over his robe, as if preparing to go outside. Unfortunately, he'd have to wait a little.

I took hold of the handles of the wheelchair.

"You're new," he said sweetly.

"Got to borrow this for a minute," I said.

"Hey!" he said to my back as I peered down the hall-way and headed out with the chair.

"Emergency," I said. "Heart attack."

I raced down the hall with the chair. The squeak of the wheels on linoleum sounded loud and furious, Revenge of the Wheelchair in Surround-Sound volume. I was really starting to sweat now. My heart was going a thousand miles an hour.

"I am not a communist, God damn it!"

Grandfather Wong's first shout.

"First they steal from me and then they say I am a communist!" I heard a crash, breaking glass. Grandfather Wong was doing a great job, but oh, God, we were sup-posed to have Lillian ready to fly out of there by now. I zipped into the room, just as I saw a flash of white pass the hallway. Nurse number one, check.

"Jesus, what took you so long?" Peach said. "Grandfather Wong is going at it."

"You try finding a wheelchair in this place."

"Only nurses are allowed to move us," Helen said.

"I got permission," I said.

Lillian clutched her purse to her as if she couldn't wait to get out of there.

"Something fishy is going on here," Helen said.

"Get your hands off me! I am a citizen!" Grandfather

Wong shouted down the hall. I heard a solid thump, another crash.

"Olivia!" a nurse shouted. "Quick!"

Nurse number two.

"Heave ho," Peach said. We pulled Lillian up. She was helping all she could. We set her down a little roughly in the chair. Our aim wasn't the greatest either—one thin butt cheek was tilted up the side of the chair.

"I'm calling the nurse," Helen said. "You two are trouble and you can't tell me different."

I acted on instinct. I ran to Helen's bed. "Look," I said, taking her hand and leaning down next to her ear. "We're getting Lillian out of this place to be with the man she loves." Helen's eyes got big behind the glasses. Big as Poe's would be in the pictures Chip Jr. just took of him. "You can be part of helping her escape." It was a gamble based on my feeling that people who most stringently adhered to rules were the ones who most enjoyed the secret thought of breaking them.

Helen shut up. She looked pleased. "I once ran an illegal gambling organization," Helen said.

For a moment, that stopped me in my tracks. You just never thought that people with crocheted Kleenex box covers could be crooks, or great successes, for that matter. Think about it next time you see someone old, wheeling around in his motorized scooter with an American flag on a pole on the back. He could have been a jewel thief. Or a concert pianist. "I'll come back to visit you," I said.

"If they ever let you back in," Peach said. She sounded a little jealous. I was supposed to be *her* granddaughter, after all.

"Let's go," I said. I ran up the hall, checked to see if the nurses' station was clear. From the entrance of the hall, I waved my okay. Poor Lillian still had one butt cheek up. Mr. Wong was still crashing around in his room. More glass breaking.

"Calm down, Mr. Wong! Get Elaine," one of the nurses shouted.

"She's in another room."

"Get her!"

Grandfather Wong was overdoing it a bit. That's all we needed, for the nurse in Mr. Fiorio's room to come wandering out right then. I held up my hand in a stop position. Peach froze the wheelchair mid-hall. Mrs. Wong knew what to do, though. "Quiet down a bit," she cooed. "It's all right." I could picture her squeezing her nails into Grandfather Wong's arm, stepping her heel onto his foot as a message. There was sudden quiet. Probably Grandfather Wong was in too much pain to talk.

We waited a few beats. No one emerged. I waved Peach forward again.

Just then Mrs. Connors emerged from Mr. Fiorio's room. Shit! I waved my hands madly at Peach. *Go back!* Peach looked struck and frozen with fear. Where could she go? Mrs. Connors was heading for her desk. If she passed the hallway, she'd be certain to see Lillian. Down the hall, Helen's head popped out of her room. She wanted to watch. I waved madly at her too. *Back inside!*

I leaned against the wall, trying to look casual. My heart was going crazy. I felt like I was trying to conduct an orchestra of lunatics. I leaned against that wall as if it was just something I did all the time. Why anyone would be leaning across the wall looking casual right there was something I hadn't figured out quite yet. I heard a huge skidding squeak of wheelchair tires behind me. If Mrs. Connors hadn't heard that, it'd be a miracle.

"Wow," I said loudly. "Whew." I scraped the toe of my tennis shoe hard against the floor, trying to replicate the sound.

Thankfully, Mrs. Connors' ears hadn't moved on yet from Grandfather Wong's squawking. "All that commotion!" Mrs. Connors said. She looked at me there, leaning against the wall. "You've probably never heard anything like it before. We get it here on occasion. Feel free to eavesdrop."

She crossed the hall to her desk. I could only hope that behind me, Lillian and Peach had made it out of sight. *Please,* I prayed. I couldn't tell if Mrs. Connors was being cruel or kind with her remark. "I was looking for a soda machine," I said stupidly. Yep, hysterical outbursts in rest homes always gave me an unquenchable thirst.

"In the reception area downstairs."

She took a pad and pen off her desk, headed back to Mr. Fiorio's. But things were quieting down in Grandfather Wong's room. God, we'd have to hurry.

My heart was thudding terribly. I ran back down the hall, looking into open doors. I saw Peach and Lillian backed up inside the room of the two owl faces. Boy, they sure were getting a show today.

"Run," I said.

Lillian clutched her purse. She held on to the arm of her chair with her one good hand. Peach passed Lillian's bag to me and we flew. I punched the button of the elevator.

Nothing.

Punch, punch, punch.

"Goddamned elevator," Peach said.

Nothing.

I heard Mrs. Wong's voice. *Sorry,* she said. *So sorry.* And the nurse: *I'm sure you'll replace the television.*

"Goddamnit, goddamnit," Peach said.

Nothing. And then finally, *ding.*

We rushed in, jostling Lillian recklessly over the edge of the elevator floor. Peach pushed the button, shutting the door behind us.

"Oh, my God," I said. My underarms were two huge masses of wetness.

"Let's hope your mother's got the front covered."

Elevator music played gentle and slow. "The Girl from Ipanema." It made you feel that every second since the beginning of eternity was passing once more. Five hundred zillion years later the doors opened. A couple waited to get on, the woman clutching her husband's elbow. They stood pleasantly aside as we left. Another woman carrying a bouquet of flowers was coming through the front doors to visit. No Delores.

"Head down and go," I whispered to Peach. There was

no sign of my mother or the receptionist. The front doors opened and *shushed* behind us. When they closed, my body felt so infused with energy, you could have hooked me up to wires and lit up a small city. Chip Jr. stood right outside the doors. He still had his camera around his neck. He took our picture.

"All clear out here."

"Jeez, put that away. We've got to move," I said.

"You got some pair of wet armpits," Chip Jr. said helpfully.

Miz June was waving her arm out the window. "Get in the car! Get in the car!" Peach and I heave-ho'd Lillian in. I felt bad, my wet shirt against her lovely sweater.

As I backed myself out of the car, Mrs. Wong appeared outside the doors. She looked exhausted, but beaming. She had a scrape mark down her arm, and her glasses, when she peered in the window, were smudged with fingerprints.

"Grandfather Wong earned his *Playboys* today!" she said.

"He was great," I agreed.

"He threw his water glass at the television," she said. She seemed proud of him.

"I hope he got his Almond Roca anyway," I said.

"The large can," she said. "And Aplets & Cotlets. Left over from Christmas, but he won't care."

Peach settled Lillian with a few of her things, then shut the door. "You know what I just realized? We're going to need that wheelchair."

She was right. "Can't we stop and get one on the way?" I said. I was thinking about the man with the plaid robe, still waiting to go outside.

"Sure, there's a Wheelchairs R Us on every corner."

"Put it in the trunk," Miz June said. "We'll figure it out later. We've got to get in the car. We can't stand around here in plain sight." I'm sure Miz June never so much as stole a sugar packet from a restaurant before.

"No problem. I've got some at home," Mrs. Wong said. Wheelchairs weren't something you thought that people would have spares of lying around, but okay. "I will bring it and leave it right here."

"How do you fold this thing?" I asked.

"Let me." Peach expertly collapsed it. "I know all about these from when Henry was sick." We lifted it into the trunk, laid it on top of our bags. Peach's chest was heaving in a worrying fashion. That Lincoln trunk was so big it could have held a marching band.

"Get in! Get in!" Miz June said. She revved the accelerator to make her point. We got in, shut the door. Mrs. Wong sat in the front seat for a moment.

Whew.

"Now we just have to wait for the others." Miz June said.

"How are you doing, Lillian?" I said. I patted her knee. "Sorry about the stinky shirt."

"Apologize to me too," Chip Jr. said. "I've got to sit next to you."

"Can't they hurry up?" Miz June said.

Our eyes were fixed on the door. I could see Anna

Bee, still on watch, standing on the lawn by the Golden Years sign, where she had a good view of any cars that might be arriving.

My mother came out. She carried a stack of pamphlets in her hands. She held them up in victory. Mrs. Wong got out of the front seat and Mom got in without missing a beat. "I almost bought a room. Hi, Lillian," she said over her shoulder. "Are you ready?"

"We're still waiting for Harold," I said.

"He'd better hurry. There's no telling how soon they'll discover Lillian is missing," Miz June said. "I've got a bad feeling about this."

"It was a brilliant plan, Mrs. Wong," my mother said. Mrs. Wong, with her smeary glasses, leaned inside my mother's window. She beamed.

But my mother should have known better than to say something like that at that moment, before we'd completely made it out of the parking lot. She knew enough about fate to know it had a thing about being taken for granted. Right then, Anna Bee waved her arms from her post. Her eyes looked alarmed. She jogged over the grass. Good thing we picked a bike rider to man that post; she was fast. She jabbed a finger in the air. First the direction of the street, then toward the back of the building.

"Delores. Oh, hell, Delores. I knew she was coming. I could feel it," Miz June said. I'd never heard her swear before. Even when something bad happened, like Beauty throwing up on the settee, or Harold spilling grape juice on the carpet, she always had impeccable manners.

"Around the back," my mother said.

Miz June shot down on the accelerator and all of us in the back veered to one side. I looked over my shoulder at the suddenly abandoned Mrs. Wong. With her ever cool head, she walked toward her own car. Peach pushed Lillian down across our laps to hide her. Lillian was counting on us. My heart was starting up again. We had to get out of there.

"Where do you hide a Lincoln?" Miz June said. We were in the back of the building, near the Dumpsters and service doors. I saw a window-cleaning truck. I wondered if it belonged to that creepy math sub with the soft drink vendetta.

"Just stay here," my mother said, although she didn't sound too sure.

"Goddamnit, where is that goddamn Harold?" Peach said.

"Maybe we should leave without him," Miz June said. "This is too dangerous."

"We've got maybe five minutes before they find out that Lillian is gone," my mother said. "Maybe less."

"What is taking him so long?" Peach said. Lillian looked worried down there on our laps.

"Okay, one minute more and we leave, Harold or no Harold," my mother said.

I thought of how happy Harold had looked on our grass that morning. He had to go. He'd be heartbroken if he missed this.

Miz June had turned the car around. We were ready to speed out of there. "Thirty seconds," my mother said.

"Delores is riding up that elevator this very minute!" Peach said. "We've got to get out of here!"

"Harold would want us to get Lillian there," Miz June said. "Above all else."

"All right, gang, it's been a minute," my mother said. "Hit it."

Miz June stepped on the gas. Right then, the service doors opened and some young guy came out to light a cigarette. He watched us as if he saw Lincolns driven wildly by old ladies every day. He probably did.

We drove around the corner to the front parking lot.

"Wait," I said.

Anna Bee had Harold by the elbow. She was running him our way across the parking lot.

Mom opened the front door and he got in. Anna Bee was breathing heavy. She had leaves and junk all in her hair. "We had to hide in the hedge," she breathed. "Go! Go!" She slammed the door.

Miz June hit the gas pedal. I saw Mrs. Wong's arm, flashing gold jewelry, waving good-bye. I was sad to leave her and Anna Bee behind. But after that day, they would be grateful for a good, long rest.

"She wouldn't let me out of her clutches, that nurse," Harold said. He was panting heavily.

"Mrs. Connors?"

"The soon to be ex-Mrs. Connors. I did what we agreed, told her that Mr. Fiorio had started breathing funny. She checked him out, said he was fine and started asking me all kinds of things."

"Like what sound Mr. Fiorio had made?" Peach asked.

"No, like what I did in my spare time. She went to get her pad to take my phone number."

"I can vouch for that," I said. "She came out and almost saw us."

"She thought you had money," Peach said.

"She had the hots for me. One thing's for sure," Harold said and snapped his fingers. "I've still got it."

"Floor it, Miz June," my mother said. "They've got to know by now that Lillian is gone."

It was what Miz June had been waiting to hear all day. She screeched down the street, ran a yellow light.

Up and over a neighboring hill, and then a crawl through town as we headed toward the beginning of Cummings Road. Once at the other side, we'd have arrived at the freeway entrance.

"What's this?" Mom said. I craned my neck over the front seat. The car in front of us had stopped, brake lights shining red. In the other lane, a semi-truck had also stopped at the head of a growing line of cars.

"Police barrier," Peach said. "We're caught."

"Don't be ridiculous," Harold said.

"It's an eagle," Chip Jr. said.

And sure enough, it was. A bald eagle, standing in the middle of Cummings Road, picking at a red scarf that had been thrown to the ground. Just picking at it, as if it had come across something so unexpected that traffic would just have to wait.

"Honk or something," Peach said.

"No," Chip Jr. said. "That would scare it."

"I think that's the point," I said.

"Delores will be on our trail!" Peach said.

"I don't know what to do," Miz June said. "It's an eagle, after all."

"This is nuts," Mom said.

"Imagine our plan failed due to a bald eagle in the middle of the road." Harold sighed as if it had already happened.

The semi-truck waited patiently. The line behind it was growing long. Cars were stacking up behind us, as well. A few people in cars leaned their heads out of the window to look. Chip Jr. did the same. He stuck his shoulders out and watched.

"Hurry up, bird," Miz June said.

The eagle continued to examine the scarf. People turned off their engines. He had all the time in the world. He had not just stolen an old lady from a rest home.

Chip Jr. remembered his camera. He stuck the lens out of the window. As he did, the eagle took the scarf in his mouth and lifted up, his wings huge and reaching, the scarf swaying, a joyful banner. The semi-truck driver started to honk in glee, and other drivers did the same. Chip Jr. started to clap, and Miz June gave the Lincoln horn a few beeps of celebration. As I've said, you never know what you're going to see on Cummings Road.

The cars started up again and we were on our way. We were filled with the giddiness of discovery and the freedom it can bring. Then, we had no idea that time was against us. We did not know that our mission required speed and the most direct route. We were not thinking big thoughts—how fate has its own reasons, how time can turn without warning into something horribly selfish, stingy. Instead Chip Jr. tore a flat stick of gum in half and handed me a piece, and Peach and Harold argued about whether or not he could roll down the window. You could still see that red scarf, getting smaller and smaller in the distance.

Chapter 12

"Mrs. Wilson-now-Mrs. Thrumond *would be jealous* enough to spit," Peach said. She kept taking a compact mirror out of her purse and reapplying her lipstick as if she were just about to be apprehended on *America's Most Wanted*. Lillian had fallen asleep. Chip Jr. took a picture of her with her mouth hanging open. Some old guy was grooving on the radio.

"I just love Tony Bennett," Miz June said.

Okay, Tony Bennett was grooving on the radio. It had been switched on as the energy for conversation had finally dwindled. We talked endlessly at first, teasing Lillian about finally being with her Charles, as she beamed and smiled and made little croaks of words and animated hand gestures as if she was coming slowly out of a long sleep. We each recounted our escapades at Golden

Years ("Considering the level of care, it is actually very reasonably priced," my mother had said), talked books ("I must confess that every year at Christmastime I read passages of *Little Women* aloud to Beauty," Miz June said), and the pros and cons of donating one's organs ("I'll donate my organ and my old saxophone, too," Harold had chuckled). But now the only ones talking were Peach and Chip Jr., who'd been infused with sugar energy after we'd stopped at a 7-Eleven for Slurpees and a bathroom break.

"Think about it," Chip Jr. said. "We're not seeing the light from right now. Stars are really pictures of the past. That light was coming to us from the time of cavemen, or before." He was getting worked up.

"That's amazing," Peach agreed.

"It's weird, don't you think? There is all this drama going on in space all the time. Explosions and stars dying, and we're just down here doing things like deciding what drink to have with our Quarter Pounder Meal."

"Just pulling weeds and clipping our toenails," Peach said.

"Harold, would you watch the elbows?" my mother said. He was eating his Slurpee with the little spoon end of the straw. I could see that my mother's jaw was tight, the way it got when she descended into crankiness. I'm not sure if it was the long car ride, or if worry had made her irritable. Back at 7-Eleven she'd had to help Peach get Lillian to the bathroom.

"God, Ruby, I don't want to get old," she'd said after

they'd emerged. Peach was as chipper as ever, but Mom looked worried, as if the truth of Lillian's deterioration had hit home. If anything happened to Lillian, if it didn't work out at Charles Whitney's, she would be the one who would feel ultimately responsible.

"You're the one that's shifting around every two seconds," Harold said.

"I'm trying to avoid your constant swirling of the Slurpee cup."

"Children," Miz June scolded.

We all retreated to our own worlds for a while. The car radio still played, but no one spoke. Mom stared out the window, and so did I. I don't know what she was seeing, but I was imagining phone booths, all of the phone booths that were out there just beyond the window. I could hear the dial tone, and then the rolling clank of coins dropping in a telephone slot. And then there would be Travis' voice. I could make sure he was okay. His voice would fill the need I had to hear it. What had happened that night at Johnson's Nursery was the most painful, shameful event of my life, and I'd like to be able to say that I never thought of him again afterward. But I did. He had a way of creeping in my mind, just like we had crept into that dark house. He walked around inside, took things that didn't belong to him.

"Maybe we should think about finding a place to stay," Miz June said. "Everyone is getting tired."

"It's only six o'clock," my mother said.

"It's been an eventful day," Miz June said. "And we

need to call Mrs. Wong to see what's happened at Golden Years since we left."

"There might be a warrant out for our arrest," Peach said. She sounded hopeful.

"We haven't done anything illegal," my mother said. "Not exactly. One doctor declared Lillian incompetent, but that doesn't mean another will. Lillian can give Charles power of attorney."

"The girls will fight that."

"I'm turning off at the next exit," Miz June said.

"We're not even over the Oregon border," my mother said. She sighed. Miz June took that as an okay, and she put on her turn signal a good half mile before the exit.

"Look, a Denny's!" Harold said. For a chef, he sure wasn't fussy about food.

"Senior meals," Miz June said.

"I love menus with pictures," Peach said.

The Denny's was right by one of those motels with the little bear in a nightcap and pajamas on its sign. Mom went to check availability and prices of rooms and to call Mrs. Wong and Charles. I wished I were the one on that phone, I admit it. Instead I followed the old people into the restaurant, and we got a table. As if we hadn't had enough closeness for one day, we sat on one of those curved booths, with Lillian and her wheelchair on one end. It took Peach a really long time to scoot around to her end of the vinyl bench. The table was sticky on the bottom of my arm, and it smelled smoky in there. An older woman with a coffeepot in one hand and a water pitcher in the other came to our table. CINDY her name tag said, a name much too cheerful for her disposition. I bet she was wearing someone else's apron. Cindy had lost her smile probably twenty years ago.

"Coffee," Cindy said. It was probably a question.

Harold held up one hand. "Keeps me awake."

She poured some for Peach, and then disappeared again, the bow of her apron looking pert and cheerful.

"The picture of happiness," Miz June said. She'd noticed too. She already had her glasses out and was staring down her nose at the large pictures of baked potatoes and breaded chicken steaks. Peach was pointing things out to Lillian, who was awake and looking chipper. Harold was on the breakfast page.

The couple next to us ate without talking to each other, which is one of the most depressing public sights, if you ask me, right up there with cars abandoned in people's yards. Two tables away, a young couple with three small children also didn't speak—he concentrated on his meal as she wiped the chin of one child and fed the baby in the high chair, and tried to get the other to stop staring at us. When Mom arrived, she looked much happier. Her cheeks were rosy from the evening air and her eyes were relaxed.

"Now, look who *is* the picture of happiness," Miz June said.

"Two double rooms, and a couch in one for Harold. In-room coffeepots." She gave herself applause and did a goofy curtsy. She slid in next to Chip Jr. "Now, for a big, juicy cheeseburger. Bacon."

"Charles Whitney is certainly looking forward to seeing *you*," she said to Lillian, who smiled.

"So did you get Mrs. Wong?"

"Oh, right. Jeez, I almost forgot I just talked to her."
Mom thunked her forehead with her fist. It was the same
thing she used to do to the television to get the color to
work before it gave up entirely and went yellow. "Yeah.
Anna Bee was over there having dinner with them."

"I'm surprised she didn't accuse Mr. Wong of hitting
on Anna Bee," I said.

"Nah. She's had enough excitement for a while. She
heard from Delores and Nadine," Mom said to Lillian.
"Also from someone at Golden Years. And Delores' attorney called."

"He can't do nothing," Harold said.

"Scare tactics," Miz June said. It seemed to be working. Lillian looked scared.

"Don't worry, Lillian," I said.

"They'll no doubt be coming to see Charles," my
mother said.

"We better get there first," Miz June said. "Get that
power of attorney signed." I suspect she also just wanted
another chance to try to break the sound barrier in the
Lincoln.

"Well, they'll be seeing Charles *eventually*," my
mother said.

"What do you mean eventually?" I said.

"Mrs. Wong told them they'd never find him. That he
was in hiding. They tried everything to get her to tell

where he was. Reason, pleading, bribery. They finally got it out of her. He was staying at the Coronado Hotel in San Diego. A place Lillian and he had a memorable weekend many years ago."

Lillian's shoulders were moving up and down. She snorted a little. Laughter.

"Never been there, huh?" Peach said. Lillian shook her head. I loved it. Victory. That day had been so great. That day was the best thing I ever did.

Cindy came to spread more sunshine and took our orders. Harold and Lillian were both having pancakes.

"If they're as sweet as you, Cindy, I'll have the pancakes," Harold said. His ego had inflated since Mrs. Connors. At this rate, we'd have to get a U-Haul to pull it behind us.

Cindy's pen stopped scratching. She looked up and withered Harold with a look. So much for his way with the ladies.

"Jesus, Harold. You're lucky she didn't jab your eyes out with her pen," Peach said.

"Or stab you repeatedly with the pin end of her name tag," Miz June said.

"That was really bad," I said.

"Couldn't Mrs. Wong have thought of somewhere a little farther away for Charles to be?" Harold said, ignoring us. "That's maybe, what, a couple hours down the coastline?" Harold said.

"She did well coming up with that, I thought," Miz June said.

"So who else did you call?" I asked Mom. "You were out there awhile."

"She called Joe Davis," Chip Jr. said. "Can't you tell by her red cheeks?" He pinched his own to make them rosy. "I like Joe Davis," Chip Jr. said.

"I had to check on Poe," she said.

"Well, you certainly have cheered up since the car," Miz June said.

"You bit Harold's head off," I said.

"She was testy all right," Miz June said.

"I'm sorry, Harold," my mom said. "I was feeling discouraged that we hadn't made much progress. We hadn't even crossed the state line."

"So that's what it was about," I said. "The state line." I was teasing, or else I thought I was. It was one of those moments where your own voice knows your feelings before you do. It had an edge to it. It was starting to move toward that joking that wasn't really funny.

"What?" My mom sipped her water. The kid who had been staring in the next booth started to jump up and down on the seat.

"It was about crossing the state line. You wanted to be past where Dad is." I swayed my hand up and down, in the motion of a roller coaster. I had only meant to indicate we were nearby the amusement park; the more cruel double meaning, that her emotions regarding men were as up and down as the Mine of Terror, only occurred to me as I put my hand down.

Chip Jr. raised his arms roller coaster–style and did a

fake scream. He hadn't yet realized that we'd tripped over into the land of the unsaid. Too late, he noticed that the table had gotten quiet. He put his arms down. He began to scoot the paper off of his straw with the intent focus of someone doing heart surgery. My mother looked down and studied her fingernails.

"It can be difficult for women to get to the point where their feelings are not based on the attention of the men around them," Miz June said. I presume she meant it kindly, but my mother flushed red.

"Who are you to talk?" my mother said to me. The vinyl of the bench seat was stuck to the back of my legs. I felt the heat rise in my own face. We were suddenly having an argument, and that's how it was done by Quiet People, anger rising and struggling for release through a red face, words of barely contained viciousness. "After we've just done the Travis Becker soap opera."

"I learned from the expert," I said. Anger flew from the place where I had tried to contain it for so long. We were book readers, trained to step around raw feelings in the name of politeness and love, and yet I was furious. Furious at her sudden happiness, after years of her periods of mourning and absence that we had tried forever to fix with our goodness and peace and humor. She was happy. Fine. Terrific. Congratulations. My voice was hateful. I didn't even care that the old people were hearing me. "He loves me, he loves me not."

"You gave your heart to a thief, Ruby, my God, and it wasn't like you didn't know what he was like." Everyone else was quiet, except for Harold, who took a noisy drink from his water glass and made a show of putting his napkin on his lap. Maybe he had his hearing aid turned off, or maybe he saw his plate of pancakes coming. The charming and bubbly Cindy must have reached the end of her shift, as walking toward us with plates stacked up his arms was RANDY, tall Randy, not much older than me and wearing a mustard-colored shirt buttoned down too low, as if he was trying to show something off. Didn't restaurants have a law about that sort of thing? After he'd unloaded the plates, I realized his object of pride was probably the one lone chest hair that was waving about frantically as he stood directly under the air-conditioning vent. It looked like a guy on a deserted island trying to signal to the rescue plane.

Harold leaned forward, giving his plate of food a long look with wide, appreciative eyes. My mother was making a snowy mountain from bits of torn-off napkin. The silence was oh so sharp. It cut. "Here you are, gang," Randy said. "Anything else I can get you?" He was staring at Lillian. You'd have thought he'd never seen an old lady in a wheelchair before.

"What happened to Cindy?" Peach said.

"She's on a break," Randy said.

"I hope it's a long one," Harold said.

Randy chuckled. "Yeah, glacial."

Whatever that meant. Randy turned away. I almost waved good-bye to the chest hair. He came back a second later with a catsup bottle, even though there was already one at our table. "There you go, gang. Tomato, tomahto."

It was quiet at our table, except for the sound of Peach's knife edge scraping the glass plate as she cut Lillian's pancakes, and Chip Jr.'s palm hitting the bottom of the catsup bottle. The people with the three kids got up to leave, a smattering of food left on the floor beneath where the baby sat. No one spoke. With Randy gone, tension sat between my mother and me like an extra person. It should have been given a menu and a water glass.

The silence sat in my stomach, making the food look bright and revolting and making guilt creep along the inside of my skin. I tried to eat a French fry.

"I dated a thief once," Peach said. Lillian's pancake, which she'd been carefully trying to skewer for the past few seconds, dropped off her fork. We all looked up at Peach. Relief eased into the crack of the broken silence. I could have hugged Peach. I tell you, those Casserole Queens were really getting to me. Tension danced out of the room like it realized it was at the wrong party.

"Sure, and you wrote to that convict, too, don't forget," Harold said.

"This was when I was sixteen. I can't remember his name. That's the funny thing you realize when you get older. People and things you think are so important right then, you can't even remember later. Billy, maybe. No. Bobby? Starts with a B."

"Burt?" Miz June suggested.

"No," Peach said. "Anyway, he stole street signs. Had a whole collection in his backyard. YIELD, STOP, NO PARKING.

No idea how he got them off. Once I was going to help him take a signboard on the corner of Front Street and Alder, but then he yanked the whole damn thing out of the ground, post and all. He'd been shaking it loose for weeks. We put it across the backseat of his car, the pole hanging out one window. He wasn't too bright. Put the bus stop sign he stole in his front yard and got caught when the bus kept stopping there." I laughed.

"Bart?" Miz June said.

"No. Jeb! That's it. Jeb."

"You said it started with a B," Harold said.

"I knew it was something that sounded like a hillbilly name," Peach said.

"I was convinced Mr. Varsuccio was in the mafia," Miz June said.

"And you dated him," Peach said.

"He was such a snappy dresser," Miz June said.

"Though Nine Mile Falls isn't exactly Mafia territory," my mom said.

"Yeah, but who would look for him there?" Chip Jr. said.

"Perfect hideout," I said.

"He didn't dress so snappy," Harold said.

"Tell us about your thief," Miz June said.

It was raw, broken-glass territory that required passing in bare feet. But right then, with darkness falling outside and our reflections beginning to show in the window, with the yellow lights of the restaurant warmly displaying the comforts of life—pies behind glass, swivel counter chairs, Miz June's purse with the pinch clasp sitting on the seat beside me—it seemed safe to venture out there. Everyone looked my way except for Chip Jr., who had lifted the bun of his hamburger and was reordering its insides. Even Lillian looked up with bright, expectant eyes. She cleared her throat, as if helping me to begin.

"He had a motorcycle," I said.

"Ah!" Peach said.

"I saw it sitting on his front lawn."

"His parents are rich," my mother said.

"Ann," Miz June warned. She put two fingers to her lips and pretended to zip them shut. A surge of joy filled me. Like when the teacher finally sees what that bad kid in your class is doing to you under his desk.

My mother took a big, rebellious bite of her hamburger.

"He liked to do dangerous things," I said.

"Like what?" Peach asked.

"Stand in the middle of Cummings Road. Drive too fast." I lowered my voice. "Sneak into people's houses."

"You ditched him, I'll bet," Peach said.

Guilt snuck around my insides. I wished I could tell them it was true, that Travis was gone from me. The door-slammed-and-locked kind of gone, no remnants of cravings. I needed to tell them the whole story, though, I knew that. Somehow it felt important to say it. Somehow it seemed critical. I wasn't sure I could do the rest of this. My voice was small, barely mine. "He broke into Johnson's Nursery. I worked there. Libby Wilson is my mom's best friend." God, I was about to cry. My voice shook. I thought I might sob in Denny's. Maybe a lot of people had sobbed in Denny's—after all, it was open all night.

"I was there with him." I heard the glass breaking in my mind. I saw the lit sign DOG KNOWS WHO YOU ARE. "I told him where she kept the key. To the cash register." The tears rolled down my cheeks. I wiped them with the back of my hand.

"I could kill him," Harold said.

"What, knock him unconscious with your flour sifter? Listen to him, Mr. Macho. You're a chef," Peach said.

"I could take that punk," Harold said.

"Hit him with your rolling pin," Mom said through another mouth of burger.

"You could chase him with your scary Halloween cookie cutters," Peach said.

"Well, it looks to me that you won't be repeating that mistake," Miz June said.

"He punished himself, anyway," my mother said. "Cracked himself up on his motorcycle on Cummings Road."

Lillian shook her head. "Oh, boy," Peach said.

"Why is it that women always like the bad boys, anyway?" Harold said. "He was probably good-looking, right?"

I nodded.

"It's not about looks," Miz June said.

"It's not?" Peach said. She'd polished off her corned

beef sandwich and was starting in on the pickle skewered with a frilly toothpick. Frilly toothpicks are one of those inventions that make you stop and think that at one point in time, it was someone's great idea. Imagine some guy in his basement, drinking Orange Crush and picking his teeth and going *Aha!*

"It's not *just* about looks, or even mostly. It's not that we want something *bad*, it's just that we want something *big*," Miz June said.

"True," Peach said.

"So you find it in some punk? That's like wanting Mexican food but going to a Chinese restaurant to get it," Harold said.

"True again, but you're missing the point," Peach said.

"The pursuit of love gets mixed up with the pursuit of life," Miz June said.

"So go climb a mountain," Harold said.

"Oh, Harold," my mother said.

"It's that easy, isn't it?" Miz June said. "I look at my grandchildren and I still see it. The boys are expected to *do*. Accomplish something. Seek adventure. Sure, they study for careers now, but what are girls still expected to seek? Boys. Boys get mountains, girls get boys."

"She's right," my mother said.

"She *is* right," Peach said.

"Girls can climb mountains if they want," I said. "We know that. I don't like this idea," I said.

"Like it or not, it happens all the time." Miz June delicately cut another piece from her veal cutlet. "A man's identity is complete through action, a woman's, when she has a man. Through him. We fall off our high heels into the narrow crevasse of what it means to be female. Let me tell you. You fall in love and you think you're finding yourself. But too often you're looking inside him for you, and that's a fact. There's only one place you can find yourself." She patted her chest.

I thought about the painting in Miz June's living room. Of the man on his knees in front of the woman with her head turned. Miz June, with her pearls and the crinkled skin of a plum left too long in the back of a refrigerator, had years of thoughts stored up on the subject of women and men.

"I thought we were supposed to be over that kind of thing. I thought feminism cured that," my mother said.

"You can't possibly believe that," Miz June said. "Look around. Look at yourself."

I never would have gotten away with saying that, but Miz June wore pearls. Pearls made everything sound polite. My mother thought about it.

"What about you?" Mom said. "You are always surrounded by men. You are the ultimate lady."

"Lady has nothing to do with it. I was raised to be a lady. After George died, all these old coots came around wanting someone to wash their socks. A lady I will be, but a man's accessory, his *handbag,* no thank you. I will not be someone's ornament. I will not just be someone's honey, baby, sweetheart." She stuck out her chin.

"June, you're preaching," Peach said.

"This is a book club. We are supposed to discuss things."

"Surrounded by feminists in Denny's," Harold said. "Sounds like a newspaper headline."

My mother wadded up her napkin and threw it at him. Another napkin sailed in the air. It came from the direction of Lillian's wheelchair. It barely made it to the salt and pepper shakers in the middle of the table, but Lillian looked pleased with herself.

"Chip Jr.," Harold said. "You, me, outta here."

"I'm not getting into this," Chip Jr. said.

"Miz June's right. We need a chance to have adventure," my mother said.

"We've certainly had one today," Peach said.

"Love can come when you're already who you are, when you are filled with you. Not when you look to someone else to fill the empty space." Miz June said. "Not when it's your definition."

"To adventure," Peach said. She lifted her Denny's water glass.

"To adventure," we all said, even Harold. We lifted our glasses. Lillian's ice cubes shook and rattled in the glass, and a sound came from her throat: *to.* Miz June's pearl bracelet slipped up her wrist as she raised her arm. I clinked my glass with everyone's, my mother's last. Her eyes said she would always forgive me.

"Here's what I think, Ruby," Miz June said after we'd put our glasses down.

"You've already told us. I agree with Peach, for once

in her miserable life. You're preaching," Harold said. "I got to put money in the collection box," he pretended to take something out of his pocket and toss it into the basket that held Miz June's bread roll.

"So I'm preaching. Fine. This is important," she said. "You didn't love that boy, Ruby. You loved his motorcycle."

Just then Randy came back. He set our check down flat on the table. "You," he pointed at Lillian. "I just saw you on TV. I told myself, 'Randy, the colossum mondo misfired.' But no, man, I'm sure it was you."

"Oh, yeah," my mother said. "I forgot to tell you that Mrs. Wong said you were on TV."

"You're kidding!" Peach said. "We were on TV? I hope she recorded it."

"Not us, just Lillian's picture," my mother said.

"How could you forget!" Harold said.

"Joe Davis Forgetting Pill," Chip Jr. said.

"Slow news day," Peach said. She was just jealous.

"They said she was missing. Wandered away from the rest home. I guess she got found. Celebration dinner, huh?" Randy said.

"No, she's still missing," Harold said. "We abducted her. We took her out of there. She's on the run. For God's sake, quit elbowing me, Peach, you lethal cow."

"Jesus, Harold," Peach said. "Don't be an idiot."

"They already know we've got her," Harold said. "I don't see what the big damn deal is. We're taking her somewhere she wants to be," he told Randy.

"Cool!" Randy said finally. "Like *Free Willy*."

Harold looked baffled. To his defense, we hadn't been able to understand anything Randy said, but I could see Harold consider all the options. Free Willy, some runaway convict? Like Free Willy, some expression of encouragement?

"It's a movie," I said.

"About a whale," my mother said.

"They steal the whale from these bad guys and set it free in the ocean," Chip Jr. said.

"Free Willy," Randy said. "Glacially maximum."

I read Charles Whitney's book while Mom was next door, settling the old people in their room. I had begun reading it after the night at Johnson's Nursery. Mom had said it had brought her back to life after my father's visit. Maybe it could cure me of Travis too, and help me remember that this was just one chapter in a long life, as Mom said. Not only did I have one of the characters asleep in the room next to me, but there was also the practical matter that Charles Whitney's book was a thick one. I would go into that other world for a long while, and let the distance of it restore me, the way a long sleep, or a vacation, does. If time heals all wounds, and a book can hold a person's entire life, then you can speed up the process with a pulp time warp.

"Harold complained about being on the pull-out couch, until Peach said he could get in with her. That shut him up," my mother said as she closed our door. I set my book down on the nightstand. Mom slipped off her shoes, fell backward onto the still-made bed closest to the door. "What a day."

I lay flat across the other bed, staring up at a painting of a Venice canal. Mom's bed had the same one over it, painted from a different angle. "It seems like it's been six days long," I said.

Chip Jr. was in the bathroom. He insisted he be the one to tear off the protective strip on the toilet seat. We could hear him try the shower—on, off. The toilet flushed with such an explosion, it sounded like a rocket taking off.

"Yikes," my mother said.

"I hope he's okay in there."

Chip Jr. was not only okay; he emerged wearing the complimentary shower cap.

"Gorgeous," my mom said.

"Your head looks like the top of a muffin," I said.

Chip Jr. pretended to soap up his armpits. "La la la," he sang.

"You can take that home if you want," my mother said. She put both pillows behind her head. Chip Jr. examined the room. He opened the drawers of the dresser, found a cable television guide.

"*Hot Sisters in Waikiki*," he read. "Girlie show."

"Pervert," I said. "You had to turn right to that."

"What do you know about girlie shows?" my mother said. Her voice sounded funny with her chin at that angle. "It could be about nuns."

"Nuns in Hawaii," I said.

"Of course they'd be hot in those outfits," my mother said. "Give me that."

Chip Jr. tossed her the booklet, pages flapping, and it landed on the bed beside her. He continued his hunt. He found a plastic bag to put dirty laundry in, stationery. He clicked the pen up and down. He moved to the table made of wood laminate and flipped through the padded book of services, opened the bedside drawer and found the Bible.

"In the beginning, God created the heavens and the earth," Chip Jr. read.

"This is going to take awhile," I said.

Chip Jr. climbed on the bed I was lying on and stood. He stuck one arm out like a great orator. He still had his shower cap on. "Now the earth was formless," Chip Jr. said in a deep voice.

"This is a little long for a bedtime story," my mom said from the other bed. I couldn't see her. All I could see was Chip Jr.'s back. He started jumping up and down. "Darkness was over the surface of the deep," he read, jumping.

"Make him stop," I said.

"I'm too tired for religion," she said.

"You can't be saying that now that you're dating a minister," I said. I gave Chip Jr. a kick in the back of the knees so that he fell on his butt on the bed.

"Hey," he protested, but not too much. He returned the Bible to the drawer, got out the phone book.

"I'm not dating a minister," she said. And then a moment later, "Okay. Maybe dating."

"It's almost funny. You with a minister," I said.

"Funny? It's hilarious," she said.

"You'll have to stop swearing."

"Damn. How in the hell am I going to be able to do that?" she said.

Chip Jr. started the jumping oration thing again, this time with the phone book. "Beauty schools, beauty supplies and equipment—sales and service. Bed and breakfast accommodation." I didn't care as much. This time he was on Mom's bed. "Beds—disappearing." He looked up from the huge book. "Beds—disappearing?"

"Don't ask me," my mom said.

"Bee removal," he read.

"Pest control. That's what we need in this room," I said.

We all got in one bed and watched old *Jetsons* cartoons, until Mom kicked us out to read for a while before we went to sleep. I got between the crispy motel sheets. I love crisp motel sheets, all tucked in tight, as long as you can train your mind not to think of all the people who might have slept in them, which can ruin it in a second.

I picked up Charles Whitney's book again.

Of course Rose was beautiful. Any man would have noticed and considered that a prize. But that is not what captivated me and made me feel the way I did. She sat me on the edge of her bed one night, and instead of loosening my tie and slipping her hands into my unbuttoned shirt, which I would have expected and wouldn't have minded, she retrieved a shoe box from her closet. She lifted the lid. The shoes were still inside; I remember them—black pumps with open toes and a slender back strap. Underneath the shoes was a stack of folded papers. Poems. She was a poet. Images leapt and flooded her mind—a boy on a dark street, a woman wading out to sea, a tree burnt in a fire, a black dog in a yellow field. And although I wanted her hands to slip around the neck of my shirt down my bare back, these sheets of paper fed me more than that ever could. One was written on a paper bag. A poem on a paper bag—that was passion. That was direction—more beautiful than her perfect face, more desirous than her skin.

I set the book down. I thought about this. The fan in the room blew in a solid, drowsy hum.

"I'm falling asleep," Mom said from the other bed.

"Me too," I said.

"I'm at the end of the chapter," Chip Jr. said. Hardy Boys. Mom gave him a few minutes—she always understood about chapter ends—then turned off the light.

Mom was a big lump in the other bed, and there was a thin sliver of light under the door.

"Quit touching my leg with your leg," I said to Chip Jr.

"Quit touching *my* leg with *your* leg," he said.

"Shush," Mom said.

I turned my pillow over to the cool side and settled into the sheets. There, in the quiet with the three of us, I felt a comfort and sureness. I willed myself not to think of Travis Becker or of my own guilt. I tried to let my confession to the Casserole Queens do its work. They'd come in and cleaned a burdensome closet for me, it seemed—hauling away all that I was too attached to to be rid of, making those firm decisions that made you feel better afterward for the lightness they bring. Maybe Travis Becker really was just one event in a long line of events that was to be my life. I felt peaceful and tired, the way you do after a day at the beach, that particular kind of tiredness that contentment brings. With the three of us together in that room with the Venice canal paintings, and glasses with paper lids that looked like French maid hats, I had that rare feeling that I was just where I belonged.

Chip Jr. began to snore. His nose was having itself a rebellious, attention-grabbing moment. It reminded me of when I used to believe that all my dolls would come alive at night and do things I'd never know about. Chip Jr. was sleeping away, but his nose was having a rock concert.

"Ruby?" my mother whispered from the other bed. "Are you asleep?"

"How can I be with that racket?"

"You'd think he'd wake himself up. Then again, he once slept through an earthquake. His piggy bank fell right on the foot of his bed, and he didn't even notice."

"I'll kick him or something."

"Wait. Ruby? I was thinking. You know, about what Miz June was saying tonight, and the rest. With all this divorce around and, I don't know, images of a sleazy sort of *rhinestone* love, I don't want you to lose faith in it. Love, I mean."

"Okay," I said. "I won't." I don't know if I meant it or not.

"Don't lose faith in the pure, sweet kind. It is out there, Ruby. I still believe it is, anyway. I just look at Charles and Lillian and I believe."

I thought about the poems in the shoe box, Charles Whitney holding them on his lap like a small chest of treasure. "Okay."

She held out her hand to me from the other bed and I took it and squeezed.

"I love you, Ruby," she said. Mom's voice was quavery. Surfing a wave of near tears.

"I love you too."

Mom cleared her throat, trying to keep the tears at bay. I could hear her in the next bed, struggling.

"Mom?"

"Hmm?" Her voice was small.

"Are you okay?"

"Yes."

"No, you're not."

"I . . . um. I'm just. Oh, jeez." A small sound escaped her throat. "I'm just sorry, is all, Ruby. I'm so sorry."

"For what?"

"For all . . ." She could barely choke out the words. "For all the wrong things I did as a mother. I wasn't very good."

"It's okay."

"It's not. It's not okay." Her chest heaved, up and down, pain escaping in a sob.

"You just . . . When you have a baby . . ." I waited. "You just want to do so *right*."

"You did great." I got out of the bed, kneeled down beside her. "Mom, you did great." She put her arms around me, kissed the top of my head. I felt her shake her head no. One of her tears rolled down and I could feel its coolness on my cheek. I felt so bad about my anger at her in the restaurant. My own eyes got hot, my throat closed. Tears rolled down my own cheeks now. I held on to her arm. We held on to each other, wrapped up in the fabric of mothers and children, the quilt of guilt and innocence, good intentions and failings, full but imperfect hearts.

"Why do we have to be so human?" my mother said.

She wiped her eyes with the back of her hand.

Just then, Chip Jr. made some sound like his tongue and larynx were having a wrestling match.

"Oh, jeez." She started to laugh, laughing and crying at the same time, trying to keep it quiet. Little muffled snorts were escaping. I started laughing too.

"It sounds like the time you turned on the garbage disposal when there was a spoon in it," I said.

"Never mind," she said, but her chest was still heaving

up and down in the dark, trying to keep the laughter in, trying to keep quiet. "Oh, jeez."

Her throat made the gasp of a laugh being strangled, and I busted up.

I took a big breath, made my face solemn. "Think death," I said, which cracked us both up again.

We quieted down. The horrendous gargling had made Chip Jr. stop snoring. Mom kissed the top of my head. I climbed back into my bed. I lay there for a long time, thinking. I whispered to the other bed in the darkness. I didn't know if she was still awake.

"Mom?"

"Yeah?" she whispered back.

"I think Miz June was right when she said I was in love with Travis Becker's motorcycle."

"That's okay, Ruby," my mother said. "I think I was in love with your father's guitar."

Chapter 13

We didn't know we were in a race against time, that's the thing. With Delores and Nadine stalled for a while we thought our biggest problems were taken care of, unaware that another, much larger villain awaited. But we just didn't know that. And no one hurried.

We were all enjoying the trip too much to want to rush. The next morning after breakfast, when Miz June turned the ignition key of the Lincoln, the radio blared on, the heater blasted high, and the windshield wipers *swunked* back and forth furiously. Miz June jumped back in surprise.

"Harold!" my mother shouted over the music until she found the knob and gave it a twist.

"Oh!" Lillian grunted in the back seat.

"You almost gave me a heart attack," Miz June said. Which wasn't exactly a joke in that car.

"Just a little something to make sure you were all awake this morning," Harold said.

"Seeing you in your pajamas this morning already did the trick. I'm afraid to close my eyes, lest I see the horror replay itself," Peach said.

"I wasn't wearing my glasses, but the pajamas did appear to have snowflakes on them," Miz June said.

Lillian made a sound of agreement. As we got closer to Charles Whitney, she was talking more and more. Peach had combed Lillian's hair and freshened her up. She even wore lipstick, Peach's own, and both their lips looked the same bright color.

"What's wrong with snowflakes?" Harold said. He was freshened up too, but he stunk up the car with too much aftershave.

"I like snowflakes," Chip Jr. said.

"Well, it is August," I said.

"It's not just that it's August," Miz June said. "It's just . . ." The three women who had witnessed Harold and the snowflakes broke up into peals of laughter.

"Tonight, we want a fashion show," my mother said.

"First, roll down the window. Someone got carried away with the fou-fou water," Peach said. She fanned her hand in front of her face. I edged the window down a bit, until we started to drive and Lillian patted her hair as if she were worried the slight breeze was ruffling it. I rolled it up again. Vanity had its own language.

We decided to drive only so far as Eureka, California, in the northern part of the state, mostly because Miz June found the name on the map and liked *the lovely sound of exclamation*, and because my mother was worried about taxing the old people, and because Harold had actually been there once and liked it. Lillian would have to wait that much longer to see Charles Whitney, but she didn't seem to mind. She seemed to be enjoying the adventure more than anyone, tapping her foot to the radio and clicking the glass with her fingernail to show us something she wanted us to see out her window—a dog staring our way out from the passenger's seat of another car, a truck with a herd of cows painted on the side. She was in that time before a big event where anticipation and all the enticing possibilities of the future are almost better than the real thing. Later I would remember the way her thin skin seemed to glow translucent, radiating happiness. It made me think of a pearl held in a gentle hand. And later, too, I would wonder. Were we wrong to have taken our time? If we'd have known, would we have slept in the car and taken turns driving and gone over the speed limit? Would we have robbed her of lingering with the deliciousness of expectation?

There was nothing fast at all about traveling with old people, except for the times Miz June's foot would suddenly become possessed by some accelerator-pushing maniac and we would make a lurch and a speed increase so sudden that you pictured all the jowls and wrinkles in the car flattened and pushed backward with breaking-the-sound-barrier force. Talk about a heart attack. Traveling with old people also meant extremes in temperature. Miz June had the air conditioning blasting. Chip Jr.'s lips were turning blue, and I had to shove my fingers in my armpits to keep them warm. When we got outside, we'd be greeted with flattening heat. Neither of these things seemed to faze the Queens—except for Harold, they all wore long pants and sweaters, shoes with socks. Just looking at those socks made my feet crawl with heat. I had never been for so many hours at such close proximity to scratchy fabrics—polyester pants squashed up against my shorts-clad legs, lamb's wool sweaters against my bare arms.

We crossed the Oregon state line. Chip Jr. sat up on his knees and looked out the back window and I looked too, imagining a snaky line firm and dark as those on the map. We drove through the curves and ramps of Portland, being very quiet so that Miz June could concentrate, while Mom asked politely over and again if Miz June was sure she didn't want her to drive, and I prayed silently that Miz June would let her. God ignored me, and Miz June's nose and the windshield were really getting to know one another. Chip Jr. was studying his watch as if time were the only thing that might save him, which I guess was the truth.

Back on the freeway again, Miz June relaxed and turned on the radio. I knew that very soon, off to the right of the freeway, we would see the sea serpentlike humps of the roller coasters of the Gold Nugget Amusement Park. I saw the signs indicating that the attraction was up ahead, but my body knew too, with that inside-body knowledge that knows when you're nearly home even when you've been sleeping in the car, and wakes you just before the alarm clock goes off. I watched my mother's face for any indication that she was feeling it too, that hum of anticipation and dread, but she wore the same blank expression that she'd had since we'd made it safely out of Portland. She looked out the window as if she were absorbed in every mattress store sign and storage facility we passed.

"There it is," Chip Jr. said. So he'd been looking for it too, and he was right—the swirls and loops rose up in the air over a bank of trees and the roofs of off-ramp gas stations.

"There what is?" Harold said.

"The Gold Nugget Amusement Park," Chip Jr. said. His voice was hushed, awed, as if we'd just passed a historic landmark, the marker of an important but brutal battle, and maybe that's exactly what we had passed. It seemed to call for a moment of silence.

But it wasn't silence that we got. Instead a strange thing happened. If I believed in signs and stuff like that, like my father, I would have thought it was one. Because right then there was the deafening sound of a motorcycle gunning its engine, and within a moment, it veered into the lane beside us, sped forward, then swerved in front of us into our lane.

"God in heaven!" Miz June exclaimed.

"Asshole," Peach said.

I watched it pass. In spite of myself, against all logic,

I looked to see that it wasn't Travis Becker. As far as signs went, this one was a bit shaky. After all, the motorcycle was one of those Harleys with studded leather that you see outside of taverns, and a hefty couple in matching black outfits was riding it. Passing us would not be an odd or unusual act, either—Miz June was driving substantially under the speed limit. Still, my mother must have been making the same connections I was. The Gold Nugget. A motorcycle. Right at that moment. She turned around and gave me a long look, then turned and faced front again.

"I've got a crazy idea," she said.

"Overtake that motorcycle and make a citizen's arrest?" Miz June said. She was one step away from road rage, if you ask me.

"The amusement park," Mom said. "We could go. I think we should go."

Chip Jr. looked at me, and I looked at him. Her desire to go, I knew, came partly because she wanted to demonstrate something important to me—the ability to overcome. But I'd been the paramedic at the accident site of her wrecked heart for too long, and I wasn't sure this was such a good idea. My brother obviously felt the same way.

"I love amusement parks!" Harold said. "They're the only place you can get a really good corn dog." The more I got to know Harold, the more miraculous I found it that he didn't weigh three hundred pounds.

"It sounds like a lovely idea," Miz June said. Lillian clapped.

"We won't make it to Eureka until late," my mother reminded.

"No reason we can't have some fun along the way," Harold said.

"More fun, anyway, than seeing you in your snowflake pajamas!" Peach said. The giddiness factor in the car was rising. Pretty soon they'd be hopping up and down in their seats.

"And I must warn you, this place isn't exactly cheap," my mother said.

"Senior discount!" Harold said. The idea of corn dogs had made him bubbly as a pot of boiling water.

"Shit," Chip Jr. whispered.

"Shit, shit," I said.

"Shit-shit. A small, fluffy dog breed," he said.

"Shit-shit with rice. Number twelve on the Japanese menu."

"We've done that one already," he said.

"Well, pardon me for not being at the top of my game," I said

"Would you two quit whispering?" Mom said. "If you're worrying, don't. Your dad's not even here today. Thursday is his day off."

Miz June slowed down and flicked on her turn signal, this time, I swear, a full mile before the next exit. We had a line of cars behind us that would make the dead body in a funeral procession envious. "All in favor," Miz June said. There was a manic chorus of agreement.

I'm surprised no one got hurt getting out of the car.

They shoved and jostled to get out, showing the crazed enthusiasm of shoppers at the half-off table of a Nordstrom sale. We waited in line at the ticket place, built to resemble a small log cabin.

"Stop that, you little beast," Peach said to a little kid in front of us who was chasing pigeons. Luckily his parents didn't hear.

We wandered through the gates decorated with fake signs. WARNING! KEEP OUT! EXPLOSIVES! Peach pushed Lillian's wheelchair. The crowd of people was a mix of visitors in their printed T-shirts and baseball caps, a few teenagers holding hands in a way that reminded me of businessmen hauling around their briefcases, and the park workers in their long period dresses and black jeans and vests, looking rushed and hot, heading off to a break or to their posts. I watched each of the workers pass, thinking for sure that this would be the one Thursday that my father actually would be there. Peach caught my eye and winked at me. *Stop worrying,* that wink said. *Let it go.* And she was right, I guess. If you've ever had those times where you've clutched a pen or something else in your hand for a long time, only to look down and be surprised that you are still holding it long after your need for it has passed, you'll understand. Sometimes our minds just make us go on clutching something. Sometimes we get so used to holding that we forget to let go.

We separated, the old ladies to find some shade and some ice cream, and Harold and us to try out the rides. Chip Jr. left his camera with the old people for safety.

Harold talked Mom, Chip Jr., and me into riding the roller coaster. The rickety all-wood one, the Mine of Terror that clambered and shuddered up high hills and zipped you down with stomach-lurching intensity, only to rocket you back up and onto a side-riding curve. My mother screamed her head off, and so did Chip Jr. and I; my throat was raw with fear and exhilaration when we got off. When I was back on the ground again, my legs shook like Miz June's hands, and Harold's hair looked like an electrified porcupine, standing on end and betraying the fear he wouldn't admit to when we were done.

"That wasn't so bad," he said, but I hadn't forgotten his voice screaming right along with Chip Jr.'s in the car behind Mom's and mine, and he looked a little green. They take your picture as you drop down into the mine, and they post the photos on the wall of the General Store after they're developed, so we went along afterward to see. Mom bought it, and we went to find the ladies to show them. In the photo, Chip Jr.'s eyes are squinched tight, and Mom and I have open mouths, but Harold looks truly petrified. Later Mom would put it up on the bookcase in the living room, where it still is to this day.

Miz June examined the photo. "You look like you've seen a ghost," she said to Harold. The three ladies sat in the shade under a tree, Lillian in her wheelchair and Peach and Miz June on a bench. They all had ice cream cones, a napkin wrapped around each cone, and someone had bought a Mylar frog balloon and tied it to the handle of Lillian's wheelchair. Chip Jr. got his camera back and took a picture of it.

"My life flashed before my eyes," Mom said. She was flushed, but looked happy.

"It wasn't so bad," Harold said again. His color was returning to normal. "Now for Destruction Junction."

"Let's go," Chip Jr. said. He had picked up Harold's hand and held it.

"I'm sitting this one out," Mom said.

"Chicken," Harold said.

"Bawk, bawk," Peach said. She put her hands under her armpits and flapped.

"Oh, all right," my mother said. Boy, those Casserole Queens could push her around. We needed them at home.

We rode the Gold Rush and then Destruction Junction. We tried out the bumper boats, and Harold's slacks got soaked. We rode the White-Water Rapids, getting in a big round boat with a few other people. Sadistic passersby could push a button outside the ride and send a geyser of water up in the air to shoot the folks zipping past in the boat. We all agreed that we were glad Peach hadn't known of this possibility.

We met back up with the ladies, who were now eating sno-cones.

"We've observed something as we've been sitting here," Peach said. "America is the land of the big butts." Hers wasn't exactly petite, and she did say this as she slurped the last bit of cherry liquid from her soggy paper triangle.

"I'm glad you have been doing some sociological research while you were here, instead of just feeding your faces," my mother said. Lillian had a red ring around her mouth.

"I think I've earned my corn dogs," Harold said.

"We've decided we'd like to ride the train," Miz June said.

Harold went for food, and the train conductor lifted Lillian and put her in the handicapped spot near the front. It was an open-air coal train that drove as slow as Miz June on the off-ramp. It traveled through a swampy area and then a wide meadow, and the Mylar frog cruised along with permanent cheer. The train platform was right outside the Palace Saloon, where my father usually performed. When we got off the train, you could hear a voice, not my father's, bound energetically from the open door of the theater, along with the overly enthusiastic strums of a guitar. Harold waited for us on the platform, drinking something from a paper cup with a straw.

"How were the corn dogs?" Chip Jr. said.

"Three," was all he could say. Jeez, he'd even loosened his belt. You could see the little white line where the buckle usually lay across the leather. "Look what I got you guys at the General Store." Harold held out a hand to Chip Jr. and me. In each palm was a rock embedded with the fossil of a fern frond. He pulled another one out of his pocket. "I got one for me too. Five hundred and fifty million years old," he said.

"Well, you share a birthday, then," Peach said.

We thanked Harold. Chip Jr. studied his. For a moment he was lost in fifty-five-million-year-old thoughts.

"A cool drink looks nice," Miz June said. She was eyeing the saloon.

"That's where Dad performs," Chip Jr. said, stating the obvious.

"So? Your mother can go anywhere she wants," Peach said.

"Yeah," Mom said.

"Besides, Lillian needs a drink," Peach said.

"She looks parched," Miz June said. Lillian fanned herself.

"I've done everything else," Mom said. "I can go in there." She was really pleased with herself, you could tell. Chip Jr. looked my way, rolled his eyes heavenward.

Harold pitched his cup into a nearby garbage can. "I'm ready for another."

The blast of air-conditioning felt good. A man in cowboy garb, Dad's fill-in, stood on the stage, smiling with wide white teeth and singing "Jubilee." He had pulled a small girl from the audience, and she was pounding a tambourine with the frozen, feared movements of a hostage at gunpoint. Her parents clapped and snapped pictures, which she'd be sure to hate when she was older. Peach steered the wheelchair to a table in the back, the frog balloon swaying and bumping into things like a drunk in a bar.

We sat down. A waitress, spilling breasts, came to

take our drink order. Miz June started to move a bit to the music.

"Is she expecting a big tip because we got to see her knockers?" Peach said loudly, over the music.

Chip Jr. clamped his hands over his ears. "He hates knocker talk," I said. We got our drinks. Harold had decided to pay the tip, judging by where his eyes were glued. The cowboy singer started in on "This Land Is Your Land." My father was a much better singer. I was hit with the sudden reminder that we had a baby sister, Chip Jr. and I. I pictured the faux cowboy on the stage with a baby, drooling on his fringe, grabbing hold of his nose with a little hand, patting the round end of the micro-phone. I shut out the image. I wanted to clap my hands over my ears, same as Chip Jr. and the knockers. The faux cowboy looked my mother's way. He winked at her, an overdone, lounge-singer wink. Peach elbowed her.

"He sure likes you," Peach said to my mother.

"Is he one of Dad's friends?" I said.

"How should I know?" she said. "I've never seen him before in my life."

My mother looked smug. I slurped my drink. Done. If the faux cowboy pulled my mother up there to play the tambourine, I was leaving. Chip Jr.'s fist was clenched tightly, the fossil still in it. He drank his Coke so fast, he'd be burping cannonballs.

Everyone finished their drinks as the faux cowboy was wrapping it up for a break. The audience broke into a smattering of applause. He started handing out signed photos of himself. I had a few of those of Dad, which he had given me.

"Ready to go, gang?" Peach said.

"Yay. Get me out of here," Chip Jr. said.

"What about you, Ann?" Miz June said.

"Yes," Mom said. "I'm ready."

"The sign says a magician is next," Harold said.

"We've got places to go," Miz June said.

We shoved our chairs back, maneuvered once more to the door.

"Bye, folks," the faux cowboy called to us.

"Bye," we said.

"Did you get your picture?" he waved a handful of his photos.

"No, thanks," my mother said. "Nothing I haven't seen before."

I have to admit. The way she went out those swinging saloon doors would have made any cowgirl proud.

After the three corn dogs he'd eaten, Harold farted halfway to Eureka, although he said it wasn't him. Both he and Lillian eventually fell asleep, and Miz June finally let my mother drive, as she said she couldn't see well in the dark. One night, she told us, she'd slammed on the brakes and skidded half a block, narrowly missing what she thought was a boy with a backpack about to cross the street, but was actually a pair of mailboxes. So glad she shared that. I felt better with Mom behind the wheel. The funny thing was, as far as the metaphorical Car of Life went, this time she really *was* driving.

When we got to the motel and opened the trunk to get the bags, the frog balloon leaped out and made my mother scream. It waved around in the night air as if pleased with its trick. It reminded me of Chip Jr.'s phase of hiding behind my bedroom door and jumping out, scaring the crap out of me.

We got ready for bed in the new motel room. My mother made her phone calls, and used her fakey voice talking to Joe Davis, her shoulders curved around the phone for privacy, while we pretended not to listen. She called our own answering machine. She listened for a long time. Five messages from Travis Becker, she said. *Five.*

My heart lurched at his name, the idea that he'd been calling. There was power in the knowledge that I hadn't been there when he did. I felt a surge of wanting, and yet his name, spoken in that motel room, made me feel that unpleasant sensation of biting into hot food and finding it cold in the middle.

"Call him," my mother said. "Deal with it."

"You just got finished saying how these calls from the motel were going to cost you a fortune," I said.

"Call him. It's worth every penny."

"I don't want to call him." I didn't want to hear his voice. I wasn't sure I could be as strong as she wanted me to be.

"I rode the roller coasters. I went into that saloon."

"Yeah, you made eyes at the singer, too," Chip Jr. said.

"I did not," she said.

Chip Jr. wiggled his eyebrows up and down, tried to give the motel dresser a sexy look. My mother threw a pillow at him.

"Call him and deal with it," she said. "Let it go. You can do it, Ruby."

I wasn't sure about that. I wondered if there were some pieces of your life that would always be too monumental to ever leave you. Some events in life that were fossils embedded in rock, the wrinkles etched on an old person's face, words imprinted in a book. Permanent, permeating. I told Mom what I was thinking.

"You're right," she said. "Yes. Words imprinted in a book. But Ruby, then you turn the page."

"I can't do it while you're both here," I said.

"We'll go in the bathroom."

Chip Jr. scurried off the bed. Mom followed him. They shut the door. "Make some noise in there, or something," I called to them.

Chip Jr. began to sing "This Land Is Your Land." My mother must have socked him. "Ow," he yelled. I tried to read the plastic card on the phone for directions. I still remembered Travis Becker's number.

The phone rang. He picked it up right away. I realized he was probably still recovering, lying in bed. I pictured a glass of water by his bed, with a bendy straw. I pictured his mother bringing him meals, little yellow-brown bottles of pills he'd swallow with his head back and his neck stretched.

His voice sounded strong as ever. He might have just been out riding his motorcycle, having just parked it on the lawn. I thought of his golden hair, nearly white in the sun. I thought of us that day by the train tracks, feeling each other's hearts. I felt like my insides had been gathered up in a fist. I was clutching on to him, and there was a sick fear of letting go. I didn't understand the feeling. It was loss, I guess.

"Where've you been? I've been trying to call you. You didn't even come see me in the hospital."

"How are you feeling?" I asked. I could imagine the groans from the bathroom. I heard Chip Jr. spinning the toilet paper roll. I couldn't help it—I started to cry.

"I can't hear you. Where are you?"

"Eureka." Tears rolled down my face. A few slid between my cheek and the phone.

"What? Shit, I can barely hear you."

"I asked how you're feeling."

"The drugs are great. When they wear off, I hurt like hell."

"I'm glad you're all right," I said. It was true. I couldn't have lived with the thought of him being permanently hurt that night, or, God forbid, dead. I touched my fossil on the nightstand, circled it around with my finger.

"Come over and see me. You can take my mind off the pain. I've been lying here thinking about the possibilities."

"The only reason I called was to tell you that I can't see you again."

"Right," he laughed.

"I mean it." I pictured those saloon doors, the way they swished closed behind my mother. I'd been so proud of her. I wanted to be as proud of myself. That thing I was clutching ripped away from me. And it hurt. But it felt good too. "Not just can't. But don't want to."

"I don't believe you. I got you wrapped around my finger," he laughed.

"I see you for what you are," I said. I was still crying. I wish I hadn't been, but I was.

"Right," he said. He chuckled again.

"Travis? Fuck off."

I slammed down the phone. I looked at it. I was surprised how beautiful it looked. Proud and strong and solid. This phone on a nightstand in a motel in Eureka, California. A fine, terrific, fantastic phone. A model among small appliances.

"I've never heard you say that," my mother said coming out of the bathroom. Chip Jr. was still in there.

"I never have said that." She put her arms around me. I wiped my tears with the back of my hand.

"Wow," she said admiringly.

"Not bad, huh?" I said into her shoulder. I suddenly felt exhausted.

"Not that I want you to go around saying it all the time or anything."

There was a knock at our door. My mother got up to answer it, opened it a crack, then wide. "Oh, my God!" she screamed. I walked over to look. Chip Jr. got up from the floor of the bathroom, where he had been sitting, try-ing to figure out how they replaced the Kleenex in those little built-in cabinets in the bathroom. The metal plate lay on the floor.

"Check out those snowflakes!" Chip Jr. said.

Peach had Harold by the elbow. Miz June rolled Lillian into our room in her wheelchair. She was already dressed for bed too, wearing a short flowered nightgown that showed her thin, veiny legs, pouchy flaps of elbow skin.

"I hardly see what the big deal is," Harold said. But it was true: He looked hysterical. The pajamas were the kind you'd see on a stuffed bear, soft and flannel, and Harold's round stomach stuck out round and hard. Chip Jr. patted it.

"Twins," Peach said, and we all cracked up.

My mother gave Chip Jr. some quarters from her purse, and we went out to the soda machine and brought back a few cans of Mountain Dew. Everyone sat in our room and drank from plastic cups and played hearts with a pack of cards Chip Jr. had thought to bring along. I often remem-ber that particular night, how strong we all were. How we were as vital and alive as a thunderstorm. Harold, with his tennis shoes worn without socks and his snowflake paja-mas; my mother with the pencil behind her ear for keep-ing score on a piece of motel stationery. Lillian, with that bow at the neck of her nightgown, small, satiny, and girl-ish. That bow was as fragile as a whisper, as tender and vul-nerable as a wave good-bye. And yet somehow, even in this, there was strength.

Chapter 14

What they say is, life goes on, and that is mostly true. The mail is delivered and the Christmas lights go up and down from the houses and the ladders get put away and you open yet another box of cereal. In time, the volume of my feelings would be turned down in gentle increments to near quiet, and yet the record would still spin, always spin. There was a place for Rose so deeply within myself that it was another country, another world, with its own light and time and its own language. A lost world. Yet its foundations and edges were permanent—the ruins of Pompeii, the glorious remnants of the Forum. A world that endured, even as it retreated into the past. A world visited, imagined, ever waiting, yet asleep.

■■■

"He's going to need Jesus, he drives like such an idiot," Miz June said about a truck that screamed past us with a huge wooden cross swaying from its rearview mirror. The driver flipped his middle finger up in that well-known gesture of religious tolerance and goodwill. I put my book down. Reading in the car made my head ache, anyway.

"That reminds me. I had this dream last night. We were all on a plane and it was being hijacked," Chip Jr. said. "Robbed, anyway. Harold gave the guy his watch. Peach reached in her pockets and a frog jumped out." Chip Jr. shivered. Obviously it was one of those dreams where you had to be there.

"It was from the train ride," I said. "The fake bandits."

"And the balloon," Mom said. The frog had been shoved back in the trunk again, in creepy jack-in-the-box style. Cheer in unimaginable proportions becomes eerie somehow.

Lillian looked beautiful. Peach had overdone it a bit with the perfume, though, which was probably contributing to my headache. For this, her reunion day, Lillian wore a lavender sweater and lavender slacks, with a scarf of various pastels tied in a carefree way around her neck, and a serene smile. Her white, white hair was tucked behind her ears in a playful fashion.

"Lillian, you look great," I said.

Peach gestured toward Lillian. "Woman, Starting a New Life," she said.

"The day we've all been waiting for," my mother said.

I wasn't sure if she meant Lillian's new life, or her own.

We had veered through farmland, tall stalks of new green corn, and small round lumps of what must have been lettuce. Orchards, too, of nut trees and oranges, which made the air smell sweet and thirst-quenching. I started to have that feeling you get when you are heading toward the sea, that knowledge of its presence nearby, the sky that feels a little wider and that hollow in your stomach that senses it will soon be filled with something large. Every time we climbed a hill, I expected to see it, but not yet, not yet, until we finally rounded a bend and saw it there, a small peek of vibrant blue, fighting its way out of a cauldron of fog. It made me gasp. I think if the sea doesn't make you gasp, I don't know what will.

"There it is," Miz June said. She must have been feeling the same. She was letting my Mom drive, thank God. The road was getting winding and narrow. She'd pulled over a few miles back and they'd swapped seats, after a hay truck passed her on the narrow road, zapping around a corner with the confidence of a loud radio, as the Lincoln shuddered.

Still, every time Mom picked up a little speed, the Queens would pipe up. *You might want to ease up on this particular road, Ann.* Miz June. Or, *Slow the hell down! Are you trying to get us killed?* Peach.

The ocean played hide-and-seek; gone for a moment, then back to shock us again with another glorious panoramic. We stopped at a scenic lookout point so that Chip Jr. could take pictures. It was deliciously cool on the bluff. A couple stood with their arms around each other, admiring the view. Their windbreakers flapped around, making the kid brother version of the sound the paragliders make when they ease into a landing at Moon Point. Looking at the ocean from up above gave me that same feeling as watching the paragliders, too—that slow fill of the heart to the point it felt like it had wings. I understood the logo of the paragliding school. Spirit liftoff.

Goose pimples sprang up on my arms. The coolness felt delicious. The air was a misty tonic of fog and salt and beach. I sniffed deeply. I felt so good, new. Waves rose and broke on kingly chunks of rock, rolled out, lifted again. Part of the water was sparkly and blue, the other part still sleeping in, reluctant and lazy with fog. Chip Jr. took too many pictures, none which would do the real scene justice. The sea and sky have a particular skill of eluding good photographs, like the tribesmen who believe their soul will be stolen if their picture is taken. Memory is the single way the experience can be captured and taken.

My mother had her arms wrapped around herself. "June is right," she said as she looked out across the ocean. I got this sudden weird sense that I was seeing just her, the essential her, not the mother her. "We all have this longing for something bigger than life." Miz June, for her part, had stayed in the car with the other ladies. Her face was stuck out the rolled-down window, eyes closed and chin tilted to best breathe the air.

"Men go to sea," Harold said. His hands were shoved down into his pockets.

"Women fall in love."

"And then they leave you because you drink out of the milk carton."

"I guess that's June's point," my mother said. "It's too much to expect that someone else can satisfy that space."

"Mary left me after I finally got out of the Navy and started working as a chef. She hated the Navy."

Chip Jr. took Harold's picture. I thought it was a pretty rude thing to do, right when Harold was remembering hard things. Mom squeezed Harold's arm. I'd never thought of Harold that way before—vulnerable, with the capacity to be hurt. He seemed too capable for hurt.

"Why didn't you marry again? I'm sure you had plenty of chances."

"Too goddamned ornery." He rubbed the stubble on his chin. In the excitement of leaving, he'd forgotten his razor at home. "Too scared, to tell the truth."

We went back to the car. Lillian had fallen asleep. It sure seemed like she slept a lot. Like babies do. Sleep was another thing that came back to us in a circle.

Peach decided that she needed to use the bathroom after all, and we waited for her to appear again on the little winding trail that led to the creaky wood stalls. The windbreaker couple ambled back to their Honda. An RV was parked beside us, CAPTAIN ED written in script on the back, though Captain Ed was nowhere to be seen. HOME OF THE BIG REDWOODS, a faded bumper sticker said. It had been stuck on with an extra layer of packing tape.

"Look." Harold snickered.

Peach appeared. She had a trail of toilet paper stuck

to her shoe, and it was following out from behind her, toilet paper with big dreams, pretending to be a bridal train.

"Those places ought to be illegal," she said, and gave a fake shiver.

The toilet paper had come loose. It looked abandoned and somehow sad lying there on the ground. "Ruby, pop out and pick that up," my mother said. Chip Jr. poked my leg to point out that I had just won the crappy job lottery, as if I hadn't noticed. I swatted him, made sure when I returned to throw the wadded-up ball into his lap. He batted it back at me. That toilet paper was having the time of its life. Sometimes it pays to make an escape attempt.

The road seemed to get narrower and curvier, as the scenery grew even more dramatic. The rocks became numerous and boastful, the crashing waves more forceful. The cypress trees that dotted the coastline were windblown into odd shapes, with branches thrust away from the sea as if they'd turned to run from the wind and gotten caught by a witch casting a frozen spell.

"We're probably only an hour or so away. Is everyone okay?" my mother asked from the driver's seat. Since the road had gone amusement park on us, everyone had gotten quiet.

"Puke fest," Chip Jr. said. I felt around the crack of the seat, where the wad of T.P. had lain, forgotten for a moment, heading down into the Land of Disgusting Crud under the seat. Saved. I lobbed it, too hard, and it landed right back where it started at Peach's foot.

"Crack the window if you feel queasy," my mom said.

"Do you need a Tic Tac?" She always offered us one if we were in the car with her and there was some kind of trouble. If I didn't know better, I'd have thought Tic Tacs could cure boredom, sibling fighting, hunger and thirst, bodily needs, and being lost without a map.

"What's that?" she said.

I looked out the window. But that wasn't what she meant. I felt it a second later. A sputtering. Little jolts. It felt like the Lincoln was gasping for air.

"Oh, shit," my mother said.

Lillian stirred, scooted up in her seat.

"What is it?" Miz June asked.

"Give it some gas," Harold said.

"I am. That's what I'm doing. Goddamn it."

The car stopped sputtering. Suddenly there was only a gliding feeling, smooth and quiet. The engine seemed to have shut off.

"Shit, shit!" my mother said. She managed to pull to the shoulder, slammed on the brakes.

"Shit-shit," Chip Jr. whispered. "Maracas played by some lady with fruit on her head."

"Not now, you moron," I said.

"Oh, my God. Oh, my God. What are we, an hour away? And just look! Look around! Goddamn it to hell."

She was right. In terms of being stranded, this wasn't exactly the best place. Isolated curves behind us, a snake of road hugging the rugged coastline before us. The most beautiful view of the ocean you'd ever want to see, not that Mom could really notice that now.

"Oh, dear," Miz June said. This was something a Tic Tac wouldn't fix.

"And me, so high and mighty about not wanting a cell phone. Not wanting to be one of those people talking on them in the grocery store—'fish sticks tonight, honey?' And now is a time when you really need one. Great. Just great." Mom put her head down on the steering wheel. It was not like Mom to get hysterical. This was bad.

"Do something, Harold," Peach said.

He slid out of the front seat. We watched him through the window as he went to the front of the car and fumbled with the front latch. A moment later he disappeared behind the slope of the lifted hood.

Mom sighed and got out too. I wasn't sure whether to follow or not. It was one of those times that either thing you do could be just as wrong. I opted to get out—I'd taken traffic safety the year before and learned how to change a tire. If one should happen to pop off while we were out there studying the engine, I'd know just what to do.

Harold was making noises as he looked at the engine, little *hmms* and *ahs*, as if he and the engine were having a little heart-to-heart talk. In my opinion, he should have been less sympathetic and more stern. We had somewhere we needed to be.

My leaving the car had apparently acted as a sign for everyone to abandon ship—Peach and Miz June and Chip Jr. all got out, leaving Lillian alone and looking as forlorn as a forgotten lunch box. Everyone made a half circle around the engine, waiting for it to do something miraculous, give birth maybe, or spout the secrets of the universe.

"Hmmm," Harold said.

"You don't know what the hell you're doing, do you?" Peach said.

"Not really," Harold admitted. "Actually, no."

Mom raked her fingers through her hair, trying to untangle the regrets that I'm sure were forming. "Okay!" she said decisively. Nothing more came, though. As a strategy, it needed some improvement.

"Excuse me," Miz June said.

We looked at her. She spun the pearls of her necklace with one hand.

"I think I may know what the trouble is," she said.

"Thank God," my mother said.

"I neglected to mention something when you took over the wheel, Ann. We were a little low on gasoline."

"We have half a tank," Mom said.

"We always have half a tank, dear." Miz June was retreating into old lady talk. She was probably afraid of being thumped by the whole gang of them. "What I mean to say is, the gauge is broken. It always stops at the halfway mark. Chester Delmore mentioned this when he gave me the car. Of course, he gave me his number to call him if I ever got stranded, which is probably why he didn't fix it beforehand. I've been counting the mileage in my head, but it slipped my mind when you took over the wheel."

"Well, Chester Delmore is a little far now for a rescue mission," Peach said.

"I'm truly sorry," Miz June said.

My mother sighed. "It was a mistake."

The wind whipped around, flapping the old people's pant legs. I knew what this meant from Cummings Road. "A truck is coming," I said.

Actually, it was a Trailways bus. It lumbered around the corner, came toward us. It was filled with lots of fuzzy gray heads, too. It looked like a giant caterpillar in there. Harold waved one arm. They all turned to look our way. I could picture the tour guide inside on his microphone. *And on your right, you'll see a stranded automobile. Notice the bunch of idiots helplessly beside it. This area is particularly noted for its abundance of stranded idiots, dating back to the stranded idiot infestation of the early 1800s . . .* He drove slowly past and disappeared out of sight.

"Thanks a lot, you old son of a gun," Harold yelled to the back of the bus.

"Boy, that sure fixed him," Peach said.

"Put a cork in it, heifer."

"Back at you, stretcher case."

"Corpse."

"'Let it snow, let it snow, let it snow,'" Peach sang. She stuck out her stomach out. "Ho, ho, ho."

"Ooh, that got me."

"Okay, enough," my mother said. She held up both hands as if she'd just been arrested. Rings of sweat were starting to form under her arms. We waited in tense silence. Moments passed. More moments.

"Car!" Miz June called.

A convertible, no less. Woman driving, the man next to her. Money. Cell phone jackpot. They probably had two.

We waved and called. Both waved back heartily and drove on.

"I can't believe it," my mother said.

"What did they think, we were the greeting committee?" Peach said.

Harold put on a blank expression. He imitated the moronic wave of the convertible drivers to imaginary passing cars.

"Oh, despair," Miz June said.

We waited for a long time. Peach and Mom finally got Lillian out of the car. It seemed like forever, to the point where everything you can't have—bathroom, food—suddenly begins to nag you with immediate need. I wished I'd gone back at the scenic lookout. The ocean roared in and out. The rocks sat patient, as they'd done forever. The road was still as a painting.

"If anyone tells Mrs. Wilson-now-Mrs. Thrumond this part, they're dead," Peach said.

"I'm thirsty," Chip Jr. whispered to me.

"Drink your spit," I said.

But I was thirsty too, and tired of looking at that dotted white line and imagining cars that weren't there. Where had everyone gone, anyway? Where was the couple in the windbreakers? Captain Ed? The people in the cars parked at every rest stop? The trucks full of farm workers?

"This isn't going to work," my mother said. "We could be here forever. Maybe I should start walking."

"I wish someone would call me a cab," Peach said.

"You're a cab," Harold said. He chuckled. At least someone still had a sense of humor.

Mom put her palms to her eyes. When she removed them, she gasped. "Motor home." She breathed. "Oh, my God, motor home!"

I looked. She was right. A huge motor home, with big wide windows and an ambling, overweight gait, a fat guy hurrying down an empty hall. Not Captain Ed, but someone else, the biggest motor home I'd ever seen, with two green stripes zipping boldly down the sides. My mother waved, a two-arm wave of desperation. Harold stood in the middle of the road, a heroic but unnecessary gesture, as the motor home swayed to a stop a few paces behind us. Then came the friendly slam of the driver's door, an unbelievably cheerful sound. Miz June clasped her hands together. Peach jumped up and down a bit with excitement, like she'd just won the washer-dryer combo on a game show.

"Hi, folks," the man said. He looked like the kind of guy who would say *hi, folks*—small and round with gray hair making a half circle on his head. He had a generous nose, belly slung over his pants, a big silver belt buckle with a deer on it trying to breathe under there. His shirt read PROUD TO BE AN AMERICAN, and featured a bald eagle with the same haircut as his own.

"Thank goodness you stopped," my mother said. "We ran out of gas."

"Well, that's not the smartest thing you ever did," the man said, and was instantly forgiven, I'm sure, by all of us. If that camper had a bathroom, he could rip us apart like a vulture if he wanted. "Frank," he said, and held out his hand. That was certainly true.

"Ann McQueen," my mother said. She introduced everyone.

The door of the camper opened and a woman stuck her head out. She had short hair Clairol-ed orange and big warm eyes and a motherly body. Well, nothing like my mother's slim curves, but how you picture other mothers—shoulders and chest as round and squishy as bread loaves. She wore the same shirt with the eagle, not tucked in, though, but smoothed over her jeans as flat as her bumpy terrain would allow.

"You can come out now, Marjorie," Frank said.

"Frank was making sure you weren't rapists," she said.

"Just fools who ran out of gas," Frank said.

My mother eyed Peach to make sure she'd keep her mouth shut, and then tried to get a peek inside the camper. She was thinking the same thing I was about the camper bathroom.

"Silly us," Miz June said. She was trying to peek in there too.

"I don't have a gas can, but I got myself one of those phones. Where you folks headed?"

"Carmel," my mother said.

"What brings you folks that way? Washington plates." Frank was a regular FBI agent.

"We're bringing Lillian here to live with an old friend of hers." Lillian smiled.

"How sweet," Marjorie said.

"Get me that cell phone, Marjorie."

Marjorie disappeared. "Where in Washington you from?" Frank asked.

"Nine Mile Falls. Just east of Seattle," Harold said.

"Woodburn, ourselves. Oregon. We're retired. Traveling the country. Best way to see the sights, right here. We got everything we need. Wife's got her sewing machine in there. VCR. Every Demi Moore movie." Frank winked at Harold. "Wife brought the china. The girls grew up and we always said we'd sell the house and just go. Well, the wife couldn't sell the house, of course. You shoulda seen the waterworks on *that*. So I figure, what the hell. You only live once."

Sometimes, I've discovered, people only ask a question so that they can answer it themselves.

"Met some helluva fine people on the way. Helluva fine people. Everywhere around the world. You wanna meet people, this is the way to go." He slapped the side of the RV. He remembered his poor belt buckle, gasping for air, and hitched it around a little.

"I can't find it, Frank." A small voice from inside the camper.

"Under the seat," he shouted. "Move the atlas."

"Atlas?" she said.

"Under the seat," he yelled.

"We met people from as far away as Japan," he said.

"Mooshie mooshie." He put one hand up. "That means hello."

"How about that," my mother said. She had practice at dealing with the public from being a librarian.

"You'd think one mooshie would do," Peach said.

Frank laughed. He shook his head. "Isn't that right. One mooshie would do." He would use that line on the next stranded motorist, I was sure.

"Found it!" Marjorie said. "Thank goodness it has enough batteries."

"Don't push anything. Last time you pushed something you erased all my messages."

"One message. I erased one."

"Hand it to me. This baby's got everything you need. I can see what time a movie starts in Idaho." I knew personally that there were many times in my life when I wondered what time a movie started in Idaho.

"It was a wrong number, anyway," Marjorie said. "Someone calling to tell us that our lawn mower repair was completed. No charge."

"Mooshie mooshie." Chip Jr. made kissy noises my way. I whacked him.

"Check this out. Name a city."

"Carmel," my mother said. She was doing her best to keep him on track.

"Carmel, okay." He looked at his phone. "Eighty-two degrees and sunny."

"Just like here," Peach said. "What a coincidence, since we're an hour away."

Mom shot her a look. "I'm thinking the best person to call would be the friend we're meeting. I've got his number."

"Okinawa. Fifty-eight and cloudy."

"Let them use the phone, Frank," Marjorie said.

"Push this here. See? You're set to go."

"Thanks." Mom walked off a ways on her own and after a moment, thankfully seemed to be talking to someone. She plugged her free ear with one finger to hear better, had her head down.

"And how old are you two?" Marjorie said to Chip Jr. and me. I told her. "I have grandchildren," she said, as if that meant we had something in common. "Justine is thirteen. David is eleven. Let me show you the pictures." She disappeared inside the camper again, ducking her head even though there was plenty of room for her. Frank was telling everyone about the time he accidentally left Marjorie behind at some rest stop by the Little Bighorn Battlefield in Montana. He went twenty miles before he realized she wasn't there. After he picked her back up, he had to take her to the gift shop and buy her a Bighorn Canyon book bag and refrigerator magnet before she stopped being mad. Mom was nodding her head and pacing. She looked stressed. It was like watching the news with the sound off. Finally Mom approached Lillian, spoke to her softly, then held the phone to her ear.

"Here they are," Marjorie said. "This was from our family trip to Santa's Village last summer. This is Justine, and this is David." She tapped the photo with her finger.

Thank goodness she pointed out which was which, since one was a boy and the other a girl. "They look very nice," I said. Two kids in shorts and tank tops stood next to a huge polka-dotted mushroom and smiled painfully.

"Why that Denise let David pierce his ear is another thing," Marjorie said. I looked closer, saw the gold stud in the boy's ear.

"Making him into a pansy," Frank said. "Looks like a fruitcake."

Lillian nodded into the phone, and Mom took it back.

"We got unlimited minutes, so don't you worry," Frank said. "We're all about giving."

"Whatever you give comes back to you twofold," Marjorie said. "Give someone a smile and they'll give you a hug."

"Gag," Chip Jr. whispered.

"Was that a yes?" Mom asked Lillian. Lillian nodded again. "Okay," Mom said. "It's a plan."

"We just love Christmas," Marjorie said. She'd lost me somewhere on the conversation trail until I realized she was looking at the picture of Santa's Village.

"We used to start decorating the house on November first, every year," Frank said. "Full train set. Inflatable Santa with sled and reindeer on the roof. So many damn lights that when the dog chewed through the power cord he was thrown across the room."

"That was before we got the Winnebago and became

vagabonds," Marjorie said. "'Bagobonds,'" I call us."

"You could make a sweatshirt. 'Bagobonds,' in puff paint," Peach said. I shot her a warning look, since Mom was off duty.

"That's what I thought. Hear that, Frank? I said the same thing."

"Thank you," my mother said to Frank and handed the phone back to him. "Well, gang," she said to us. "Charles will be arriving as soon as he can. And when he arrives, we'll be having a wedding."

"A wedding!" Marjorie said.

"Here?" I said.

"What's the hurry—is the bride pregnant?" Frank chortled, while that innocent deer on the belt buckle was pummeled rhythmically with flab.

"Delores and Nadine were quicker than we thought," Mom said. "They're staying in a motel in Carmel and claim to have a court order that puts Lillian in their care. She meets the requirements for incompetence, and they have several people saying so. Unless Charles is her legal spouse, Lillian will be going back to the Golden Years. They wanted to marry anyway. It'll just be a little sooner than we expected. Charles is bringing a minister who lives down the street. It's got to happen now."

"We were hoping to get to the Steinbeck Festival in Monterrey," Marjorie said. "But I don't want to miss a wedding. This would be perfect for the Bagabond Newsletter."

"I love that *Heart of Darkness*. Steinbeck's a genius," Frank said.

"Joseph Conrad," my mother said. "*Heart of Darkness* is by Joseph Conrad."

"I'm sure it's Steinbeck," Frank said. "I remember it from high school."

"She's a librarian," Harold said.

"Joseph Conrad? Didn't he sing 'It's Only Make Believe'?" Marjorie said.

"That's Conway Twitty," Miz June said.

"Never heard of Joseph Conrad," Frank said.

"Well, if it's not John Steinbeck, we might as well stay for the wedding," Marjorie said. "Frank, a *wedding*."

"Oh, all right," Frank said.

"Do you all want a drink of something while we wait? Fresca? Perhaps you all need to use the ladies and gentleman's room?"

Finally.

While we waited for Charles, Marjorie took us inside the Winnebago and showed us her Forever Christmas collection, little glass snowy houses and groups of glass carolers with earmuffs or top hats, and glass children kneeling under glass Christmas trees. The statues were stuck to every flat surface with duct tape so that they wouldn't slide around during those tight curves. She showed us the Christmas outfits she was making for Justine and David—red plaid dress with green bric-a-brac trim for Justine, green plaid vest with red bric-a-brac trim for David. I wasn't sure who to hurt for—

well-intentioned grandmother, embarrassed grandchildren, or the store that still sold bric-a-brac.

Frescas were offered all around, and we saw pictures of Marjorie and Frank's trip to John Day Fossil Beds in Oregon. After all the time we had waited for the moment, it was hard to believe that it was really Charles Whitney finally driving up that road. In preparation for Lillian and her wheelchair, he had recently purchased a van; the registration was still just a numbered piece of paper in the back window. The minister, Chuck Lindley, sat in the passenger's seat, and when he emerged holding the orange gasoline jug, we discovered that he'd been pulled straight from painting his house; his overalls were paint-splattered, and a quick hand washing had left moons of blue under his fingernails.

Lillian held her hand to her heart when Charles stepped from the car. He wore a denim shirt and a tie, not his usual attire, I guessed, since the top button of the shirt was undone, as if he could no longer stand the strangling. His captain's beard was paper white and trimmed, his eyes pure beams of joy, sun glints. He greeted my mother, then clasped his hands together and just looked at Lillian for a while with the sweet delight and moment of reverence you feel when you've awoken to a snowfall. Then he went to her, knelt down. Took her hands, which were trembling. And then the great man, author of eleven books, masterpieces like *White Rain* and *Hawk's Daughters* and a collection of poetry of distinction, and two-time national Book Award winner, laid his cheek down upon the knees of the woman he loved, who was now nineteen and thirty and eighty-two and every age in between. In front of us played the story of a woman and a man, the most simple and most complex story that exists, and she set her hand on his head with the gentleness of a blessing.

It was a beautiful wedding, a radiant wedding. The groom's voice shook, the minister held his Bible away from his paint-splattered overalls. When Charles bent down to kiss Lillian, we all heard him as he whispered only one word. *Grateful.* Lillian's face was glowing. Harold cleared his throat again and again to keep from crying. Afterward Marjorie got a frozen Sara Lee cheesecake from her kitchen and put a glass couple in glass earmuffs on the top, and we toasted Charles and Lillian with our Fresca cans. The hot wind from a passing semi-truck made my mother's hair spin around and catch in her mouth. Chip Jr. caught it all on film.

Behind Charles and Lillian was the backdrop of the ocean, blue and white and both turbulent and serene. The perfect setting for a wedding. Better than a church, even. Because what is more like love than the ocean? You can play in it, drown in it. It can be clear and bright enough to hurt your eyes, or covered in fog; hidden behind a curve of road, and then suddenly there in full glory. Its waves come like breaths, in and out, in and out, body stretched to forever in its possibilities, and yet its heart lies deep, not fully knowable, inconceivably majestic.

Chapter 15

"*That dog,*" Chip Jr. said. "*I can't help but think of him.*"

"What dog?"

"The one that was thrown across the room when he chewed through the electrical cord. Frank and Marjorie's dog."

"They stuffed him," Harold said.

"Don't be morbid," Peach said.

"I'm not the one that stuffed him," Harold said.

We were heading home. We'd said good-bye to Frank and Marjorie and had gone back briefly to Charles's house, a shingled cottage with stepping stones making a path to the door, and a back deck that looked over the sea. I didn't mind leaving Lillian in Carmel. The houses there were out of a fairy tale, lacking only the thatched roofs, and the salty clean air was wet and fresh. Charles had a birdhouse hanging in his tree, and tomato plants and a dish of milk for the neighbor's cat. Inside he had a round teapot and a violet plant by the kitchen sink, roomy wood floors, and enough books to make it feel like a wise, warm place. We didn't stay long, even though I wanted to. We agreed on the drive there that we wouldn't. We kissed and hugged Lillian good-bye and promised to call the next day. Delores and Nadine would soon be there, and Chuck Lindley would stay for support. Charles's attorney would be arriving any minute, as would his daughter. This drama, Mom said, was not ours, and we believed, really believed, that all was well. Harold pouted for a while after we were back in the car. He wanted to see the look on Delores's face when Lillian lifted up her hand to show her the ring they'd temporarily borrowed from Chuck Lindley's wife's jewelry box.

"How do you know they stuffed him?"

"I saw him. When Frank showed me his golf trophy after the wedding. The dog was in their bedroom. If you could call it a bedroom."

"More like a bed cubby," Miz June said.

"Did they duct tape him down so he didn't slide around?" my mother said, and laughed. She cracked herself up.

"No, but they should have. He was on his side with his legs sticking out when we went in, and Frank had to set him upright again. He knocked the dog over when he opened the door."

"So he was electrocuted," Chip Jr. said. "By Christmas lights."

Mom busted up. Relief that our mission was accomplished had her in a good mood.

"It's not funny," Chip Jr. said.

Miz June stuck her arms out stiffly and opened her eyes wide, frozen-dog-style.

"Nah, he wasn't electrocuted. He must have survived that. Frank told me that he died of old age."

We all got quiet on that one. Mom had been right. The old people had grown on me in ways I couldn't explain. The feeling in my stomach that grew right then, hollow dread, gnawing sadness, made me realize that I loved those Casserole Queens.

DOG WORKS MIRACLES, the sign said when we came home. And for a while that felt true. Our kitchen was fixed, coated with fresh paint, and Poe had become a near gentleman, aside from his one lapse of peeing on the floor from excitement when he first saw us. Four days after we returned home, we had a wedding reception at Miz June's for Lillian and Charles, even though the honorary guests, who were still in Carmel, were absent.

"Try these," Mrs. Wong said. "Longevity noodles. It is bad luck to cut a strand, as the noodle indicates long life." She insisted on being in charge of the food. She had gone over early that morning with her own grocery bags, and rooted around in Miz June's well-stocked cupboards for the rest of the ingredients. You could live for weeks after a nuclear war with the stuff in Miz June's cupboards and the overflow onto the shelves in her garage. She'd lived through the depression, Mom explained. That's why you could build a fortress with the amount of canned goods she had.

The table was filled with Mrs. Wong's foods. Red cooked chicken, red for the color of happiness. A whole fish, with buggy eyes, which made Anna Bee shiver. Buns with lotus seeds, indicating many children, though I thought we could have skipped those for Lillian and Charles. Chip Jr. had brought the pictures from the trip and hung them around Miz June's house. Images from our adventure—Lillian waving, parked next to the newspaper box outside Denny's; a field of orange trees; the eagle with the red scarf; Mom's eyes peering over a fan of playing cards—were stuck along the walls and other various places. A row of three heads shot from the back, Miz June's, then Mom's, then Harold's, our view the whole trip, dangled on the stair rail. A nice shot of the Mylar frog hung on one of Miz June's fringe lampshades. The photo of Harold, caught in reflection at the scenic look-out, was stuck on the toilet bowl. In it, he looked caught in one of those honest and unadorned moments, like when you've just woken up, or have come in from the cold after raking leaves. Halfway through the party I noticed that the photo had disappeared, snatched, I first guessed, by Harold himself, as it was a particularly hand-some shot, though later I discovered the corner of it peek-ing from the open zipper of Peach's purse.

More guests arrived. Joe Davis came, bringing a wed-ding gift wrapped in white paper with silver bells, which

Mom opened to reveal a box of chocolates later set on the table and pounced on by the Queens like lions on a zebra carcass. Fowler the librarian arrived with a date, a slim woman with long dark hair and dark eyeliner and a shirt with sleeves made of fishnet. *Floozy*, Peach whispered in the kitchen. Bernice Rawlins, who worked at the library, was spotted knocking on Miz June's neighbor's door, and Mom rushed out to guide her to the right house, the one with all of the cars parked in front of it. Miz June had invited a new suitor, Mr. Kingsley, who arrived in a hat and suit, and Mom invited Lizbeth and Sydney and Libby Wilson. My heart dropped when I saw Libby, batik skirt swinging in a whirl of color as she came in the door. I focused on a pair of plates of appetizers that had previously been shaped like a dragon and a phoenix and now looked like they'd survived a bomb blast.

Libby was not one for indirect social dramas. She strode directly toward me and took a pinch of my sleeve and drew me to a corner by Miz June's china cabinet. I studied a cup that looked like it was made from a lettuce leaf, and a miniature tea set with apples on it.

"Ruby," Libby said. "Look at me. It's still me."

"That's the problem." Her kindness was doing its work, loosening the tears that had gathered in readiness the moment I saw her. The smallest kindness is an arrow in the heart of a guilty person, that I'd learned.

"Listen," she said. "Your mother and I have been friends for too long to let this come between us. She called me up on your first day of kindergarten, crying her eyes out." She reached out to hug me. "I needed a little time, is all." I put my arms around her, smelled her cinnamon smell.

"I am so sorry," I said to her. Tears rolled down my face, landed on her shoulder.

"I know you are."

"I am so, so sorry."

"Don't blow your nose on my dress," she said, making me laugh. She gave me a squeeze. "Ruby, remember that man I told you about, who I missed my mother's chemotherapy for?"

I nodded.

"He stole my credit card. I got the bill. He went out to dinner a lot, bought a new computer, and a subscription to *Christian Computing* magazine."

"You're kidding."

"Dead serious."

"Jeez." I thought about this. "*Christian Computing?*"

"What I want to know is, how is Christian computing any different than any other computing?" Libby said.

"Willing to spend more when the Holy Grail comes up for sale on eBay," Mom said as she came and put her arms around both of us. "Friends," she said. She put her cheek on Libby's shoulder.

Miz June put on some music. A two-record set of Benny Goodman. Chip Jr. watched the needle of the record player collect a ball of dust, and Miz June started to dance with Mr. Kingsley. Anna Bee had worn her hooded sweatshirt with the butterflies on it, and Harold

put things in her hood when she wasn't looking—a napkin, one of Mrs. Wong's lotus seed buns. Fowler's girlfriend sat beside him on the settee, petting Beauty with
her foot. Lizbeth waltzed Sydney in a circle, as Sydney
stuck her tongue out at me. Miz June and Mr. Kingsley
were spinning and dancing hard. Mr. Kingsley bumped
into the sofa, which bumped into the wall and tipped to
an angle Miz June's painting of the couple in the boat.

"Oh, my," Miz June said when the song was over. "You
are a marvelous dancer, Mr. Kingsley."

He pulled her waist toward him as the music slowed.
"And you, my dear, are Ginger Rogers," he said.

Joe Davis took my mom's hand and led her in a dance.
She looked happy, and was talking in that tight-lipped
way that meant she was trying not to blow her garlic
prawn breath on him. She held him there when the song
changed to a fast one, and Joe Davis stomped too hard
and skidded the needle of the record player, making
everyone miss the beat for a moment. Mrs. Wong took
Chip Jr. out on the floor for a spin, and he wiggled his
hips and stepped on the cat's tail when Mrs. Wong spun
him around. Sydney, Lizbeth, Mom, and I formed a line
and kicked our legs cancan style.

I imagined Lillian and Charles sitting peacefully on
their deck in Carmel, looking at the ocean, touched by its
salty breeze as we sang and toasted them with champagne
and ate a real wedding cake that Harold made. I imagined
them holding hands in sweet quiet as we danced, danced.

■■■

"Jeez, Poe, what are you watching?" Poe sat upright on the couch, looking straight at the television, where there was some soap opera couple half naked in bed. She had her soap opera tongue down his soap opera throat. Poe turned to look at me for a moment and then kept watching.

The phone rang. In the three weeks that we'd been back, Travis Becker had called four times. It gave me a perverse pleasure to see his name on the caller ID and to ignore it. I wondered if he could sense me there on the other end, my heart lurching, training my newly strong self to look at his name and see what I should: something ugly and dangerous, a cigarette butt, an ambulance siren, a slick road, a poisonous spider best hit with a shoe.

But it wasn't Travis Becker on the phone this time. It was Charles Whitney's daughter, Joelle. Lillian was in the hospital. She'd had another stroke. She was in intensive care.

Mom was expected home from work soon, but I called her there anyway and told her. Then I went into Chip Jr.'s room, where he sat on the floor with Mom's old magic kit that she'd had since she was a kid laid out in front of him—orange cups, green dragon coin case, cards, and string.

"Check this out," he said. He held up a dollar bill and then rolled it up. He stuck a small square of purple scarf down inside it, opened the dollar to reveal that the scarf was gone.

"Wow, that was great," I said. It was.

"Now I'll make it come back," he said.

"I've got some bad news. About Lillian." He stopped his trick. Looked up at me and waited. "She's in the hospital."

"Why?"

"She had another stroke."

"She's not dead, though," he said.

"No," I said. "But she's not doing very well."

"She wouldn't be dead. She just got to California."

We had a quiet dinner, did the dishes. The dishwasher, squeaking and groaning with its odd rhythm, was the only noisy thing. We opened the door and a rush of steam poured out. We used three hot bowls for ice cream, the scoops quickly melting a soft layer into the bowl. Mom changed into her robe. We played a halfhearted game of Masterpiece while Poe sat in the box lid like a cat. By the end of the evening, Mom had gotten another phone call. Lillian had died, just two hours before. It seemed unbelievable that in one place someone could be opening a steamy dishwasher, and in another someone could be dying.

Chip Jr. sobbed against my mother, into her terry cloth shoulder. She held him in one arm, reached her other out to me, and took my hand.

"It's not how it's supposed to be," he cried.

Chapter 16

This is what I know: We are all a volume on the shelf of the Nine Mile Falls Library, a story unto ourselves, never possibly described with one word or even very accurately with thousands. A person is never as quiet or unrestrained as they seem, or as bad or good, as vulnerable or as strong, as sweet or as feisty; we are thickly layered, page lying upon page, behind simple covers. And love—it is not the book itself, but the binding. It can rip us apart or hold us together. My mother has always said that a book is worthy of a strong embrace, but, too, you must be gentle with one. Careful in whose hands you put it. Layers, by their nature, are fragile things.

We gathered with the Queens once more, this time in Joe Davis's church. An enlarged photo of Lillian holding a red sno-cone sat in a frame on a table in the front of the church, next to a stack of Charles Whitney's books and a vase of white roses. There was a note from Charles, in his strong, tender handwriting:

Know that, whatever has happened, you have all done a marvelous and meaningful thing. I will always believe that she waited for us to be together before she let go. It was the happiest few weeks of my life, and she died holding my hand.

My mother read a Robert Browning poem, about love found and lost and remembered, and Joe Davis talked about God in a way that made Him sound kind and understanding and there for us. The church was full of Lillian's friends and bittersweet feelings and the sound of Harold blowing his nose. Somewhere in Carmel that same day, on a cliffside dotted with wind-frozen cypress trees, Charles Whitney was saying a final good-bye to his soul mate.

My father called just before we were to go back to school. Chip Jr.'s new school clothes were already laid out on his floor, like a flattened cartoon character, in readiness. My father wanted us to come and visit, Chip Jr. and me. There was someone we should meet, he said. A sister. A baby girl. Someone who shared some part of us, though who could say which part. Eye color? A way with words? Some obscure piece of genetic material that sat quietly in our blood? Family was the people around you who you loved and who loved you back. When that phone call came, I was more related to Mrs. Wong than a stranger I hadn't even met. The first definition for the word *relative* is "relevant," after all.

"Call me when you're heading home," Mom said.

"You know we're coming back tomorrow," I said.

"I still want you to call. That way I'll know to worry if it gets late."

I sighed, but I didn't really mind. I was glad, actually, that she was in full mother mode, with both feet firmly on the ground.

"I'm bringing my lucky fossil," Chip Jr. said.

"Full tank of gas and a lucky fossil," I said. "We're set."

We played the license plate game, talked about birds and how they decided who was the leader of the triangle, stopped for some fries. Chip Jr. read the directions to Dad's house. While I was there with Dad and his fiancée, Cilla, and baby, I kept trying to make the dad I knew fit with this new place and new people. Dad's same voice, a refrigerator full of foods I didn't know he liked. Dad's coat, in a closet I'd never seen before, hanging next to strange coats. Dad's familiar hands holding a baby that smelled like peaches, his own hair smelling like a shampoo I didn't know the brand of. His fiancée—the word was strange enough—with a high laugh and a face much plainer than I imagined, a Midwest accent that said she'd had a whole life somewhere else before then.

Chip Jr. and I whispered in the dark, glad for each other's familiarity. We said good-bye the next morning, my father expressing his desire to see us more, as if this baby made him remember that we were here too. It would take many more trips before it would feel right that my father knew how to work that particular remote control in that particular house, mow that lawn, sing to that baby, Olivia, who would finally become herself to us.

We called Mom when we headed home, just after we crossed the state line. Chip Jr. and I both squeezed inside the phone booth.

"Guess where we are," I said to Mom.

"In a Mexican jail," she said.

"Nope."

"I give up, then."

"The same phone booth outside the Denny's we went to with the Queens. The one you called Mrs. Wong and Joe from."

"Tell her a big fat guy is sitting in our booth. Tell her he's eating the same bacon cheeseburger she ate," Chip Jr. said.

"Ha, ha, very funny. I heard that," she said.

I craned my neck to look through the windows blasted with advertisements for breakfast specials. "He's not kidding," I said.

"Do you see Randy the Colossally Cool Waiter?"

"Mmm, not yet," I said.

"How'd it go?" she asked. "How was the baby?"

"Fine. Cute. Cilla was a lot plainer than I thought she'd be." Avoid the word *fiancée*. Avoid the fact that Cilla was a lot nicer than I'd thought too. We'd had a long history of protecting each other, my mother and I. I'm sure we'd keep protecting each other forever. We cared too much for each other to have between us the recklessness of complete honesty.

"So get home safely," she said.

"We will, as long as we get out of this phone booth before we catch some deadly disease," I said. The phone felt sticky, and there was a little nest of cigarette butts in one corner that my shoe was keeping its distance from, like those circles of kids you worry are doing drugs just outside of school property. Someone had written JASON ROCKS in permanent marker on the glass; another had crossed out ROCKS and replaced it with SUCKS DIX. If you are going to be crude, in my opinion, you at least ought to spell correctly.

"Put your brother on for a minute," she said. "And I'll let you go. See you soon, and drive carefully."

"I will."

I stepped out of the booth, examined the juniper plants and the newspaper boxes full of real estate magazines. When I went back to the booth, Chip Jr. was holding the receiver to his ear but wasn't saying anything.

"What are you doing?" I mouthed.

Chip Jr. held his hand over the receiver. "Poe was sitting by Mom so she put him on the phone. I'm listening to him breathe."

He held the phone out to me. I heard what sounded like a loud gust of static from a television, quiet, and then the gust of static again.

Chip Jr. took the phone back. "I missed you, boy," he said.

School started. I kept going to the Casserole Queen's book club. The surprise was, no one noticed that I was no longer who I had always been. At least not at first. But it didn't matter. I felt it. A core of something solid, not the water or sand or clay that had been there before, but something firm and permanent.

There were other surprises. Joe Davis had returned to his home very late one night from a date with my mother, only to see Anna Bee running across the church lawn, holding up her pant legs from the dewy grass, her socks flashing white in the darkness. LET DOG BE YOUR GUIDE.

"Is he sure it was her?" I asked Mom.

"Well, he's sure it was her that he saw. Unless he catches her again with black letters in her hand, it still could be half the town. For a while, Joe thought it *was* half the town, everyone taking turns on different days."

"Anna Bee, though? That's just too strange." I always thought it was Renny Powell, the guy that helped Joe with the church grounds.

"It fits, if you think about it. Anna Bee, animal lover, naturalist. Rebellious vandal." She laughed. "He doesn't want to know who it is, you realize. He has a great fondness for the dog vandal."

"So maybe she was just doing tai chi on the lawn."

"At midnight," my mother said.

■■■

The air was starting to have that fall feeling—I'm not sure what it is, because even if it is a hot leftover summer day, you still feel it—that sense of things ending and others beginning at the same time. There is some kind of resignation in the air, a bittersweet smell that comes, maybe just as the leaves begin to change, before you even notice the subtle shift in colors that will burst like wildfire onto the hillsides just a week or two later. What I am sure of, though, is that even if we didn't have the calendar, or the trees, to help us, we would sense that it was still early September, because September comes to you like a pull in your stomach. And the feeling got to me a little, I confess, as I walked home that day, one of the early days back at school my senior year. That pull makes you want to find a reason for it, and as I passed Travis Becker's house, which I passed with focused disinterest the days prior, I looked long and hard at those gates and decided again that I did not want to go through them. Sometimes a decision is not one monumental event, but many small, slightly unsteady ones.

Instead I went to Moon Point and watched the paragliders, who would still have another month of good weather, if they were lucky. The day was too autumn-glorious to resist soaring in, I guess, and the parking lot and roadside was filled with cars, including the funny van with the whale and I LOVE POTHOLES bumper sticker. I sat down and watched them awhile, listening to the flapping, book pages turning, turning with sharp speed, and watching them make butterfly circles against the mountainside.

I watched two people land, their parachutes collapsing sumptuously around them once their feet touched ground, their faces so exhilarated that it made you feel it too.

I walked to the small house that acted as the office of the paragliding school. As Charles Whitney said, when your life changes, a definite action is called for. I had never been there before, even though I had come to the field so many times. The door was half open. I was surprised to see the whale van guy behind the desk, talking on the phone. I couldn't believe it was him. He was wearing a T-shirt with the school logo on it, a heart with wings. I waited for him to finish.

"I know you," he said when he got off the phone.

"I know you."

"The girl with the shiny hair and the good sense of humor."

"The guy with the squirting whale van. You work here."

"I do."

"That is so great."

He grinned. "I think so too." He nodded at me as if we both understood something about each other. "Well," he said finally. "What can I do for you?"

Here is what happened then. I heard the voices of the Queens. I heard the clinking of their glasses, raised in a toast. *To adventure*, they said.

And I listened.

"I want to fly," I said.

Honey, Baby, Sweetheart

BY DEB CALETTI

About the Book

Ruby McQueen has never had trouble being good—getting along with her family, doing well in school, and making good decisions. Which is why nobody is more surprised than she when bad boy Travis Becker sucks her into his world of privilege and lawlessness and she follows so willingly. But when Ruby does the unthinkable, she sets in motion a madcap multigenerational adventure, as those close to her do everything they can to save her from herself. Can one summer change what Ruby knows about true love, family, fate, and her own heart?

Discussion Questions

- Ruby's involvement with Travis Becker is out of character for her, but she says, "It was about the way a moment, a single moment, could change things and make you decide to try to be someone different." What does Ruby feel is her pivotal moment? Do you agree? Who else in the story has moments like the one Ruby describes?

- Travis believes that Ruby is fearless, and so she becomes that way around him. How much of our personalities is defined by how others see us? Does Ruby succeed in becoming truly fearless? On what do you think Travis is basing his vision of Ruby?

- In what ways are Ruby and her mother similar when it comes to romantic relationships? In what ways are they different? What do they learn about romance over the course of the summer?

- Discuss Ruby's relationship with Chip Jr. What role does Chip Jr. play in her life? What role does he play within the family as a whole?

- How is Joe Davis different from Ruby's father? What does he bring to the McQueen family? How do his struggles with the church sign reflect his beliefs about spirituality?

- How do the members of the Casserole Queens feel about Ruby? About each other? Why does Ruby enjoy her time with them so much?

- Why is it so important to the Casserole Queens that Charles and Lillian be reunited? What does each member of the group contribute to the plan? What does each member gain from the reunion?

- Ruby says that, had they known Lillian had so little time left, they would have hurried their trip along. Do you think this is true? What did they gain by taking their time on the way to meet Charles? Do you think that Lillian would have wanted them to hurry?

- Why is Ruby so fascinated by the paragliders? What do they represent to her? Does anything else in her life make her feel this way?

- Ruby says, "I guess for one summer, just one summer . . . I did have passion and adventure in my life." To which events do you think she is referring? Do you think that there was any adventure in her life before this summer? Do you think she will continue to have passion and adventure in her life?

Activities

- Start your own book group, like the Casserole Queens. Invite all your friends, decide how often you would like to meet, and have someone bring snacks.

- The story behind Lillian and Charles's relationship inspired the Casserole Queens to strike out on their adventure. What stories are hidden in your family tree? Interview your parents, grandparents, aunts, and uncles about their lives. Write down this oral history and share it with other family members.

- Look into volunteering at a nursing home or retirement community in your neighborhood.

- Is there something in your life that you've been wanting to learn—like Ruby and paragliding—that you could take up now? See if there's anywhere in your town you could take lessons.

Simon & Schuster Children's Publishing www.SimonSaysTeach.com

Here's a peek at another novel by Deb Caletti:

wild roses

To say my life changed when my mother married Dino Cavalli (yes, *the* Dino Cavalli) would be like saying that the tornado changed things for Dorothy. There was only one other thing that would impact my life so much, and that was when Ian Waters drove up our road on his bicycle, his violin case sticking out from a compartment on the side, and his long black coat flying out behind him.

My stepfather was both crazy and a genius, and I guess that's where I should start. If you've read about him recently, you already know this. He was a human meteor. Supposedly there's an actual, researched link between extreme creativity and mental illness, and I believe it because I've seen it with my own eyes. Sure, you have the artists and writers and musicians like my mom, say, who are talented and calm and get things done without much fuss. The closest she gets to madness is when she gets flustered and calls me William, which is our dog's name. But then there are the van Goghs and Hemingways and Mozarts, those who feel a hunger so deep, so far down, that greatness lies there too, nestled somewhere within it. Those who get their inner voice and direction from the cool, mysterious insides of the moon, and not from the earth like the rest of us. In other words, brilliant nuts.

I guess we should also begin with an understanding, and that is, if you are one of those easily offended people who insist that every human breath be politically correct, it's probably best we just part company now. I'll loan you my copy of *Little House in the Big Woods* (I actually loved it when I was eight) and you can disappear into prairie perfection, because I will not dance around this topic claiming that Dino Cavalli was joy-impaired (hugely depressed), excessively imaginative (delusional), abundantly security conscious (paranoid as hell) or emotionally challenged (wacko). I'm not talking about your mentally ill favorite granny or sick best uncle—I'm not judging anyone else who's ill. This is my singular experience. I've lived it; I've earned the right to describe how it felt from inside my own skin. So if your life truths have to be protected the same way some people keep their couches in plastic, then ciao. Have a nice life. If we bump into each other at Target, I'm the one buying the sour gummy worms, and that's all you need to know about me.

Anyway, madness and genius. They're the disturbed pals of the human condition. The Bonnie and Clyde, the

Thelma and Louise, the baking soda and vinegar. Insanity just walks alongside the brilliant like some creepy, insistent shadow. Edgar Allan Poe, Virginia Woolf, Charles Dickens. William Faulkner, Dostoevsky, Cézanne, Gauguin. Tolstoy, Sylvia Plath, Keats, and Shelley. Walt Whitman and F. Scott Fitzgerald and Michelangelo. All wacko. And we can't forget the musicians, because this story is about them, especially. Schumann and Beethoven, Chopin and Handel and Rachmaninov and Liszt. Tchaikovsky and Wagner.

And, of course, Dino Cavalli.

In that group you've got every variety of creation: the ceiling of the Sistine Chapel and *Farewell to Arms* and the epic poem, "Ode on a Grecian Urn," which, if you ask me, finds its true greatness as a cure for insomnia. You've also got every variety of crazy act. You've got the gross—van Gogh slicing off his earlobe and giving it to a woman (you can just hear her—*Damn, I was hoping for chocolates*), and the unimaginable—Virginia Woolf filling her pockets with stones to hold her down in the river so that she could do an effective job of drowning. And even the funny—the reason our dog is named William, for example, is because Dino Cavalli bought him during a particularly bad bout of paranoia and named him for his enemy and former manager and agent, William Tiero. He liked the idea of this poor, ugly dog named William that would eat used Kleenex if he had the chance. He liked yelling at William for getting too personal with guests. I can hear his voice even now, in his Italian accent. *Get your nose out of Mrs.*

Kadinsky's crotch, William, he'd say with mock seriousness, and everyone would picture William Tiero with his bald head and beetle eyes, and they would laugh. Man, oh, man. You didn't want to get on Dino Cavalli's bad side.

Some people think the brilliant have been touched by God, and if this is true then Dino Cavalli got God on the day he was wearing black leather and listening to his metal CDs, feeling a bit twisted and in the kind of mood where you laugh at people when they fall down. God wearing a studded collar. Because, sure, Dino Cavalli was a world-renowned composer and violinist, a combination of talent virtually unheard of, but there were days he didn't get out of bed, even to shower. And, sure, he wrote and performed *Amore Innamorato,* said to, "have moments of such brutal tenderness and soulful passion that it will live forever in both the hearts of audience members and the annals of modern composing,"[1] as well as the unforgettable *Artemisia* ("breathtaking and heart-stopping work with the brilliance of the seventeenth-century masters."[2]), but he also had the ability to make you feel small to the point of disappearance. His perfectionism could shatter your joy like a bullet through a stained glass window.

What I'm saying is, he possessed magnificent and destructive layers. Either that or he was just plain possessed. I mean, it all got toned down in the papers, but we all know what could have happened to William Tiero that day. We all now know what happens when you self-

---

[1] Dawson Cook, "Cavalli Strikes a Perfect Note" *Strad Magazine* (April 1996): 12–15.
[2] Alice Lambert, "The Season's Best" *Strad Magazine* (May 1989): 20–22.

destruct. Yet I've got to say, listening to his music can make you cry. Goose bumps actually rise up along your arms.

Everyone wants to get close to genius and fame, claim pieces of it, mostly because it's the closest they'll ever get to fame themselves. You learn this when you live with someone renowned. Those who know that Dino Cavalli was my stepfather think I'm near enough to fame to call it good. Fame, the nearness of it, the possibility of it rubbing off, seems to turn people into obsessed Tolkien characters, hypnotized not by a ring but by the thought of getting on TV. Luckily at my school, most of the kids who hear the name Dino Cavalli will think it's some brand of designer shoes. To the majority I am just Cassie Morgan, regular seventeen-year-old trying to figure out what to do with my life and hoping my jeans are clean and swearing at myself for cutting my own bangs again. Few know my stepfather was once on the cover of *Time* magazine, or was also well known for the journals in which he wrote of his sexual adventures as a young composer in Paris. Everyone is too involved in the school game of How Orange Is Tiffany Morris's Makeup Today to care, even if they did. But the teachers and orchestra students, they know who I am, and I see what it means to them. Once during a school concert this kid was staring so hard at me that he accidentally stepped into an open viola case and wore it like an overgrown shoe for a few seconds on the gym floor.

And then there's Siang Chibo, who used to follow me home every day. She would walk far behind me and duck behind trees when I turned around, like some cartoon spy. She once tripped over a tree root in the process and spewed the contents of her backpack all over the place. You couldn't find a more incompetent stalker. I went over to her after she fell, and her palms even had those little pockmarks on them from landing on gravel. Now we have a Scrooge-Tiny Tim partnership of reluctant giving and nauseating gratitude. To Siang, I'm second in line in the worship chain of command, right after Dino. If people look at the famous as if they've been touched by God, then they look at those close to the famous as the ones who have seen Jesus' face in the eggplant.

You would have never recognized the Dino I lived with in the books that had been written about him before the "incident." No one had a clue. No one seemed to see what was coming. His demons were the real truth, but those who clutched at his fame made him into someone else. Just listen to Irma Lattori, a villager from Sabbotino Grappa, interviewed in Edward Reynolds's *Dino Cavalli—The Early Years: An Oral History,* the much-quoted source of Dino's childhood. It's his only authorized biography, in which the people who knew him then tell the events of his life.

Everyone in Sabbotino Grappa knew Dino Cavalli had that special light, Irma says in the book. *From the time he was an infant. I would see his mother, Maria, walk him around in his carriage. She was a beautiful woman with round, warm eyes. She always dressed elegantly, oh, so rich. She had tucked a peacock feather in the back of his carriage. It rose up, like a grand flag. You want to know where he got* Un Cielo Delle

Piume Del Peacock? *That was his inspiration. Maria always appreciated the unusual. She wore hats, even when no one wore hats. Stunning. No wonder he became a ladies' man. He was born, you see, taking in the world and using it in his work. Born to beauty and greatness. He couldn't have been more than six months old, this time I am remembering. He reached his hands up to me when I bent to look at him. He wanted me to hold him. He wouldn't let my sister Camille go near him.*[3]

And Frank Mancini, gardener, another one of the villagers from tiny Sabbotino Grappa: *A beautiful garden, beautiful. Four hundred years old. Magnolias in the spring. Plumbagos, hibiscus in the summer. Lemon trees and figs. An olive garden. I worked my fingers to the bone. Now I cannot tie my own shoe, my fingers are so crippled. But it was a beautiful garden, and you could hear the child playing the violin through the open window. Small boy, not more than four years old, and he played the violin! A divine gift. His mother played the piano. Music was in his veins. And the smell of lemon trees. I didn't mind that the father was cheap and barely paid me enough to buy food.*[4]

All in all, as gagging as a dental X ray.

"No one ever mentions that he is a wife-stealing psycho," my father said once after Dino was featured in the entertainment section of the newspaper—FAMED MUSICIAN SEEKS LOCAL INSPIRATION. He tossed the paper down on his kitchen table. "With bad breath."

---

[3] Dino Cavalli—*The Early Years: An Oral History.* From Edward Reynolds, New York, N.Y. Aldine Press, 1999.
[4] *Dino Cavalli—The Early Years: An Oral History.* From Edward Reynolds, New York, N.Y. Aldine Press, 1999.

"You haven't even been close enough to him to smell his breath," I said.

"Who says you have to be close," my father said. Let's just say my father didn't read the divorce books that say you are not supposed to talk badly about the other parent and the other parent's partner. Actually, I think he probably did read them, but has somehow convinced himself that only my mother is required to follow these rules. He ignores the other Divorced Parenting Don'ts too, the ones where you aren't supposed to grill your kid about what happens in the other home. Sometimes he tries to be casual about his fishing around, and other times it's like I'm in one of those movies where the criminal sits under the bare light-bulb in a room and after twelve hours confesses to a crime he didn't commit.

My parents were divorced three years ago, and my mother married Dino five days after the divorce was final. Do the math and figure out what happened. If you've been through this, you know the vocabulary. Parenting plan, custody evaluation, visitation, court orders, mediation, transfer time. And can anyone say *restraining order*? I can talk with my friend Zebe about these things. Ever since I met her in Beginning Spanish we've spoken the same language, in more ways than one. Her new stepfather may not be famous, but we understand the most important things about each other. She knows that you really don't give a crap about who gets you on Labor Day, that *no-fault divorce* are the three stupidest words ever spoken, and that you are not split as easily as your parents' old

Commodores albums, and there was even a war over those.

"Barry Manilow, in my house. Not Commodores," Zebe told me once. "Which they both hated, by the way. For a week they were flying e-mails at each other over the goddamn F-ing *Copacabana* LP. They each accused the other of taking it. 'Did your mother find my "missing" album yet?' 'Next time you go to your father's, look for my stolen record.' God."

"Was anyone hurt?" I asked.

"Aside from the e-mail bloodbath, the only thing that was hurt was both of their egos when one of them finally remembered that they brought the album to some party back in the seventies and left it there on purpose."

"You wonder why they ever got married."

"*Mi mono toca la guitarra,*" she said. *My monkey plays the guitar.* It's what she wrote on every Spanish test question she didn't know the answer to. I cracked up. Zebe's the greatest.

If my father treated my time at my mother's house as if he were the gold miner panning for The Dirt of Wrongdoing, my mother, on the other hand, would listen to any news of my father the same way someone who had plans to stay inside listens to a weather forecast. Hearing just enough to make sure there was no tornado coming. This is one difference between the leaver and the left, the dumper and the dumpee. The dumpee has the moral righteousness, and the desire to hear every dirty fact that will prove that *You get what you deserve in the end.* The dumper has the guilt, and wants to know as little about the other party as possible, in case they hear something that will make them feel even more guilty.

"Dad's got a new client. Some big Microsoft person," I told Mom once. It was after she and Dino had first gotten married, and I was starting to get a real clear picture of what she'd gotten us into. I guess I was hoping she was seeing, too, and that a little nudge in Dad's direction might help along the underdog. I hadn't learned yet that in terms of divorce, your only real hope is not to play team sports.

"Oh, really. Good for him," she said. She was braiding her long hair. She had a rubber band in her teeth. *Oh, weewy. Ood for him.* She finished the braid, put her arms down. "I need to find my overalls. I'm planting tulip bulbs today. Planting just calls for overalls." She went to her closet, flung open the doors.

"It'll bring him a lot of money," I said. My father was an accountant. He was a white undershirt in a world of silk ties and berets and pashmina. He was a potato amongst pad Thai and curry and veal scallopini. He was still madly in love with my mother. He didn't have a chance.

"Great," she said. "My God, look at this mess. The man is incapable of hanging anything up." She said this with a great deal of affection, poked a toe at a pile of Dino's shirts. "Overalls, overalls. Bingo." She held them up.

"You're not even listening."

"I'm listening, I'm listening. You're just making me feel like I'm in some *Parent Trap* movie. You're not going to put frogs in Dino's shoes or something, are you?"

Mom's unwillingness to get involved may have also had to do with her own experience of her parent's divorce. Thirty-two years after the end of their marriage, she still can't tell one of her parents that she's visiting the other, or she'll be punished with coldness, hurt, and upset. Thirty-two years later, and her mother still refers to her father's wife as That Tramp.

"I thought you'd like to know. Jesus, Mom."

"Good. Thanks for telling me. You're not the *Parent Trap* type anyway. What was the name of that actress? Started with an H. Heather. Hayley! Mills. God, how'd I remember that? You, girl, are not Hayley Mills. I'd like to see them put you in a remake. Disney'd ditch the hemp bracelet. Don't you think? Too edgy."

"I hope squirrels dig up your tulip bulbs," I said.

She socked my arm. "You know how much I respect you. I *like* your hemp bracelet."

Respect—that was what was lacking in the other member of our household. Dino didn't respect me, or my mother, either, for that matter. Or anyone who wasn't his own perfect self. See, Dino hadn't always acted crazy. For a while, he was just plain arrogant. Dino was fluent in criticism, as generous in spirit as those people who keep their porch lights off all Halloween. If my mom was dressed up to go out and looking beautiful, he'd point out her pimple. If you opened the wrong end of the milk carton, he'd make you feel you were incapable to the point of needing to be institutionalized. After I'd bought this jacket with fur around the collar and cuffs at Old Stuff, Dino had pointedly told me that people who tried to make some statement of individuality were still only conventional among those of their group.

"I'm not trying to make a statement," I said. I was trying to keep the sharpness out of my voice, but it was like trying to hold water in your hands—my tone was seeping through every crack and opening possible.

"I didn't say you were. Did I say you were? It was a commentary on dress and group behavior," he said in his Italian accent. He chewed a bite of chicken. He was a loud, messy eater. You could hear the chicken in there smacking around against his tongue. His words were offhand, casually bragging that they meant more to me than they did to him. "By avoiding conventions, one falls into other conventions." He plucked a bit of his shirt to indicate someone's clothing choice. I felt the ugly curl of anger starting in my stomach.

"I'm sorry, I just don't want to be one of those See My Thong girls who bat their eyelashes at boys, rah rah rah, wearing a demoralizing short skirt and bending over so a crowd sees their butt," I said. "That's convention." Anger made my face get hot.

"Be who you like. I was simply making an observation. You don't need to bite me with your feminist teeth."

Honestly, I don't know how my mother didn't poison his coffee. Certainly I wondered what the hell she was thinking by loving him. If this is what could happen to a supposedly charming, romantic guy, then no, thank you. And this was before everything happened, even. Before

Dino's craziness became like a roller coaster car, rising to unbelievable heights, careening down with frightening speed; before he started teaching Ian Waters; before he began composing again and preparing for his comeback after a three-year dry spell. But in spite of what must have been perfect attendance in asshole classes, Dino was one of those people who got under your skin because you cared what they thought when you wished you didn't. So after that conversation I did the only thing I could. I wore the coat the next day, too. The truth was, I wasn't sure I liked it either. It was vaguely Wilma Flintstone and Saber Tooth Tiger. Little hairs fell into my Lucky Charms.

Because I wanted his approval and hated that fact, I did what I could to make sure I didn't get it at all. One of those things you should be in therapy for. Before I met Ian Waters, for example, I had no interest in music, which was an act of will living in a house where my mother was a cellist and my stepfather a prominent violinist and composer. But Ian Waters changed that about me, and everything else, too. Before I met Ian the music I liked best was something that sounded, if Dino was right, *like your mother hunting for the meat thermometer in the drawer of kitchen utensils.* My interest was in astronomy—science, something that was mine and that was definite and exact. I felt that the science of astronomy existed within certain boundaries that were firm and logical. If you think about how vast the universe is, this gives you some idea of how huge and wild I thought the arts were.

After three years of living with Dino Cavalli, I had had enough of people of passion. Passion seemed dangerous.

I'd seen the tapes of his performances, the way he had his chin to his violin as if he were about to consume it, the way his black hair would fly out as he played, reaching crescendo, eyes closed. It made you feel like you needed to hold on to something. I'd never felt that kind of letting go before. It all seemed one step away from some ancient tribal possession. And that crescent scar on his neck. That brown gash that had burned into him from hours and hours and hours of the violin held against his skin. He had played until the instrument had made a permanent mark, had become part of his own body. If Chuck and Bunny are right, and everyone should *hunger for life and its banquet,* I would rather have the appetite of my neighbor Courtney and her two brothers, over Dino's. All Courtney and her brothers hungered for in life was a box of Junior Mints and MTV, fed straight through the veins. Dino, he could inhale an emotional supermarket and still be ravenous.

Right then, the only thing I was hungry for was to have Dino Cavalli, this flaming, dying star, out of my universe. It was the only thing I would dare be passionate about. That is, until Ian Waters veered into our driveway on his bike, his tires scrunching in the gravel, scaring Otis, the neighbors' cat, who ran across the grass like his tail was on fire. Otis was running for his life. In a way, that was when I began finally running to mine.

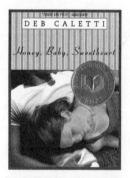
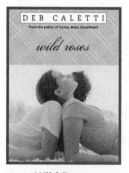

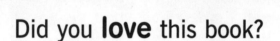